ABOVE THE BLEAT OF SHEEP AND TRAMPLE OF MANY HOOFS RANG OUT MESCAL'S CRY, DESPAIRING.

She had turned, her hands over her breast. Wolf spread his legs before her and crouched to spring, mane erect, jaws wide.

By some lightning flash of memory, August Naab's words steadied Jack's shaken nerves. He aimed low and ahead of the running bear. Down the beast went in a sliding sprawl with a muffled roar of rage. Up he sprang, dangling a useless leg, yet leaping swiftly forward. One blow sent the attacking dog aside. Jack fired again. The bear became a wrestling, fiery demon, death-stricken, but full of savage fury. Jack aimed low and shot again.

THE
HERITAGE
OF THE
DESERT

ZANE GREY

A TOM DOHERTY ASSOCIATES BOOK
NEW YORK

This is a work of fiction. All the characters and events portrayed in this book are fictitious, and any resemblance to real people or events is purely coincidental.

THE HERITAGE OF THE DESERT

All new material copyright © 1977 by Tom Doherty Associates, LLC.

A Forge Book
Published by Tom Doherty Associates, LLC
175 Fifth Avenue
New York, NY 10010

www.tor-forge.com

Forge® is a registered trademark of Tom Doherty Associates, LLC.

ISBN-13: 978-0-7653-6313-8
ISBN-10: 0-7653-6313-5

First Forge Edition: December 1997
Second Forge Edition: March 2009

Printed in the United States of America

0 9 8 7 6 5 4 3 2 1

CONTENTS

CHAPTER I

The Sign of the Sunset

"But the man's almost dead."

The words stung John Hare's fainting spirit into life. He opened his eyes. The desert still stretched before him the appalling thing that had overpowered him with its deceiving purple distance. Near by stood a sombre group of men.

"Leave him here," said one, addressing a gray-bearded giant. "He's the fellow sent into southern Utah to spy out the cattle thieves. He's all but dead. Dene's outlaws are after him. Don't cross Dene."

The stately answer might have come from a Scottish Covenanter or a follower of Cromwell.

"Martin Cole, I will not go a hair's-breadth out of my way for Dene or any other man. You forget your religion. I see my duty to God."

"Yes, August Naab, I know," replied the little man, bitterly. "You would cast the Scriptures in my teeth, and liken this man to one who went down from Jerusalem to Jericho and fell among thieves. But I've suffered enough at the hands of Dene."

The formal speech, the Biblical references, recalled to the reviving Hare that he was still in the land of the Mormons. As he lay there the strange words of the Mormons linked the hard experience of the last few days with the stern reality of the present.

"Martin Cole, I hold to the spirit of our fathers," replied Naab, like one reading from the Old Testament. "They came into this desert land to worship and multiply in peace. They conquered the desert; they prospered with the years that brought settlers, cattle-men, sheep-herders, all hostile to their religion and their livelihood. Nor did they ever fail to succor the sick and unfortunate. What are our toils and perils compared to theirs? Why should we forsake the path of duty, and turn from mercy because of a cut-throat outlaw? I like not the sign of the times, but I am a Mormon; I trust in God."

"August Naab, I am a Mormon too," returned Cole, "but my hands are stained with blood. Soon yours will be if you keep your water-holes and your cattle. Yes, I know. You're strong, stronger than any of us, far off in your desert oasis, hemmed in by walls, cut off by cañons, guarded by your Navajo friends. But Holderness is creeping slowly on you. He'll ignore your water rights and drive your stock. Soon Dene will steal cattle under your very eyes. Don't make them enemies."

"I can't pass by this helpless man," rolled out August Naab's sonorous voice.

Suddenly, with livid face and shaking hand, Cole pointed westward. "There! Dene and his band! See, under the red wall; see the dust, not ten miles away. See them?"

The desert, gray in the foreground, purple in the distance, sloped to the west. Eyes keen as those of hawks searched the waste, and followed the red mountain rampart, which sheer in bold height and processional in its craggy sweep shut out the north. Far away little puffs of dust rose above the white sage, and creeping specks moved at a snail's pace.

"See them? Ah! then look, August Naab, look in the heavens above for my prophecy," cried Cole, fanatically. "The red sunset—the sign of the times—blood!"

A broad bar of dense black shut out the April sky, except in the extreme west, where a strip of pale blue formed background for several clouds of striking color and shape. They alone, in all that expanse, were dyed in the desert's sunset crimson. The largest projected from behind the dark cloud-bank in the shape of a huge fist, and the others, small and round, floated below. To Cole it seemed a giant hand, clutching, with inexorable strength, a bleeding heart. His terror spread to his companions as they stared.

Then, as light surrendered to shade, the sinister color faded; the tracing of the closed hand softened; flush and glow paled, leaving the sky purple, as if mirroring the desert floor. One golden shaft shot up, to be blotted out by sudden darkening change, and the sun had set.

"That may be God's will," said August Naab. "So be it. Martin Cole, take your men and go."

There was a word, half oath, half prayer, and then rattle of stirrups, the creak of saddles, and clink of spurs, followed by the driving rush of fiery horses. Cole and his men disappeared in a pall of yellow dust.

A wan smile lightened John Hare's face as he spoke weakly: "I fear your—generous act—can't save me and may bring you harm. I'd rather you left me—seeing you have women in your party."

"Don't try to talk yet," said August Naab. "You're

faint. Here—drink." He stooped to Hare, who was leaning against a sage-bush, and held a flask to his lips. Rising, he called to his men: "Make camp, sons. We've an hour before the outlaws come up, and if they don't go round the sand-dune we'll have longer."

Hare's flagging senses rallied, and he forgot himself in wonder. While the bustle went on, unhitching of wagon-teams, hobbling and feeding of horses, unpacking of camp-supplies, Naab appeared to be lost in deep meditation or prayer. Not once did he glance backward over the trail on which peril was fast approaching. His gaze was fastened on a ridge to the east where desert line, fringed by stunted cedars, met the pale-blue sky, and for a long time he neither spoke nor stirred. At length he turned to the camp-fire; he raked out red coals and placed the iron pots in position, by way of assistance to the women who were preparing the evening meal.

A cool wind blew in from the desert, rustling the sage, sifting the sand, fanning the dull coals to burning opals. Twilight failed and night fell; one by one great stars shone out, cold and bright. From the zone of blackness surrounding the camp burst the short bark, the hungry whine, the long-drawn-out wail of desert wolves.

"Supper, sons," called Naab, as he replenished the fire with an armful of grease-wood.

Naab's sons had his stature, though not his bulk. They were wiry, rangy men, young, yet somehow old. The desert had multiplied their years. Hare could not have told one face from another, the bronze skin and steel eye and hard line of each were so alike. The women, one middle-aged, the others young, were of comely, serious aspect.

"Mescal," called the Mormon.

A slender girl slipped from one of the covered wagons; she was dark, supple, straight as an Indian.

August Naab dropped to his knees, and, as the members of his family bowed their heads, he extended his hands over them and over the food laid on the ground.

"Lord, we kneel in humble thanksgiving. Bless this food to our use. Strengthen us, guide us, keep us as Thou hast in the past. Bless this stranger within our gates. Help us to help him. Teach us Thy ways, O Lord—Amen."

Hare found himself flushing and thrilling, found himself unable to control a painful binding in his throat. In forty-eight hours he had learned to hate the Mormons unutterably; here, in the presence of this austere man, he felt that hatred wrenched from his heart, and in its place stirred something warm and living. He was glad, for if he had to die, as he believed, either from the deed of evil men or from this last struggle of his wasted body, he did not want to die in bitterness. That simple prayer recalled the home he had long since left in Connecticut, and the time when he used to tease his sister and anger his father and hurt his mother while grace was being said at the breakfast-table. Now he was alone in the world, sick and dependent upon the kindness of these strangers. But they were really friends—it was a wonderful thought.

"Mescal, wait on the stranger," said August Naab, and the girl knelt beside him, tendering meat and drink. His nerveless fingers refused to hold the cup, and she put it to his lips while he drank. Hot coffee revived him; he ate and grew stronger, and readily began to talk when the Mormon asked for his story.

"There isn't much to tell. My name is Hare. I am twenty-four. My parents are dead. I came West because the doctors said I couldn't live in the East. At first I got better. But my money gave out and work became a necessity. I tramped from place to place, ending up ill in Salt Lake City. People were kind to me there. Some one got me a job with a big cattle company, and sent me to Marysvale, southward over the bleak plains. It was cold; I was ill when I reached Lund. Before I even knew what my duties were—for at Lund I was to begin work—men called me a spy. A fellow named Chance threatened me. An innkeeper led me out the back way, gave me bread and water, and said: 'Take this road to Bane; it's sixteen miles. If you make it some one'll give you a lift North.' I walked all night, and all the next day. Then I wandered on till I dropped here where you found me."

"You missed the road to Bane," said Naab. "This is the trail to White Sage. It's a trail of sand and stone that leaves no tracks, a lucky thing for you. Dene wasn't in Lund while you were there—else you wouldn't be here. He hasn't seen you, and he can't be certain of your trail. Maybe he rode to Bane, but still we may find a way—"

One of his sons whistled low, causing Naab to rise slowly, to peer into the darkness, to listen intently.

"Here, get up," he said, extending a hand to Hare. "Pretty shaky, eh? Can you walk? Give me a hold—there.... Mescal, come." The slender girl obeyed, gliding noiselessly like a shadow. "Take his arm." Between them they led Hare to a jumble of stones on the outer edge of the circle of light.

"It wouldn't do to hide," continued Naab, lowering his voice to a swift whisper; "that might be fatal. You're in sight from the camp-fire, but indistinct. By-and-by the outlaws will get here, and if any of them prowl around close, you and Mescal must pretend to be sweethearts. Understand? They'll pass by Mormon love-making without a second look. Now, lad, courage.... Mescal, it may save his life."

Naab returned to the fire, his shadow looming in gigantic proportions on the white canopy of a covered wagon. Fitful gusts of wind fretted the blaze; it roared and crackled and sputtered, now illuminating the still forms, then enveloping them in fantastic obscurity. Hare shivered, perhaps from the cold air, perhaps from growing dread. Westward lay the desert, an impenetrable black void; in front, the gloomy mountain wall lifted jagged peaks close to the stars; to the right rose the ridge, the rocks and stunted cedars of its summit standing in weird relief. Suddenly Hare's fugitive glance descried a dark object; he watched intently as it moved and rose from behind the summit of the ridge to make a bold black figure silhouetted against the cold clearness of the sky. He saw it distinctly, realized it was close, and breathed hard as the wind-swept mane and tail, the lean, wild shape and single plume resolved themselves into the unmistakable outline of an Indian mustang and rider.

"Look!" he whispered to the girl. "See, a mounted Indian, there on the ridge—there, he's gone—no, I see him again. But that's another. Look! there are more." He ceased in breathless suspense and stared fearfully at a line of mounted Indians moving in single file over the ridge to become lost to view in the intervening blackness. A faint rattling of gravel and the peculiar crack of unshod hoof on stone gave reality to that shadowy train.

"Navajos," said Mescal.

"Navajos!" he echoed. "I heard of them at Lund; 'desert hawks' the men called them, worse than Piutes. Must we not alarm the men?—You—aren't you afraid?"

"No."

"But they are hostile."

"Not to him." She pointed at the stalwart figure standing against the firelight.

"Ah! I remember. The man Cole spoke of friendly Navajos. They must be close by. What does it mean?"

"I'm not sure. I think they are out there in the cedars, waiting."

"Waiting! For what?"

"Perhaps for a signal."

"Then they were expected?"

"I don't know; I only guess. We used to ride often to White Sage and Lund; now we go seldom, and when we do there seem to be Navajos near the camp at night, and riding the ridges by day. I believe Father Naab knows."

"Your father's risking much for me. He's good. I wish I could show my gratitude."

"I call him Father Naab, but he is not my father."

"A niece or granddaughter, then?"

"I'm no relation. Father Naab raised me in his family. My mother was Navajo, my father a Spaniard."

"Why!" exclaimed Hare. "When you came out of the wagon I took you for an Indian girl. But the moment you spoke—you talk so well—no one would dream—"

"Mormons are well educated and teach the children they raise," she said, as he paused in embarrassment.

He wanted to ask if she were a Mormon by religion, but the question seemed curious and unnecessary. His interest was aroused; he realized suddenly that he had found pleasure in her low voice; it was new and strange, unlike any woman's voice he had ever heard; and he regarded her closely. He had only time for a glance at her straight, clean-cut profile, when she turned startled eyes on him, eyes black as the night. And they were eyes that looked through and beyond him. She held up a hand, slowly bent toward the wind, and whispered:

"Listen."

Hare heard nothing save the barking of coyotes and the breeze in the sage. He saw, however, the men rise from round the camp-fire to face the north, and the women climb into the wagon and close the canvas flaps And he prepared himself, with what fortitude he could command, for the approach of the outlaws. He waited, straining to catch a sound. His heart throbbed audibly, like a muffled drum, and for an endless moment his ears seemed deadened to aught else. Then a stronger puff of wind whipped in, bringing the rhythmic beat of flying hoofs. Suspense ended. Hare felt the easing of a weight upon him. Whatever was to be his fate, it would be soon decided. The sound grew into a clattering roar. A black mass hurled itself over the border of opaque circle, plunged into the light, and halted.

August Naab deliberately threw a bundle of grease-wood upon the camp-fire. A blaze leaped up, sending abroad a red flare. "Who comes?" he called.

"Friends, Mormons, friends," was the answer.

"Get down—friends—and come to the fire."

Three horsemen advanced to the foreground; others, a troop of eight or ten, remained in the shadow, a silent group.

Hare sank back against the stone. He knew the foremost of those horsemen, though he had never seen him.

"Dene," whispered Mescal, and confirmed his instinctive fear.

Hare was nervously alive to the handsome presence of the outlaw. Glimpses that he had caught of "bad" men returned vividly as he noted the clean-shaven face, the youthful, supple body, the cool, careless mien. Dene's eyes glittered as he pulled off his gauntlets and beat the sand out of them; and but for that quick fierce glance his leisurely friendly manner would have disarmed suspicion.

"Are you the Mormon Naab?" he queried.

"August Naab, I am."

"Dry camp, eh? Hosses tired, I reckon. Shore it's a sandy trail. Where's the rest of you fellers?"

"Cole and his men were in a hurry to make White Sage to-night. They were travelling light; I've heavy wagons."

"Naab, I reckon you shore wouldn't tell a lie?"

"I have never lied."

"Heerd of a young feller that was in Lund—pale chap—lunger, we'd call him back West?"

"I heard that he had been mistaken for a spy at Lund and had fled toward Bane."

"Hain't seen nothin' of him this side of Lund?"

"No."

"Seen any Navvies?"

"Yes."

The outlaw stared hard at him. Apparently he was about to speak of the Navajos, for his quick uplift of head at Naab's blunt affirmative suggested the impulse. But he checked himself and slowly drew on his gloves.

"Naab, I'm shore comin' to visit you some day. Never been over thet range. Heerd you hed fine water, fine cattle. An' say, I seen thet little Navajo girl you have, an' I wouldn't mind seein' her again."

August Naab kicked the fire into brighter blaze. "Yes, fine range," he presently replied, his gaze fixed on Dene. "Fine water, fine cattle, fine browse. I've a fine graveyard, too; thirty graves, and not one a woman's. Fine place for graves, the cañon country. You don't have to dig. There's one grave the Indians never named; it's three thousand feet deep."

"Thet must be in hell," replied Dene, with a smile, ignoring the covert meaning. He leisurely surveyed Naab's four sons, the wagons and horses, till his eye fell upon Hare and Mescal. With that he swung in his saddle as if to dismount.

"I shore want a look around."

"Get down, get down," returned the Mormon.

The deep voice, unwelcoming, vibrant with an odd ring, would have struck a less suspicious man than Dene. The outlaw swung his leg back over the pommel, sagged in the saddle, and appeared to be pondering the question. Plainly he was uncertain of his ground. But his indecision was brief. "Two-Spot, you look 'em over," he ordered.

The third horseman dismounted and went toward the wagons.

Hare, watching this scene, became conscious that his fear had intensified with the recognition of Two-Spot as Chance, the outlaw whom he would not soon forget. In his excitement he moved against Mescal and felt her trembling violently.

"Are you afraid?" he whispered.

"Yes, of Dene."

The outlaw rummaged in one of the wagons, pulled aside the canvas flaps of the other, laughed harshly, and then with clinking spurs tramped through the camp, kicking the beds, overturning a pile of saddles, and making disorder generally, till he spied the couple sitting on the stone in the shadow.

As the outlaw lurched that way, Hare, with a start of recollection, took Mescal in his arms and leaned his head against hers. He felt one of her hands lightly brush his shoulder and rest there, trembling.

Shuffling footsteps scraped the sand, sounded nearer and nearer, slowed and paused.

"Sparkin'! Dead to the world. Haw! Haw! Haw!"

The coarse laugh gave place to moving footsteps. The rattling clink of stirrup and spur mingled with the restless stamp of horse. Chance had mounted. Dene's voice drawled out: "Good-bye, Naab. I shore will see you all some day." The heavy thuds of many hoofs evened into a roar that diminished as it rushed away.

In unutterable relief Hare realized his deliverance.

He tried to rise, but power of movement had gone from him.

He was fainting, yet his sensations were singularly acute. Mescal's hand dropped from his shoulder; her cheek, that had been cold against his, grew hot; she quivered through all her slender length. Confusion claimed his senses. Gratitude and hope flooded his soul. Something sweet and beautiful, the touch of this desert girl, rioted in his blood; his heart swelled in exquisite agony. Then he was whirling in darkness; and he knew no more.

CHAPTER II

White Sage

THE NIGHT was as a blank to Hare; the morning like a drifting of hazy clouds before his eyes. He felt himself moving; and when he awakened clearly to consciousness he lay upon a couch on the vine-covered porch of a cottage. He saw August Naab open a garden gate to admit Martin Cole. They met as friends; no trace of scorn marred August's greeting, and Martin was not the same man who had shown fear on the desert. His welcome was one of respectful regard for his superior.

"Elder, I heard you were safe in," he said, fervently. "We feared—I know not what. I was distressed till I got the news of your arrival. How's the young man?"

"He's very ill. But while there's life there's hope."

"Will the Bishop administer to him?"

"Gladly, if the young man's willing. Come, let's go in."

"Wait, August," said Cole. "Did you know your son Snap was in the village?"

"My son here!" August Naab betrayed anxiety. "I left him home with work. He shouldn't have come. Is—is he—"

"He's drinking and in an ugly mood. It seems he traded horses with Jeff Larsen, and got the worst of the deal. There's pretty sure to be a fight."

"He always hated Larsen."

"Small wonder. Larsen is mean; he's as bad as we've got and that's saying a good deal. Snap has done worse things than fight with Larsen. He's doing a worse thing now, August—he's too friendly with Dene."

"I've heard—I've heard it before. But, Martin, what can I do?"

"Do? God knows. What can any of us do? Times have changed, August. Dene is here in White Sage, free, welcome in many homes. Some of our neighbors, perhaps men we trust, are secret members of this rustler's band."

"You're right, Cole. There are Mormons who are cattle-thieves. To my eternal shame I confess it. Under cover of night they ride with Dene, and here in our midst they meet him in easy tolerance. Driven from Montana, he comes here to corrupt our young men. God's mercy!"

"August, some of our young men need no one to corrupt them. Dene had no great task to win them. He rode in here with a few outlaws and now he has a strong band. We've got to face it. We haven't any law, but he can be killed. Someone must kill him. Yet bad as Dene is, he doesn't threaten our living as Holderness does. Dene steals a few cattle, kills a man here and there. Holderness reaches out and takes our springs. Because we've no law to stop him, he steals the blood of our life—water—water—

God's gift to the desert! Some one must kill Holderness, too!"

"Martin, this lust to kill is a fearful thing. Come in; you must pray with the Bishop."

"No, it's not prayer I need, Elder," replied Cole, stubbornly. "I'm still a good Mormon. What I want is the stock I've lost, and my fields green again."

August Naab had no answer for his friend. A very old man with snow-white hair and beard came out on the porch.

"Bishop, brother Martin is railing again," said Naab, as Cole bared his head.

"Martin, my son, unbosom thyself," rejoined the Bishop.

"Black doubt and no light," said Cole, despondently. "I'm of the younger generation of Mormons, and faith is harder for me. I see signs you can't see. I've had trials hard to bear. I was rich in cattle, sheep, and water. These Gentiles, this rancher Holderness and this outlaw Dene, have driven my cattle, killed my sheep, piped my water off my fields. I don't like the present. We are no longer in the old days. Our young men are drifting away, and the few who return come with ideas opposed to Mormonism. Our girls and boys are growing up influenced by the Gentiles among us. They intermarry, and that's a death-blow to our creed."

"Martin, cast out this poison from your heart. Return to your faith. The millennium will come. Christ will reign on earth again. The ten tribes of Israel will be restored. The Book of Mormon is the Word of God. The creed will live. We may suffer here and die, but our spirits will go marching on; and the City of Zion will be builded over our graves."

Cole held up his hands in a meekness that signified hope if not faith.

August Naab bent over Hare. "I would like to have the Bishop administer to you," he said.

"What's that?" asked Hare.

"A Mormon custom, 'the laying on of hands.' We know its efficacy in trouble and illness. A Bishop of the Mormon Church has the gift of tongues, of prophecy, of revelation, of healing. Let him administer to you. It entails no obligation. Accept it as a prayer."

"I'm willing," replied the young man.

Thereupon Naab spoke a few low words to some one through the open door. Voices ceased; soft footsteps sounded without; women crossed the threshold, followed by tall young men and rosy-cheeked girls and round-eyed children. A white-haired old woman came forward with solemn dignity. She carried a silver bowl which she held for the Bishop as he stood close by Hare's couch. The Bishop put his hands into the bowl, anointing them with fragrant oil; then he placed them on the young man's head, and offered up a brief prayer, beautiful in its simplicity and tremulous utterance.

The ceremony ended, the onlookers came forward with pleasant words on their lips, pleasant smiles on their faces. The children filed by his couch, bashful yet sympathetic; the women murmured, the young men grasped his hand. Mescal flitted by with downcast eye, with shy smile, but no word.

"Your fever is gone," said August Naab, with his hand on Hare's cheek.

"It comes and goes suddenly," replied Hare. "I feel better now, only I'm oppressed. I can't breathe freely. I want air, and I'm hungry."

"Mother Mary, the lad's hungry. Judith, Esther, where are your wits? Help your mother. Mescal, wait on him, see to his comfort."

Mescal brought a little table and a pillow, and the

other girls soon followed with food and drink; then they hovered about, absorbed in caring for him.

"They said I fell among thieves," mused Hare, when he was once more alone. "I've fallen among saints as well." He felt that he could never repay this August Naab. "If only I might live!" he ejaculated. How restful was this cottage garden! The greensward was a balm to his eyes. Flowers new to him, though of familiar springtime hue, lifted fresh faces everywhere; fruit-trees, with branches intermingling, blended the white and pink of blossoms. There was the soft laughter of children in the garden. Strange birds darted among the trees. Their notes were new, but their song was the old delicious monotone—the joy of living and love of spring. A green-bowered irrigation ditch led by the porch and unseen water flowed gently, with gurgle and tinkle, with music in its hurry. Innumerable bees murmured amid the blossoms.

Hare fell asleep. Upon returning drowsily to consciousness he caught through half-open eyes the gleam of level shafts of gold sunlight low down in the trees; then he felt himself being carried into the house to be laid upon a bed. Some one gently unbuttoned his shirt at the neck, removed his shoes, and covered him with a blanket. Before he had fully awakened he was left alone, and quiet settled over the house. A languorous sense of ease and rest lulled him to sleep again. In another moment, it seemed to him, he was awake; bright daylight streamed through the window, and a morning breeze stirred the faded curtain.

The drag in his breathing which was always a forerunner of a coughing-spell warned him now; he put on coat and shoes and went outside, where his cough attacked him, had its sway, and left him.

"Good-morning," sang out August Naab's cheery voice. "Sixteen hours of sleep, my lad!"

"I did sleep, didn't I? No wonder I feel well this morning. A peculiarity of my illness is that one day I'm down, the next day up."

"With the goodness of God, my lad, we'll gradually increase the days up. Go in to breakfast. Afterward I want to talk to you. This'll be a busy day for me, shoeing the horses and packing supplies. I want to start for home to-morrow."

Hare pondered over Naab's words while he ate. The suggestion in them, implying a relation to his future, made him wonder if the good Mormon intended to take him to his desert home. He hoped so, and warmed anew to this friend. But he had no enthusiasm for himself; his future seemed hopeless.

Naab was waiting for him on the porch, and drew him away from the cottage down the path toward the gate.

"I want you to go home with me."

"You're kind—I'm only a sort of beggar. I've no strength left to work my way. I'll go—though it's only to die."

"I haven't the gift of revelation—yet somehow I see that you won't die of this illness. You will come home with me. It's a beautiful place, my Navajo oasis. The Indians call it the Garden of Eschtah. If you can get well anywhere it'll be there."

"I'll go—but I ought not. What can I do for you? Nothing."

"No man can ever tell what he may do for another. The time may come—well, John, is it settled?" He offered his huge broad hand.

"It's settled—I—" Hare faltered as he put his hand in Naab's. The Mormon's grip straightened his frame and braced him. Strength and simplicity flowed from the giant's toil-hardened palm. Hare swallowed his thanks along with his emotion, and for what he had intended to say he substituted: "No

one ever called me John. I don't know the name.
Call me Jack."

"Very well, Jack, and now let's see. You'll need
some things from the store. Can you come with me?
It's not far."

"Surely. And now what I need most is a razor to
scrape the alkali and stubble off my face."

The wide street, bordered by cottages peeping out
of green and white orchards, stretched in a straight
line to the base of the ascent which led up to the
Pink Cliffs. A green square enclosed a gray church, a
school-house and public hall. Farther down the main
thoroughfare were several weather-boarded white-
washed stores. Two dusty men were riding along,
one on each side of the wildest, most vicious little
horse Hare had ever seen. It reared and bucked and
kicked, trying to escape from two lassoes. In front of
the largest store were a number of mustangs all
standing free, with bridles thrown over their heads
and trailing on the ground. The loungers leaning
against the railing and about the doors were lank
brown men very like Naab's sons. Some wore sheep-
skin "chaps," some blue overalls; all wore boots and
spurs, wide soft hats, and in their belts, far to the
back, hung large Colt's revolvers.

"We'll buy what you need, just as if you expected
to ride the ranges for me to-morrow," said Naab.
"The first thing we ask a new man is, can he ride?
Next, can he shoot?"

"I could ride before I got so weak. I've never handled a revolver, but I can shoot a rifle. Never shot at
anything except targets, and it seemed to come natural for me to hit them."

"Good. We'll show you some targets—lions,
bears, deer, cats, wolves. There's a fine forty-four
Winchester here that my friend Abe has been trying
to sell. It has a long barrel and weighs eight pounds.
Our desert riders like the light carbines that go

easy on a saddle. Most of the mustangs aren't weight-carriers. This rifle has a great range; I've shot it, and it's just the gun for you to use on wolves and coyotes. You'll need a Colt and a saddle, too."

"By-the-way," he went on, as they mounted the store steps, "here's the kind of money we use in this country." He handed Hare a slip of blue paper, a written check for a sum of money, signed, but without register of bank or name of firm. "We don't use real money," he added. "There's very little coin or currency in southern Utah. Most of the Gentiles lately come in have money, and some of us Mormons have a bag or two of gold, but scarcely any of it gets into circulation. We use these checks, which go from man to man sometimes for six months. The roundup of a check means sheep, cattle, horses, grain, merchandise or labor. Every man gets his real money's value without paying out an actual cent."

"Such a system at least means honest men," said Hare, laughing his surprise.

They went into a wide door to tread a maze of narrow aisles between boxes and barrels, stacks of canned vegetables, and piles of harness and dry goods; they entered an open space where several men leaned on a counter.

"Hello, Abe," said Naab; "seen anything of Snap?"

"Hello, August. Yes, Snap's inside. So's Holderness. Says he rode in off the range on purpose to see you." Abe designated an open doorway from which issued loud voices. Hare glanced into a long narrow room full of smoke and the fumes of rum. Through the haze he made out a crowd of men at a rude bar. Abe went to the door and called out: "Hey, Snap, your dad wants you. Holderness, here's August Naab."

A man staggered up the few steps leading to the store and swayed in. His long face had a hawkish cast, and it was gray, not with age, but with the sage–gray of the desert. His eyes were of the same hue, cold yet burning with little fiery flecks in their depths. He appeared short of stature because of a curvature of the spine, but straightened up he would have been tall. He wore a blue flannel shirt, and blue overalls; round his lean hips was a belt holding two Colt's revolvers, their heavy, dark butts projecting outward, and he had on high boots with long, cruel spurs.

"Howdy, father?" he said.

"I'm packing to-day," returned August Naab. "We ride out to-morrow. I need your help."

"All right. When I get my pinto from Larsen."

"Never mind Larsen. If he got the better of you let the matter drop."

"Jeff got my pinto for a mustang with three legs. If I hadn't been drunk I'd never have traded. So I'm looking for Jeff."

He bit out the last words with a peculiar snap of his long teeth, a circumstance which caused Hare instantly to associate the savage clicking with the name he had heard given this man. August Naab looked at him with gloomy eyes and stern shut mouth, an expression of righteous anger, helplessness and grief combined, the look of a man to whom obstacles had been nothing, at last confronted with crowning defeat. Hare realized that this son was Naab's first-born, best-loved, a thorn in his side, a black sheep.

"Say, father, is that the spy you found on the trail?" Snap's pale eyes gleamed on Hare and the little flames seemed to darken and leap.

"This is John Hare, the young man I found. But he's not a spy."

"You can't make any one believe that. He's down as a spy. Dene's spy! His name's gone over the ranges as a counter of unbranded stock. Dene has

named him and Dene has marked him. Don't take
him home, as you've taken so many sick and hunted
men before. What's the good of it? You never made
a Mormon of one of them yet. Don't take him—
unless you want another grave for your cemetery.
Ha! Ha!"

Hare recoiled with a shock. Snap Naab swayed to
the door and stepped down, all the time with his
face over his shoulder, his baleful glance on Hare;
then the blue haze swallowed him.

The several loungers went out; August engaged
the storekeeper in conversation, introducing Hare
and explaining their wants. They inspected the various needs of a range-rider, selecting, in the end, not
the few suggested by Hare, but the many chosen by
Naab. The last purchase was the rifle Naab had
talked about. It was a beautiful weapon, finely polished and carved, entirely out of place among the
plain coarse-sighted and coarse-stocked guns in the
rack.

"Never had a chance to sell it," said Abe. "Too
long and heavy for the riders. I'll let it go cheap,
half price, and the cartridges also, two thousand."

"Taken," replied Naab, quickly, with a satisfaction
which showed he liked a bargain.

"August, you must be going to shoot some?" queried Abe. "Something bigger than rabbits and coyotes. It's about time—even if you are an Elder. We
Mormons must—" he broke off, continuing in a low
tone: "Here's Holderness now."

Hare wheeled with the interest that had gathered
with the reiteration of this man's name. A new-
comer stooped to get in the door. He outtopped
even Naab in height, and was a superb blond-
bearded man, striding with the spring of a moun-
taineer.

"Good-day to you, Naab," he said. "Is this the
young fellow you picked up?"

"Yes. Jack Hare," rejoined Naab.

"Well, Hare, I'm Holderness. You'll recall my name. You were sent to Lund by men interested in my ranges. I expected to see you in Lund, but couldn't get over."

Hare met the proffered hand with his own, and as he had recoiled from Snap Naab so now he received another shock, different indeed but impelling in its power, instinctive of some great portent. Hare was impressed by an indefinable subtlety, a nameless distrust, as colorless as the clear penetrating amber lightness of the eyes that bent upon him.

"Holderness, will you right the story about Hare?" inquired Naab.

"You mean about his being a spy? Well, Naab, the truth is that was his job. I advised against sending a man down here for that sort of work. It won't do. These Mormons will steal each other's cattle, and they've got to get rid of them; so they won't have a man taking account of stock, brands, and all that. If the Mormons would stand for it the rustlers wouldn't. I'll take Hare out to the ranch and give him work, if he wants. But he'd do best to leave Utah."

"Thank you, no," replied Hare, decidedly.

"He's going with me," said August Naab.

Holderness accepted this with an almost imperceptible nod, and he swept Hare with eyes that searched and probed for latent possibilities. It was the keen intelligence of a man who knew what development meant on the desert; not in any sense an interest in the young man at present. Then he turned back.

Hare, feeling that Holderness wished to talk with Naab, walked to the counter and began assorting his purchases, but he could not help hearing what was said.

"Lungs bad?" queried Holderness.

"One of them," replied Naab.

"He's all in. Better send him out of the country. He's got the name of Dene's spy and he'll never get another on this desert. Dene will kill him. This isn't good judgment, Naab, to take him with you. Even your friends don't like it, and it means trouble for you."

"We've settled it," said Naab, coldly.

"Well, remember, I've warned you. I've tried to be friendly with you, Naab, but you won't have it. Anyway, I've wanted to see you lately to find out how we stand."

"What do you mean?"

"How we stand on several things—to begin with, there's Mescal."

"You asked me several times for Mescal, and I said no."

"But I never said I'd marry her. Now I want her, and I will marry her."

"No," rejoined Naab, adding brevity to his coldness.

"Why not?" demanded Holderness. "Oh, well, I can't take that as an insult. I know there's not enough money in Utah to get a girl away from a Mormon. . . . About the offer for the water-rights— how do we stand? I'll give you ten thousand dollars for the rights to Seeping Springs and Silver Cup."

"Ten thousand!" ejaculated Naab. "Holderness, I wouldn't take a hundred thousand. You might as well ask to buy my home, my stock, my range, twenty years of toil, for ten thousand dollars!"

"You refuse? All right. I think I've made you a fair proposition," said Holderness, in a smooth, quick tone. "The land is owned by the Government, and though your ranges are across the Arizona line they really figure as Utah land. My company's spending big money, and the Government won't let you have a monopoly. No one man can control the water-supply of a hundred miles of range. Times are changing. You want to see that. You ought to protect yourself before it's too late."

"Holderness, this is a desert. No men save Mormons could ever have made it habitable. The Government scarcely knows of its existence. It'll be fifty years before there's any law here. Listen. This desert belongs to the Mormons. We found the springs, dug the ditches. No man can come in here to take our water."

"Why can't he? The water doesn't belong to anyone. Why can't he?"

"Because of the unwritten law of the desert. No Mormon would refuse you or your horse a drink, or even a reasonable supply for your stock. But you can't come in here and take our water for your own use, to supplant us, to parch our stock. Why, even an Indian respects desert law!"

"Bah! I'm not a Mormon or an Indian. I'm a cattleman. It's plain business with me. Once more I make you the offer."

Naab scorned to reply. The men faced each other for a silent moment, their glances scintillating. Then Holderness whirled on his heel, jostling into Hare.

"Get out of my way," said the rancher, in the disgust of intense irritation. He swung his arm, and his open hand sent Hare reeling against the counter.

"Jack," said Naab, breathing hard, "Holderness showed his real self to-day. I always knew it, yet I gave him the benefit of the doubt. . . . For him to strike you! I've not the gift of revelation, but I see— Let us go."

On the return to the Bishop's cottage Naab did not speak once; the transformation which had begun with the appearance of his drunken son had reached a climax of gloomy silence after the clash with Holderness. Naab went directly to the Bishop, and presently the quavering voice of the old minister rose in prayer.

Hare dropped wearily into the chair on the porch; and presently fell into a doze, from which he awakened with a start. Naab's sons, with Martin Cole and several other men, were standing in the yard. Naab himself was gently crowding the women into the house. When he got them all inside he closed the door and turned to Cole.

"Was it a fair fight?"

"Yes, an even break. They met in front of Abe's. I saw the meeting. Neither was surprised. They stood for a moment watching each other. Then they drew—only Snap was quicker. Larsen's gun went off as he fell. That trick you taught Snap saved his life again. Larsen was no slouch on the draw."

"Where's Snap now?"

"Gone after his pinto. He was sober. Said he'd pack at once. Larsen's friends are ugly. Snap said to tell you to hurry out of the village with young Hare, if you want to take him at all. Dene has ridden in; he swears you won't take Hare away."

"We're all packed and ready to hitch up," returned Naab. "We could start at once, only until dark I'd rather take chances here than out on the trail."

"Snap said Dene would ride right into the Bishop's after Hare."

"No. He wouldn't dare."

"Father!" Dave Naab spoke sharply from where he stood high on a grassy bank. "Here's Dene now, riding up with Culver, and some man I don't know. They're coming in. Dene's jumped the fence! Look out!"

A clatter of hoofs and rattling of gravel preceded the appearance of a black horse in the garden path. His rider bent low to dodge the vines of the arbor, and reined in before the porch to slip out of the saddle with the agility of an Indian. It was Dene, dark, smiling, nonchalant.

"What do you seek in the house of a Bishop?" challenged August Naab, planting his broad bulk square before Hare.

"Dene's spy!"

"What do you seek in the house of a Bishop?" repeated Naab.

"I shore want to see the young feller you lied to me about," returned Dene, his smile slowly fading.

"No speech could be a lie to an outlaw."

"I want him, you Mormon preacher!"

"You can't have him."

"I'll shore get him."

In one great stride Naab confronted and towered over Dene.

The rustler's gaze shifted warily from Naab to the quiet Mormons and back again. Then his right hand quivered and shot downward. Naab's act was even quicker. A Colt gleamed and whirled to the grass, and the outlaw cried out as his arm cracked in the Mormon's grasp.

Dave Naab leaped off the bank directly in front of Dene's approaching companions, and faced them, alert and silent, his hand on his hip.

August Naab swung the outlaw against the porch-post and held him there with brawny arm.

"Whelp of an evil breed!" he thundered, shaking his gray head. "Do you think we fear you and your gun-sharp tricks? Look! See this!" He released Dene and stepped back with his hand before him. Suddenly it moved, quicker than sight, and a Colt revolver lay in his outstretched palm. He dropped it back into the holster. "Let that teach you never to draw on me again." He doubled his huge fist and shoved it before Dene's eyes. "One blow would crack your skull like an egg-shell. Why don't I deal it? Because, you mindless hell-hound, because there's a higher law than man's—God's law—Thou shalt not kill! Understand that if you can. Leave me and mine alone from this day. Now go!"

He pushed Dene down the path into the arms of his companions.

"Out with you!" said Dave Naab. "Hurry! Get your horse. Hurry! I'm not so particular about God as Dad is!"

CHAPTER III

The Trail of the Red Wall

AFTER THE departure of Dene and his comrades Naab decided to leave White Sage at nightfall. Martin Cole and the Bishop's sons tried to persuade him to remain, urging that the trouble sure to come could be more safely met in the village. Naab, however, was obdurate, unreasonably so, Cole said, unless there were some good reason why he wished to strike the trail in the night. When twilight closed in Naab had his teams ready and the women shut in the canvas-covered wagons. Hare was to ride in an open wagon, one that Naab had left at White Sage to be loaded with grain. When it grew so dark that objects were scarcely discernible a man vaulted the cottage fence.

"Dave, where are the boys?" asked Naab.

"Not so loud! The boys are coming," replied Dave in a whisper. "Dene is wild. I guess you snapped a bone in his arm. He swears he'll kill us all. But Chance and the rest of the gang won't be in till late.

We've time to reach the Coconina Trail, if we hustle."

"Any news of Snap?"

"He rode out before sundown."

Three more forms emerged from the gloom.

"All right, boys. Go ahead, Dave, you lead."

Dave and George Naab mounted their mustangs and rode through the gate; the first wagon rolled after them, its white dome gradually dissolving in the darkness; the second one started; then August Naab stepped to his seat on the third with a low cluck to the team. Hare shut the gate and climbed over the tail-board of the wagon.

A slight swish of weeds and grasses brushing the wheels was all the sound made in the cautious advance. A bare field lay to the left; to the right low roofs and sharp chimneys showed among the trees; here and there lights twinkled. No one hailed; not a dog barked.

Presently the leaders turned into a road where the iron hoofs and wheels cracked and crunched the stones.

Hare thought he saw something in the deep shade of a line of poplar-trees; he peered closer, and made out a motionless horse and rider, just a shade blacker than the deepest gloom. The next instant they vanished, and the rapid clatter of hoofs down the road told Hare his eyes had not deceived him.

"Getup," growled Naab to his horses. "Jack, did you see that fellow?"

"Yes. What was he doing there?"

"Watching the road. He's one of Dene's scouts."

"Will Dene—"

One of Naab's sons came trotting back. "Think that was Larsen's pal. He was laying in wait for Snap."

"I thought he was a scout for Dene," replied August.

"Maybe he's that too."

"Likely enough. Hurry along and keep the gray team going lively. They've had a week's rest."

Hare watched the glimmering lights of the village vanish one by one, like Jack-o'-lanterns. The horses kept a steady even trot on into the huge windy hall of the desert night. Fleecy clouds veiled the stars, yet transmitted a wan glow. A chill crept over Hare. As he crawled under the blankets Naab had spread for him his hand came into contact with a polished metal surface cold as ice. It was his rifle. Naab had placed it under the blankets. Fingering the rifle, Hare found the spring opening on the right side of the breech, and, pressing it down, he felt the round head of a cartridge. Naab had loaded the weapon, he had placed it where Hare's hand must find it, yet he had not spoken of it. Hare did not stop to reason with his first impulse. Without a word, with silent insistence, disregarding his shattered health, August Naab had given him a man's part to play. The full meaning lifted Hare out of his self-abasement; once more he felt himself a man.

Hare soon yielded to the warmth of the blankets; a drowsiness that he endeavored in vain to throw off smothered his thoughts; sleep glued his eyelids tight. They opened again some hours later. For a moment he could not realize where he was; then the whip of the cold wind across his face, the woolly feel and smell of the blankets, and finally the steady trot of horses and the clink of a chain swinging somewhere under him, recalled the actuality of the night ride. He wondered how many miles had been covered, how the drivers knew the direction and kept the horses in the trail, and whether the outlaws were in pursuit. When Naab stopped the team and, climbing down, walked back some rods to listen, Hare felt sure that Dene was coming. He listened, too, but the movements of the horses and the rattle of their harness were all the sounds he could hear. Naab returned to his seat; the team started, now no longer in a trot; they were climbing. After that Hare fell into a slumber in which he could hear the slow grating whirr of wheels, and when it ceased he awoke to raise himself and turn his ear to the back trail. By-and-by he discovered that the black night had changed to gray; dawn was not far distant; he dozed and wakened to clear light. A rose-red horizon lay far below and to the eastward; the intervening descent was like a rolling sea with league-long swells.

"Glad you slept some," was Naab's greeting. "No sign of Dene yet. If we can get over the divide we're safe. That's Coconina there, Fire Mountain in Navajo meaning. It's a plateau low and narrow at this end, but it runs far to the east and rises nine thousand feet. It forms a hundred miles of the north rim of the Grand Cañon. We're across the Arizona line now."

Hare followed the sweep of the ridge that rose to the eastward, but to his inexperienced eyes its appearance carried no sense of its noble proportions.

"Don't form any ideas of distance and size yet a while," said Naab, reading Hare's expression. "They'd only have to be made over as soon as you learn what light and air are in this country. It looks only half a mile to the top of the divide; well, if we make it by midday we're lucky. There, see a black spot over this way, far under the red wall? Look sharp. Good! That's Holderness's ranch. It's thirty miles from here. Nine Mile Valley heads in there. Once it belonged to Martin Cole. Holderness stole it. And he's begun to range over the divide."

The sun rose and warmed the chill air. Hare began to notice the increased height and abundance of the sage-brush, which was darker in color. The first cedar-tree, stunted in growth, dead at the top, was the half-way mark up the ascent, so Naab said; it was also the forerunner of other cedars which increased in number toward the summit. At length Hare, tired of looking upward at the creeping white wagons, closed his eyes. The wheels crunched on the stones; the horses heaved and labored. Naab's "Getup" was the only spoken sound; the sun beamed down warm, then hot; and the hours passed. Some unusual noise roused Hare out of his lethargy. The wagon was at a standstill. Naab stood on the seat with outstretched arm. George and Dave were close by their mustangs, and Snap Naab, mounted on a cream-colored pinto, reined him under August's arm, and faced the valley below.

"Maybe you'll make them out," said August. "I can't and I've watched those dust-clouds for hours. George can't decide, either."

Hare, looking at Snap, was attracted by the eyes from which his fathers and brothers expected so much. If ever a human being had the eyes of a hawk Snap Naab had them. The little brown flecks danced in clear pale yellow. Evidently Snap had not located the perplexing dust-clouds, for his glance drifted. Suddenly the remarkable vibration of his pupils ceased, and his glance grew fixed, steely, certain.

"That's a bunch of wild mustangs," he said.

Hare gazed till his eyes hurt, but could see neither clouds of dust nor moving objects. No more was said. The sons wheeled their mustangs and rode to the fore; August Naab reseated himself and took up the reins; the ascent proceeded. But it proceeded leisurely, with more frequent rests. At the end of an hour the horses toiled over the last rise to the summit and entered a level forest of cedars; in another hour they were descending gradually.

"Here we are at the tanks," said Naab.

Hare saw that they had come up with the other wagons. George Naab was leading a team down a rocky declivity to a pool of yellow water. The other boys were unharnessing and unsaddling.

"About three," said Naab, looking at the sun. "We're in good time. Jack, get out and stretch yourself. We camp here. There's the Coconina Trail where the Navajo go in after deer."

It was not a pretty spot, this little rock-strewn glade where the white hard trail forked with the road. The yellow water with its green scum made Hare sick. The horses drank with loud gulps. Naab and his sons drank of it. The women filled a pail and portioned it out in basins and washed their faces and hands with evident pleasure. Dave Naab whistled as he wielded an axe vigorously on a cedar. It came home to Hare that the tension of the past night and morning had relaxed. Whether to attribute that fact to the distance from White Sage or to the arrival at the water-hole he could not determine. But the certainty was shown in August's cheerful talk to the horses as he slipped bags of grain over their noses, and in the subdued laughter of the women. Hare sent up an unspoken thanksgiving that these good Mormons had apparently escaped from the dangers incurred for his sake. He sat with his back to a cedar and watched the kindling of fires, the deft manipulating of biscuit dough in a basin, and the steaming of pots. The generous meal was spread on a canvas cloth, around which men and women sat cross-legged, after the fashion of Indians. Hare found it hard to adapt his long legs to the posture, and he wondered how these men, whose legs were longer than his, could sit so easily. It was the crown of a cheerful dinner after hours of anxiety and abstinence to have Snap Naab speak civilly to him, and to see him bow his head meekly as his father asked the blessing. Snap ate as though he had utterly forgotten that he had recently killed a man; to hear the others talk to him one would suppose that they had forgotten it also.

All had finished eating, except Snap and Dave Naab, when one of the mustangs neighed shrilly. Hare would not have noticed it but for looks exchanged among the men. The glances were explained a few minutes later when a pattering of hoofs came from the cedar forest, and a stream of mounted Indians poured into the glade.

The ugly glade became a place of color and action. The Navajos rode wiry, wild-looking mustangs and drove ponies and burros carrying packs, most of which consisted of deer-hides. Each Indian dismounted, and unstrapping the blanket which had served as a saddle headed his mustang for the water-hole and gave him a slap. Then the hides and packs were slipped from the pack-train, and soon the pool became a kicking, splashing mêlée. Every cedar-tree circling the glade and every branch served as a peg for deer-meat. Some of it was in the haunch, the bulk in dark dried strips. The Indians laid their weapons aside. Every sage-bush and low stone held a blanket. A few of these blankets were of solid color, most of them had bars of white and gray and red, the last color predominating. The mustangs and burros filed out among the cedars, nipping at the sage and the scattered tufts of spare grass. A group of fires, sending up curling columns of blue smoke, and surrounded by a circle of lean, half-naked, bronze-skinned Indians, cooking and eating, completed a picture which afforded Hare the satisfying fulfillment of boyish dreams. What a contrast to the memory of a camp-site on the Connecticut shore, with boy friends telling tales in the glow of the fire, and the wash of the waves on the beach!

The sun sank low in the west, sending gleams through the gnarled branches of the cedars, and turning the green into gold. At precisely the moment of sunset, the Mormon women broke into soft song which had the element of prayer; and the lips of the men moved in silent harmony. Dave Naab, the only one who smoked, removed his pipe for the moment's grace to dying day.

This simple ceremony over, one of the boys put wood on the fire, and Snap took a jews'-harp out of his pocket and began to extract doleful discords from it, for which George kicked at him in disgust, finally causing him to leave the circle and repair to the cedars, where he twanged with supreme egotism.

"Jack," said August Naab, "our friends the Navajo chiefs, Scarbreast and Eschtah, are coming to visit us. Take no notice of them at first. They've great dignity, and if you entered their hogans they'd sit for some moments before appearing to see you. Scarbreast is a war-chief. Eschtah is the wise old chief of all the Navajos on the Painted Desert. It may interest you to know he is Mescal's grandfather. Some day I'll tell you the story."

Hare tried very hard to appear unconscious when two tall Indians stalked into the circle of Mormons; he set his eyes on the white heart of the camp-fire and waited. For several minutes no one spoke or even moved. The Indians remained standing for a time; then seated themselves. Presently August Naab greeted them in the Navajo language. This was a signal for Hare to use his eyes and ears. Another interval of silence followed before they began to talk. Hare could see only their blanketed shoulders and black heads.

"Jack, come round here," said Naab at length. "I've been telling them about you. These Indians do not like the whites, except my own family. I hope you'll make friends with them."

"Howdo?" said the chief whom Naab had called

Eschtah, a stately, keen-eyed warrior, despite his age.

The next Navajo greeted him with a guttural word. This was a warrior whose name might well have been Scarface, for the signs of conflict were there. It was a face like a bronze mask, cast in the one expression of untamed desert fierceness.

Hare bowed to each and felt himself searched by burning eyes, which were doubtful, yet not unfriendly.

"Shake," finally said Eschtah, offering his hand.

"Ugh!" exclaimed Scarbreast, extending a bare silver-braceleted arm.

This sign of friendship pleased Naab. He wished to enlist the sympathies of the Navajo chieftains in the young man's behalf. In his ensuing speech, which was plentifully emphasized with gestures, he lapsed often into English, saying "weak—no strong" when he placed his hand on Hare's legs, and "bad" when he touched the young man's chest, concluding with the words "sick—sick."

Scarbreast regarded Hare with great earnestness, and when Naab had finished he said: "Chineago—ping!" and rubbed his hand over his stomach.

"He says you need meat—lots of deer-meat," translated Naab.

"Sick," repeated Eschtah, whose English was intelligible. He appeared to be casting about in his mind for additional words to express his knowledge of the white man's tongue, and, failing, continued in Navajo: "Tohodena—moocha—malocha."

Hare was nonplussed at the roar of laughter from the Mormons. August shook like a mountain in an earthquake.

"Eschtah says, 'you hurry, get many squaws—many wives.'"

Other Indians, russet-skinned warriors, with black hair held close by bands round their foreheads, joined the circle, and sitting before the fire clasped their knees and talked. Hare listened awhile, and then, being fatigued, he sought the cedar-tree where he had left his blankets. The dry mat of needles made an odorous bed. He placed a sack of grain for a pillow, and doubling up one blanket to lie upon, he pulled the others over him. Then he watched and listened. The cedar-wood burned with a clear flame, and occasionally snapped out a red spark. The voices of the Navajos, scarcely audible, sounded "toa's" and "taa's"—syllables he soon learned were characteristic and dominant—in low, deep murmurs. It reminded Hare of something that before had been pleasant to his ear. Then it came to mind: a remembrance of Mescal's sweet voice, and that recalled the kinship between her and the Navajo chieftain. He looked about, endeavoring to find her in the ring of light, for he felt in her a fascination akin to the charm of this twilight hour. Dusky forms passed to and fro under the trees; the tinkle of bells on hobbled mustangs rang from the forest; coyotes had begun their night quest with wild howls; the camp-fire burned red, and shadows flickered on the blanketed Indians; the wind now moaned, now lulled in the cedars.

Hare lay back in his blankets and saw lustrous stars through the network of branches. With their light in his face and the cold wind waving his hair on his brow he thought of the strangeness of it all, of its remoteness from anything ever known to him before, of its inexpressible wildness. And a rush of emotion he failed wholly to stifle proved to him that he could have loved this life if—if he had not of late come to believe that he had not long to live. Still Naab's influence exorcised even that one sad thought; and he flung it from him in resentment.

Sleep did not come so readily; he was not very well this night; the flush of fever was on his cheek, and the heat of feverish blood burned his body. He raised himself and, resolutely seeking for distraction, once more stared at the camp-fire. Some time must have passed during his dreaming, for only three persons were in sight. Naab's broad back was bowed and his head nodded. Across the fire in its ruddy flicker sat Eschtah beside a slight, dark figure. At second glance Hare recognized Mescal. Surprise claimed him, not more for her presence there than for the white band binding her smooth black tresses. She had not worn such an ornament before. That slender band lent her the one touch which made her a Navajo. Was it worn in respect to her aged grandfather? What did this mean for a girl reared with Christian teaching? Was it desert blood? Hare had no answers for these questions. They only increased the mystery and romance. He fell asleep with the picture in his mind of Eschtah and Mescal, sitting in the glow of the fire, and of August Naab, nodding silently.

"Jack, Jack, wake up." The words broke dully into his slumbers; wearily he opened his eyes. August Naab bent over him, shaking him gently.

"Not so well this morning, eh? Here's a cup of coffee. We're all packed and starting. Drink now, and climb aboard. We expect to make Seeping Springs to-night."

Hare rose presently and, laboring into the wagon, lay down on the sacks. He had one of his blind, sickening headaches. The familiar lumbering of wheels began, and the clanking of the wagon-chain. Despite jar and jolt he dozed at times, awakening to the scrape of the wheel on the leathern brake. After a while the rapid descent of the wagon changed to a roll, without the irritating rattle. He saw a narrow valley; on one side the green, slow-swelling cedar slope of the mountain; on the other the perpendicular red wall, with its pinnacles like spears against

the sky. All day this backward outlook was the
same, except that each time he opened aching eyes
the valley had lengthened, the red wall and green
slope had come closer together in the distance. By
and by there came a halt, the din of stamping
horses and sharp commands, the bustle and confusion of camp. Naab spoke kindly to him, but he refused any food, lay still and went to sleep.

Daylight brought him the relief of a clear head
and cooled blood. The camp had been pitched
close under the red wall. A lichen-covered cliff, wet
with dripping water, overhung a round pool. A ditch
led the water down the ridge to a pond. Cattle
stood up to their knees, drinking; others lay on the
yellow clay, which was packed as hard as stone; still
others were climbing the ridge and passing down
on both sides.

"You look as if you enjoyed that water," remarked
Naab, when Hare presented himself at the fire.
"Well, it's good, only a little salty. Seeping Springs
this is, and it's mine. This ridge we call The Saddle;
you see it dips between wall and mountain and sep-
arates two valleys. This valley we go through to-day
is where my cattle range. At the other end is Silver
Cup Spring, also mine. Keep your eyes open now,
my lad."

How different was the beginning of this day! The
sky was as blue as the sea; the valley snuggled deep
in the embrace of wall and mountain. Hare took a
place on the seat beside Naab and faced the descent. The line of Navajos, a graceful straggling
curve of color on the trail, led the way for the
white-domed wagons.

Naab pointed to a little calf lying half hidden
under a bunch of sage. "That's what I hate to see.
There's a calf, just born; its mother has gone in for
water. Wolves and lions range this valley. We lose
hundreds of calves that way."

As far as Hare could see red and white and black cattle speckled the valley.

"If not overstocked, this range is the best in Utah," said Naab. "I say Utah, but it's really Arizona. The Grand Cañon seems to us Mormons to mark the line. There's enough browse here to feed a hundred thousand cattle. But water's the thing. In some seasons the springs go almost dry, though Silver Cup holds her own well enough for my cattle."

Hare marked the tufts of grass lying far apart on the yellow earth; evidently there was sustenance enough in every two feet of ground to support only one tuft.

"What's that?" he asked, noting a rolling cloud of dust with black bobbing borders.

"Wild mustangs," replied Naab. "There are perhaps five thousand on the mountain, and they are getting to be a nuisance. They're almost as bad as sheep on the browse; and I should tell you that if sheep pass over a range once the cattle will starve. The mustangs are getting too plentiful. There are also several bands of wild horses."

"What's the difference between wild horses and mustangs?"

"I haven't figured that out yet. Some say the Spaniards left horses in here three hundred years ago. Wild? They are wilder than any naturally wild animal that ever ran on four legs. Wait till you get a look at Silvermane or Whitefoot."

"What are they?"

"Wild stallions. Silvermane is an iron gray, with a silver mane, the most beautiful horse I ever saw. Whitefoot's an old black shaggy demon, with one white foot. Both stallions ought to be killed. They fight my horses and lead off the mares. I had a chance to shoot Silvermane on the way over this trip, but he looked so splendid that I just laid down my rifle."

"Can they run?" asked Hare, eagerly, with the eyes of a man who loved a horse.

"Run? Whew! Just you wait till you see Silvermane cover ground! He can look over his shoulder at you and beat any horse in this country. The Navajos have given up catching him as a bad job. Why—here! Jack! quick, get out your rifle—coyotes!"

Naab pulled on the reins, and pointed to one side. Hare discerned three grayish sharp-nosed beasts sneaking off in the sage, and he reached back for the rifle. Naab whistled, stopping the coyotes; then Hare shot. The ball cut a wisp of dust above and beyond them. They loped away into the sage.

"How that rifle spangs!" exclaimed Naab. "It's good to hear it. Jack, you shot high. That's the trouble with men who have never shot at game. They can't hold low enough. Aim low, lower than you want. Ha! There's another—this side—hold ahead of him and low, quick!—too high again."

It was in this way that August and Hare fell far behind the other wagons. The nearer Naab got to his home the more genial he became. When he was not answering Hare's queries he was giving information of his own accord, telling about the cattle and the range, the mustangs, the Navajos, and the desert. Naab liked to talk; he had said he had not the gift of revelation, but he certainly had the gift of tongues.

The sun was in the west when they began to climb a ridge. A short ascent, and a long turn to the right brought them under a bold spur of the mountain which shut out the northwest. Camp had been pitched in a grove of trees of a species new to Hare. From under a bowlder gushed the sparkling spring, a grateful sight and sound to desert travellers. In a niche of the rock hung a silver cup.

"Jack, no man knows how old this cup is, or anything about it. We named the spring after it—Silver

Cup. The strange thing is that the cup has never been lost nor stolen. But—could any desert man, or outlaw or Indian, take it away, after drinking here?"

The cup was nicked and battered, bright on the sides, moss-green on the bottom. When Hare drank from it he understood.

That evening there was rude merriment around the camp-fire. Snap Naab buzzed on his jews'-harp and sang. He stirred some of the younger braves to dancing, and they stamped and swung their arms, singing, "hoya-heeya-howya," as they moved in and out of the firelight.

Several of the braves showed great interest in Snap's jews'-harp and repeatedly asked him for it. Finally the Mormon grudgingly lent it to a curious Indian, who in trying to play it went through such awkward motions and made such queer sounds that his companions set upon him and fought for possession of the instrument. Then Snap, becoming solicitous for its welfare, jumped into the fray. They tussled for it amid the clamor of a delighted circle. Snap, passing from jest to earnest, grew so strenuous in his efforts to regain the harp that he tossed the Navajos about like shuttle-cocks. He got the harp and, concealing it, sought to break away. But the braves laid hold upon him, threw him to the ground, and calmly sat astride him while they went through his pockets. August Naab roared his merriment and Hare laughed till he cried. The incident was as surprising to him as it was amusing. These serious Mormons and silent Navajos were capable of mirth.

Hare would have stayed up as late as any of them, but August's saying to him, "Get to bed: to-morrow will be bad!" sent him off to his blankets, where he was soon fast asleep. Morning found him well, hungry, eager to know what the day would bring.

"Wait," said August, soberly.

They rode out of the gray pocket in the ridge and began to climb. Hare had not noticed the rise till they were started, and then, as the horses climbed steadily he grew impatient at the monotonous ascent. There was nothing to see; frequently it seemed that they were soon to reach the summit, but still it rose above them. Hare went back to his comfortable place on the sacks.

"Now, Jack," said August.

Hare gasped. He saw a red world. His eyes seemed bathed in blood. Red scaly ground, bare of vegetation, sloped down, down, far down to a vast irregular rent in the earth, which zigzagged through the plain beneath. To the right it bent its crooked way under the brow of a black-timbered plateau; to the left it straightened its angles to find a V-shaped vent in the wall, now uplifted to a mountain range. Beyond this earth-riven line lay something vast and illimitable, a far-reaching vision of white wastes, of purple plains, of low mesas lost in distance. It was the shimmering dust-veiled desert.

"Here we come to the real thing," explained Naab. "This is Windy Slope; that black line is the Grand Cañon of Arizona; on the other side is the Painted Desert where the Navajos live; Coconina Mountain shows his flat head there to the right, and the wall on our left rises to the Vermillion Cliffs. Now, look while you can, for presently you'll not be able to see."

"Why?"

"Wind, sand, dust, gravel, pebbles—watch out for your eyes!"

Naab had not ceased speaking when Hare saw that the train of Indians trailing down the slope was enveloped in red clouds. Then the white wagons disappeared. Soon he was struck in the back by a gust which justified Naab's warning. It swept by; the air grew clear again; once more he could see. But presently a puff, taking him unawares, filled his eyes with dust difficult of removal. Whereupon he turned his back to the wind.

The afternoon grew apace; the sun glistened on the white patches of Coconina Mountain; it set; and the wind died.

"Five miles of red sand," said Naab. "Here's what kills the horses. Getup."

There was no trail. All before was red sand, hollows, slopes, levels, dunes, in which the horses sank above their fetlocks. The wheels ploughed deep, and little red streams trailed down from the tires. Naab trudged on foot with the reins in his hands. Hare essayed to walk also, soon tired, and floundered behind till Naab ordered him to ride again. Twilight came with the horses still toiling.

"There! thankful I am when we get off that strip! But, Jack, that trailless waste prevents a night raid on my home. Even the Navajos shun it after dark. We'll be home soon. There's my sign. See? Night or day we call it the Blue Star."

High in the black cliff a star-shaped, wind-worn hole let the blue sky through.

There was cheer in Naab's "Getup," now, and the horses quickened with it. Their iron-shod hoofs struck fire from the rocky road. "Easy, easy—soho!" cried Naab to his steeds. In the pitchy blackness under the shelving cliff they picked their way cautiously, and turned a corner. Lights twinkled in Hare's sight, a fresh breeze, coming from water, dampened his cheek, and a hollow rumble, a long roll of distant thunder, filled his ears.

"What's that?" he asked.

"That, my lad, is what I always love to hear. It means I'm home. It's the roar of the Colorado as she takes her first plunge into the Cañon."

CHAPTER IV

The Oasis

AUGUST NAAB'S oasis was an oval valley, level as a floor, green with leaf and white with blossom, enclosed by a circle of colossal cliffs of vivid vermilion hue. At its western curve the Colorado River split the red walls from north to south. When the wind was west a sullen roar, remote as of some far-off driving mill, filled the valley; when it was east a dreamy hollow hum, a somnolent song, murmured through the cottonwoods; when no wind stirred, silence reigned, a silence not of serene plain or mountain fastness, but shut in, compressed, strange, and breathless. Safe from the storms of the elements as well as of the world was this Garden of Eschtah.

Naab had put Hare to bed on the unroofed porch of a log house, but routed him out early, and when Hare lifted the blankets a shower of cotton-blossoms drifted away like snow. A grove of gray-barked trees spread green canopy overhead, and through the intricate web shone crimson walls,

soaring with resistless onsweep up and up to shut
out all but a blue lake of sky.

"I want you to see the Navajos cross the river,"
said Naab.

Hare accompanied him out through the grove to a
road that flanked the first rise of the red wall; they
followed this for half a mile, and turning a corner
came into an unobstructed view. A roar of rushing
waters had prepared Hare, but the river that he saw
appalled him. It was red and swift; it slid onward
like an enormous slippery snake; its constricted
head raised a crest of leaping waves, and disappeared in a dark chasm, whence came a bellow and
boom.

"That opening where she jumps off is the head of
the Grand Cañon," said Naab. "It's five hundred feet
deep there, and thirty miles below it's five thousand. Oh, once in, she tears in a hurry! Come, we
turn up the bank here."

Hare could find no speech, and he felt immeasur-
ably small. All that he had seen in reaching this
isolated spot was dwarfed in comparison. This
"Crossing of the Fathers," as Naab called it, was the
gateway of the desert. This roar of turbulent waters
was the sinister monotone of the mighty desert
symphony of great depths, great heights, great
reaches.

On a sandy strip of bank the Navajos had halted.
This was as far as they could go, for above the wall
jutted out into the river. From here the head of the
Cañon was not visible, and the roar of the rapids
was accordingly lessened in volume. But even in
this smooth water the river spoke a warning.

"The Navajos go in here and swim their mustangs
across to that sand-bar," explained Naab. "The current helps when she's high, and there's a three-foot
raise on now."

"I can't believe it possible. What danger they must run—those little mustangs!" exclaimed Hare.

"Danger? Yes, I suppose so," replied Naab, as if it were a new idea. "My lad, the Mormons crossed here by the hundreds. Many were drowned. This trail and crossing were unknown except to Indians before the Mormon exodus."

The mustangs had to be driven into the water. Scarbreast led, and his mustang, after many kicks and reluctant steps, went over his depth, wetting the stalwart chief to the waist. Bare-legged Indians waded in and urged their pack-ponies. Shouts, shrill cries, blows mingled with snorts and splashes.

Dave and George Naab in flat boats rowed slowly on the down-stream side of the Indians. Presently all the mustangs and ponies were in, the procession widening out in a triangle from Scarbreast, the leader. The pack-ponies appeared to swim better than the mounted mustangs, or else the packs of deer-pelts made them more buoyant. When one-third way across the head of the swimming train met the current, and the line of progress broke. Mustang after mustang swept down with a rapidity which showed the power of the current. Yet they swam steadily with flanks shining, tails sometimes afloat, sometimes under, noses up, and riders holding weapons aloft. But the pack-ponies labored when the current struck them, and whirling about, they held back the Indians who were leading them, and blocked those behind. The orderly procession of the start became a broken line, and then a rout. Here and there a Navajo slipped into the water and swam, leading his mustang; others pulled on pack-ponies and beat their mounts; strong-swimming mustangs forged ahead; weak ones hung back, and all obeyed the downward will of the current.

While Hare feared for the lives of some of the Navajos, and pitied the laden ponies, he could not but revel in the scene, in its vivid action and varying color, in the cries and shrill whoops of the Indians, and the snorts of the frightened mustangs, in Naab's hoarse yells to his sons, and the ever-present menacing roar from around the bend. The wildness of it all, the necessity of peril and calm acceptance of it, stirred within Hare the call, the awakening, the spirit of the desert.

August Naab's stentorian voice rolled out over the river. "Ho! Dave—the yellow pinto—pull him loose— George, back this way—there's a pack slipping—down now, downstream, turn that straggler in— Dave, in that tangle—quick! There's a boy drowning—his foot's caught—he's been kicked— Hurry! Hurry!—pull him in the boat— There's a pony under— Too late, George, let that one go—let him go, I tell you!"

So the crossing of the Navajos proceeded, never an instant free from danger in that churning current. The mustangs and ponies floundered somewhat on the sand-bar, and then parted the willows and appeared on a trail skirting the red wall. Dave Naab moored his boat on that side of the river, and returned with George.

"We'll look over my farm," said August, as they retraced their steps. He led Hare through fields of alfalfa, in all stages of growth, explaining that it yielded six crops a year. Into one ten-acre lot pigs and cows had been turned to feed at will. Everywhere the ground was soggy; little streams of water trickled down ditches. Next to the fields was an orchard, where cherries were ripe, apricots already large, plum-trees shedding their blossoms, and apple-trees just opening into bloom. Naab explained that the products of his oasis were abnormal; the ground was exceedingly rich and could be kept always wet; the reflection of the sun from the walls robbed even winter of any rigor, and the spring, summer, and autumn were tropical. He pointed to grape-vines as large as a man's thigh and told of bunches of grapes four feet long; he showed sprouting plants on which watermelons and pumpkins would grow so large that one man could not lift them; he told of one pumpkin that held a record of taking two men to roll it.

"I can raise any kind of fruit in such abundance that it can't be used. My garden is prodigal. But we get little benefit, except for our own use, for we cannot transport things across the desert."

The water which was the prime factor in all this richness came from a small stream which Naab, by making a dam and tunnelling a corner of cliff, had diverted from its natural course into his oasis.

Between the fence and the red wall there was a wide bare plain which stretched to the house. At its farthest end was a green enclosure, which Hare recognized as the cemetery mentioned by Snap. Hare counted thirty graves, a few with crude monuments of stone, the others marked by wooden head-pieces.

"I've the reputation of doctoring the women, and letting the men die," said Naab, with a smile. "I hardly think it's fair. But the fact is no women are buried here. Some graves are of men I fished out of the river; others of those who drifted here, and who were killed or died keeping their secrets. I've numbered those unknown graves and have kept a description of the men, so, if the chance ever comes, I may tell someone where a father or brother lies buried. Five sons of mine, not one of whom died a natural death, found graves here—God rest them! Here's the grave of Mescal's father, a Spaniard. He was an adventurer. I helped him over in Nevada when he was ill; he came here with me, got well, and lived nine years, and he died without speaking one word of himself or telling his name."

"What strange ends men come to!" mused Hare. Well, a grave was a grave, wherever it lay. He wondered if he would come to rest in that quiet nook, with its steady light, its simple dignity of bare plain graves fitting the brevity of life, the littleness of man.

"We break wild mustangs along this stretch," said Naab, drawing Hare away. "It's a fine run. Wait till you see Mescal on Black Bolly tearing up the dust! She's a Navajo for riding."

Three huge corrals filled a wide curved space in the wall. In one corral were the teams that had hauled the wagons from White Sage; in another upward of thirty burros, drooping, lazy little fellows, half asleep; in the third a dozen or more mustangs and some horses which delighted Hare. Snap Naab's cream pinto, a bay, and a giant horse of mottled white attracted him most.

"Our best stock is out on the range," said Naab. "The white is Charger, my saddle-horse. When he was a yearling he got away and ran wild for three years. But we caught him. He's a weight-carrier and he can run some. You're fond of a horse—I can see that."

"Yes," returned Hare, "but I—I'll never ride again." He said it brightly, smiling the while; still the look in his eyes belied the cheerful resignation.

"I've not the gift of revelation, yet I seem to see you on a big gray horse with a shining mane." Naab appeared to be gazing far away.

The cottonwood grove, at the western curve of the oasis, shaded the five log huts where August's grown sons lived with their wives, and his own cabin, which was of considerable dimensions. It had a covered porch on one side, an open one on the other, a shingle roof, and was a roomy and comfortable habitation.

Naab was pointing out the school-house when he

was interrupted by childish laughter, shrieks of glee, and the rush of little feet.

"It's recess-time," he said.

A frantic crowd of tousled-headed little ones were running from the log school-house to form a circle under the trees. There were fourteen of them, from four years of age up to ten or twelve. Such sturdy, glad-eyed children Hare had never seen. In a few moments, as though their happy screams were signals, the shady circle was filled with hounds, and a string of puppies stepping on their long ears, and ruffling turkey-gobblers, that gobbled and gobbled, and guinea-hens with their shrill cries, and cackling chickens and a lame wild goose that hobbled along alone. Then there were shiny peafowls screeching clarion calls from the trees overhead, and flocks of singing blackbirds, and pigeons hovering over and alighting upon the house. Last to approach were a woolly sheep that added his baa-baa to the din, and a bald-faced burro that walked in his sleep. These two became the center of clamor. After many tumbles four chubby youngsters mounted the burro; and the others, with loud acclaim, shouting, "Noddle, Noddle, getup getup!" endeavored to make him go. But Noodle nodded and refused to awaken or budge. Then an ambitious urchin of six fastened his hands in the fur of the sheep and essayed to climb to his back. Willing hands assisted him. "Ride him, Billy, ride him. Getup, Navvy, getup!"

Navvy evidently had never been ridden, for he began a fair imitation of a bucking broncho. Billy held on, but the smile vanished and the corners of his mouth drew down.

"Hang on, Billy, hang on," cried August Naab, in delight. Billy hung on a moment longer, and then Navvy, bewildered by the pestering crowd about him, launched out and, butting into Noddle, spilled the four youngsters and Billy also into a wriggling heap.

This recess-time completed Hare's introduction to the Naabs. There were Mother Mary, and Judith and Esther, whom he knew, and Mother Ruth and her two daughters, very like their sisters. Mother Ruth, August's second wife, was younger than Mother Mary, more comely of face, and more sad and serious of expression. The wives of the five sons, except Snap Naab's frail bride, were stalwart women, fit to make homes and rear children.

"Now, Jack, things are moving all right," said August. "For the present you must eat and rest. Walk some, but don't tire yourself. We'll practise shooting a little every day; that's one thing I'll spare time for. I've a trick with a gun to teach you. And if you feel able, take a burro and ride. Anyway, make yourself at home."

Hare found eating and resting to be matters of profound enjoyment. Before he had fallen in with these good people it had been a year since he had sat down to a full meal; longer still since he had eaten wholesome food. And now he had come to a "land overflowing with milk and honey," as Mother Ruth smilingly said. He could not choose between roast beef and chicken, and so he waived the question by taking both; and what with the biscuits and butter, apple-sauce and blackberry jam, cherry pie and milk like cream, there was danger of making himself ill. He told his friends that he simply could not help it, which shameless confession brought a hearty laugh from August and beaming smiles from his women-folk.

For several days Hare was remarkably well, for an invalid. He won golden praise from August at the rifle practice, and he began to take lessons in the quick drawing and rapid firing of a Colt revolver. Naab was wonderfully proficient in the use of both firearms; and his skill in drawing the smaller weapon, in which his movement was quicker than the eye, astonished Hare. "My lad," said August, "it doesn't follow because I'm a Christian that I don't know how to handle a gun. Besides, I like to shoot."

In these few days Hare learned what conquering the desert made of a man. August Naab was close to threescore years; his chest was wide as a door, his arm like the branch of an oak. He was a blacksmith, a mechanic, a carpenter, a cooper, a potter. At his forge and in his shop, everywhere were crude tools, wagons, farming implements, sets of buckskin harness, odds and ends of nameless things, eloquent and pregnant proof of the fact that necessity is the mother of invention. He was a mason; the levee that buffeted back the rage of the Colorado in flood, the wall that turned the creek, the irrigation tunnel, the zigzag trail cut on the face of the cliff— all these attested his eye for line, his judgment of distance, his strength in toil. He was a farmer, a cattle-man, a grafter of fruit-trees, a breeder of horses, a herder of sheep, a preacher, a physician. Best and strangest of all in this wonderful man was the instinct and the heart to heal. "I don't combat the doctrine of the Mormon church," he said, "but I administer a little medicine with my healing. I learned that from the Navajos." The children ran to him with bruised heads, and cut fingers, and stubbed toes; and his blacksmith's hands were as gentle as a woman's. A mustang with a lame leg claimed his serious attention; a sick sheep gave him an anxious look; a steer with a gored skin sent him running for a bucket of salve. He could not pass by a crippled quail. The farm was overrun by Navajo sheep which he had found strayed and lost on the desert. Anything hurt or helpless had in August Naab a friend. Hare found himself looking up to a great and luminous figure, and he loved this man.

As the days passed Hare learned many other things. For a while illness confined him to his bed on the porch. At night he lay listening to the roar of the river and watching the stars. Twice he heard a distant crash and rumble heavy as thunder, and he knew that somewhere along the cliffs avalanches were slipping. By day he watched the cotton snow down upon him and listened to the many birds and waited for the merry show at recess-time. After a short time the children grew less shy and came readily to him. They were the most wholesome children he had ever known. Hare wondered about it, and decided it was not so much Mormon teaching as isolation from the world. These children had never been out of their cliff-walled home, and civilization was for them as if it were not. He told them stories, and after school hours they would race to him and climb on his bed and beg for more.

He exhausted his supply of fairy-stories and animal-stories; and had begun to tell about the places and cities which he had visited when the eager-eyed children were peremptorily called within by Mother Mary. This pained him and he was at a loss to understand it. Enlightenment came, however, in the way of an argument between Naab and Mother Mary which he overheard. The elder wife said that the stranger was welcome to the children, but she insisted that they hear nothing of the outside world, and that they be kept to the teachings of the Mormon geography—which made all the world outside Utah an untrodden wilderness. August Naab did not hold to the letter of the Mormon law; he argued that if the children could not be raised as Mormons with a full knowledge of the world, they would only be lost in the end to the Church.

Other developments surprised Hare. The house of this good Mormon was divided against itself. Precedence was given to the first and elder wife—Mother Mary; Mother Ruth's life was not without pain. The men were out on the ranges all day, usually two or more of them for several days at a time, and this left the women alone. One daughter taught the school, the other daughters did all the chores about the house, from feeding the stock to chopping wood. The work was hard, and the girls would rather have been in White Sage or Lund. They disliked Mescal, and said things inspired by jealousy. Snap Naab's wife was vindictive, and called Mescal "that Indian!"

It struck him on hearing this gossip that he had missed Mescal. What had become of her? Curiosity prompting him, he asked little Billy about her.

"Mescal's with the sheep," piped Billy.

That she was a shepherdess pleased Hare, and he thought of her as free on the open range, with the wind blowing her hair.

One day when Hare felt stronger he took his walk round the farm with new zest. Upon his return to the house he saw Snap's cream pinto in the yard, and Dave's mustang cropping the grass near by. A dusty pack lay on the ground. Hare walked down the avenue of cottonwoods and was about to turn the corner of the old forge when he stopped short.

"Now mind you, I'll take a bead on this white-faced spy if you send him up there."

It was Snap Naab's voice, and his speech concluded with the click of teeth characteristic of him in anger.

"Stand there!" August Naab exclaimed in wrath. "Listen. You have been drinking again or you wouldn't talk of killing a man. I warned you. I won't do this thing you ask of me till I have your promise. Why won't you leave the bottle alone?"

"I'll promise," came the sullen reply.

"Very well. Then pack and go across to Bitter Seeps."

"That job'll take all summer," growled Snap.

"So much the better. When you come home I'll keep my promise."

Hare moved away silently; the shock of Snap's first words had kept him fast in his tracks long enough to hear the conversation. Why did Snap threaten him? Where was August Naab going to send him? Hare had no means of coming to an understanding of either question. He was disturbed in mind and resolved to keep out of Snap's way. He went to the orchard, but his stay of an hour availed nothing, for on his return, after threading the maze of cottonwoods, he came face to face with the man he wanted to avoid.

Snap Naab, at the moment of meeting, had a black bottle tipped high above his lips.

With a curse he threw the bottle at Hare, missing him narrowly. He was drunk. His eyes were bloodshot.

"If you tell father you saw me drinking I'll kill you!" he hissed, and, rattling his Colt in its holster, he walked away.

Hare walked back to his bed, where he lay for a long time with his whole inner being in a state of strife. It gradually wore off as he strove for calm. The playground was deserted; no one had seen Snap's action, and for that he was glad. Then his attention was diverted by a clatter of ringing hoofs on the road; a mustang and a cloud of dust were approaching.

"Mescal and Black Bolly!" he exclaimed, and sat up quickly. The mustang turned in the gate, slid to a stop, and stood quivering, restive, tossing its thoroughbred head, black as a coal, with freedom and fire in every line. Mescal leaped off lightly. A gray form flashed in at the gate, fell at her feet, and rose to leap about her. It was a splendid dog, huge in frame, almost white, wild as the mustang.

This was the Mescal whom he remembered, yet somehow different. The sombre homespun garments had given place to fringed and beaded buckskin.

"I've come for you," she said.

"For me?" he asked, wonderingly, as she approached with the bridle of the black over her arm.

"Down, Wolf!" she cried to the leaping dog. "Yes. Didn't you know? Father Naab says you're to help me tend the sheep. Are you better? I hope so— You're quite pale."

"I—I'm not so well," said Hare.

He looked up at her, at the black sweep of her hair under the white band, at her eyes, like jet; and suddenly realized, with a gladness new and strange to him, that he liked to look at her, that she was beautiful.

CHAPTER V

Black Sage and Juniper

AUGUST NAAB appeared on the path leading from his fields.

"Mescal, here you are," he greeted. "How about the sheep?"

"Piute's driving them down to the lower range. There are a thousand coyotes hanging about the flock."

"That's bad," rejoined August. "Jack, there's evidently some real shooting in store for you. We'll pack to-day and get an early start to-morrow. I'll put you on Noddle; he's slow, but the easiest climber I ever owned. He's like riding ... What's the matter with you? What's happened to make you angry?"

One of his long strides spanned the distance between them.

"Oh, nothing," said Hare, flushing.

"Lad, I know of few circumstances that justify a lie. You've met Snap."

Hare might still have tried to dissimulate; but one

glance at August's stern face showed the useless-
ness of it. He kept silent.

"Drink makes my son unnatural," said Naab. He
breathed heavily as one in conflict with wrath.
"We'll not wait till to-morrow to go up on the plateau; we'll go at once."

Then quick surprise awakened for Hare in the
meaning in Mescal's eyes; he caught only a fleeting
glimpse, a dark flash, and it left him with a glow of
an emotion half pleasure, half pain.

"Mescal," went on August, "go into the house,
and keep out of Snap's way. Jack, watch me pack.
You need to learn these things. I could put all this
outfit on two burros, but the trail is narrow, and a
wide pack might bump a burro off. Let's see, I've got
all your stuff but the saddle; that we'll leave till we
get a horse for you. Well, all's ready."

Mescal came at his call and, mounting Black
Bolly, rode out toward the cliff wall, with Wolf trotting before her. Hare bestrode Noddle. August, waving good-bye to his women-folk, started the train of
burros after Mescal.

How they would be able to climb the face of that
steep cliff puzzled Hare. Upon nearer view he discovered the yard-wide trail curving upward in cork-
screw fashion round a projecting corner of cliff. The
stone was a soft red shale and the trail had been
cut in it at a steep angle. It was so steep that the
burros appeared to be climbing straight up. Noddle
pattered into it, dropped his head and his long ears,
and slackened his pace to patient plodding. August
walked in the rear.

The first thing that struck Hare was the way the
burros in front of him stopped at the curves in the
trail, and turned in a space so small that their four
feet were close together; yet as they swung their
packs they scarcely scraped the wall. At every turn
they were higher than he was, going in the opposite

direction, yet he could reach out and touch them. He glanced up to see Mescal right above him, leaning forward with her brown hands clasping the pommel. Then he looked out and down; already the green cluster of cottonwoods lay far below. After that sensations pressed upon him. Round and round, up and up, steadily, surely, the beautiful mustang led the train; there were sounds of rattling stones, and click of hoofs, and scrape of pack. On one side towered the iron-stained cliff, not smooth or glistening at close range, but of dull, dead, rotting rock. The trail changed to a zigzag along a seamed and cracked buttress where ledges leaned outward waiting to fall. Then a steeper incline, where the burros crept upward warily, led to a level ledge heading to the left.

Mescal halted on a promontory. She, with her wind-blown hair, the gleam of white band about her head, and a dash of red along the fringed leggings, gave inexpressible life and beauty to that wild, jagged point of rock, sharp against the glaring sky.

"This is Lookout Point," said Naab. "I keep an Indian here all the time during daylight. He's a peon, a Navajo slave. He can't talk, as he was born without a tongue, or it was cut out, but he has the best eyes of any Indian I know. You see this point commands the farm, the crossing, the Navajo Trail over the river, the Echo Cliffs opposite, where the Navajos signal to me, and also the White Sage Trail."

The oasis shone under the triangular promontory; the river with its rising roar wound in bold curve from the split in the cliffs. To the right white-sloped Coconina breasted the horizon. Forward across the Cañon line opened the many-hued desert.

"With this peon watching here I'm not likely to be surprised," said Naab. "That strip of sand protects me at night from approach, and I've never had anything to fear from across the river."

Naab's peon came from a little cave in the wall and grinned the greeting he could not speak. To Hare's uneducated eye all Indians resembled each other. Yet this one stood apart from the others, not differing in blanketed leanness, or straggling black hair, or bronze skin, but in the bird-of-prey cast of his features and the wildness of his glittering eyes. Naab gave him a bag from one of the packs, spoke a few words in Navajo, and then slapped the burros into the trail.

The climb thenceforth was more rapid because less steep, and the trail now led among broken fragments of cliff. The color of the stones had changed from red to yellow, and small cedars grew in protected places. Hare's judgment of height had such frequent cause for correction that he gave up trying to estimate the altitude. The ride had begun to tell on his strength, and toward the end he thought he could not manage to stay longer upon Noddle. The air had grown thin and cold, and though the sun was yet an hour high, his fingers were numb.

"Hang on, Jack," cheered August. "We're almost up."

At last Black Bolly disappeared, likewise the bobbing burros, one by one, then Noddle, wagging his ears, reached a level. Then Hare saw a gray-green cedar forest, with yellow crags rising in the background, and a rush of cold wind smote his face. For a moment he choked; he could not get his breath. The air was thin and rare, and he inhaled deeply, trying to overcome the suffocation. Presently he realized that the trouble was not with the rarity of the atmosphere, but with the bitter-sweet penetrating odor it carried. He was almost stifled. It was not like the smell of pine, though it made him think of pine-trees.

"Ha! that's good!" said Naab, expanding his great chest. "That's air for you, my lad. Can you taste it? Well, here's camp, your home for many a day, Jack. There's Piute. How do? how're the sheep?"

A short, squat Indian, good-humored of face, shook his black head till the silver rings danced in his ears, and replied: "Bad—damn coyotee!"

"Piute—shake with Jack. Him shoot coyote—got big gun," said Naab.

"How-do-Jack?" replied Piute, extending his hand, and then straightaway began examining the new rifle. "Damn—heap big gun!"

"Jack, you'll find this Indian one you can trust, for all he's a Piute outcast," went on August. "I've had him with me ever since Mescal found him on the Coconina Trail five years ago. What Piute doesn't know about this side of Coconina isn't worth learning."

In a depression sheltered from the wind lay the camp. A fire burned in the centre; a conical tent, like a tepee in shape, hung suspended from a cedar branch and was staked at its four points; a leaning slab of rock furnished shelter for camp supplies and for the Indian, and at one end a spring gushed out. A gray-sheathed cedar-tree marked the entrance to this hollow glade, and under it August began preparing Hare's bed.

"Here's the place you're to sleep, rain or shine or snow," he said. "Now I've spent my life sleeping on the ground, and mother earth makes the best bed. I'll dig out a little pit in this soft mat of needles; that's for your hips. Then the tarpaulin so; a blanket so. Now the other blankets. Your feet must be a little higher than your head; you really sleep down hill, which breaks the wind. So you never catch cold. All you need do is to change your position according to the direction of the wind. Pull up the blankets, and then the long end of the tarpaulin. If it rains or snows cover your head, and sleep, my lad, sleep to the song of the wind!"

From where Hare lay, resting a weary body, he could see down into the depression which his position guarded. Naab built up the fire; Piute peeled potatoes with deliberate care; Mescal, on her knees, her brown arms bare, kneaded dough in a basin; Wolf crouched on the ground and watched his mistress; Black Bolly tossed her head, elevating the bag on her nose so as to get all the grain.

Naab called him to supper, and when Hare set to with a will on the bacon and eggs and hot biscuits, he nodded approvingly. "That's what I want to see," he said approvingly. "You must eat. Piute will get deer, or you may shoot them yourself; eat all the venison you can. Remember what Scarbreast said. Then rest. That's the secret. If you eat and rest you will gain strength."

The edge of the wall was not a hundred paces from the camp; and when Hare strolled out to it after supper, the sun had dipped the under side of its red disc behind the desert. He watched it sink, while the golden-red flood of light grew darker and darker. Thought seemed remote from him then; he watched and watched, until he saw the last spark of the fire die from the snow-slopes of Coconina. The desert became dimmer and dimmer; the oasis lost its outline in a bottomless purple pit, except for a faint light, like a star.

The bleating of sheep aroused him and he returned to camp. The fire was still bright. Wolf slept close to Mescal's tent; Piute was not in sight; and Naab had rolled himself in blankets. Crawling into his bed, Hare stretched aching legs and lay still, as if he would never move again. Tired as he was, the bleating of the sheep, the clear ring of the bell on Black Bolly, and the faint tinkle of lighter bells on some of the rams, drove away sleep for a while. Ac-

companied by the sough of the wind through the
cedars the music of the bells was sweet, and he listened till he heard no more.

A thin coating of frost crackled on his bed when
he awakened; and out from under the shelter of the
cedar all the ground was hoar-white. As he slipped
from his blankets the same strong smell of black
sage and juniper smote him, almost like a blow. His
nostrils seemed glued together by some rich piny
pitch; and when he opened his lips to breathe a
sudden pain, as of a knife-thrust, pierced his lungs.
The thought following was as sharp as the pain.
Pneumonia! What he had long expected! He sank
against the cedar, overcome by the shock. But he
rallied presently, for with the re-establishment of
the old settled bitterness, which had been forgotten
in the interest of his situation, he remembered that
he had given up hope. Still, he could not get back at
once to his former resignation. He hated to ac-
knowledge that the wildness of this desert cañon
country, and the spirit it sought to instil in him, had
wakened a desire to live. For it meant only more to
give up. And after one short instant of battle he was
himself again. He put his hand under his flannel
shirt and felt of the soreness of his lungs. He found
it not at the apex of the right lung, always the one
sensitive spot, but all through his breast. Little
panting breaths did not hurt; but the deep inhala-
tion, which alone satisfied him, filled his whole
chest with thousands of pricking needles. In the
depth of his breast was a hollow that burned.

When he had pulled on his boots and coat, and
had washed himself in the runway of the spring, his
hands were so numb with cold they refused to hold
his comb and brush; and he presented himself at
the roaring fire half-frozen, dishevelled, trembling,
but cheerful. He would not tell Naab. If he had to
die to-day, to-morrow, or next week, he would lie

down under a cedar and die; he could not whine about it to this man.

"Up with the sun!" was Naab's greeting. His cheerfulness was as impelling as his splendid virility. Following the wave of his hand, Hare saw the sun, a pale-pink globe through a misty blue, rising between the golden crags of the eastern wall.

Mescal had a shy "good-morning" for him, and Piute a broad smile and familiar "how-do"; the peon slave, who had finished breakfast and was about to depart, moved his lips in friendly greeting that had no sound.

"Did you hear the coyotes last night?" inquired August. "No! Well, of all the choruses I ever heard. There must be a thousand on the bench. Jack, I wish I could spare the time to stay up here with you and shoot some. You'll have practice with the rifle, but don't neglect the Colt. Practice particularly the draw I taught you. Piute has a carbine, and he shoots at the coyotes, but who ever saw an Indian that could hit anything?"

"Damn—gun no good!" growled Piute, who evidently understood English pretty well. Naab laughed, and while Hare ate breakfast he talked of the sheep. The flock he had numbered three thousand. They were a goodly part of them Navajo stock; small, hardy sheep that could live on anything but cactus, and needed little water. This flock had grown from a small number to its present size in a few years. Being remarkably free from the diseases and pests which retard increase in low countries, the sheep had multiplied almost one for one every year. But for the ravages of wild beasts Naab believed he could raise a flock of many thousands and in a brief time be rich in sheep alone. In the winter he drove them down into the oasis; the other seasons he herded them on the high ranges where the cattle could not climb. There was grass enough on this plateau for a million sheep. After the spring thaw in early March, occasional snows fell till the end of May, and frost hung on until early summer; then the July rains made the plateau a garden.

"Get the forty-four," concluded Naab, "and we'll go out and break it in."

With the long rifle in the hollow of his arm Jack forgot that he was a sick man. When he came within gunshot of the flock the smell of sheep effectually smothered the keen, tasty odor of black sage and juniper. Sheep ranged everywhere under the low cedars. They browsed with noses in the frost, and from all around came the tinkle of tiny bells on the curly-horned rams, and an endless variety of bleats.

"They're spread now," said August. "Mescal drives them on every little while and Piute goes ahead to pick out the best browse. Watch the dog, Jack; he's all but human. His mother was a big shepherd dog that I got in Lund. She must have had a strain of wild blood. Once while I was hunting deer on Coconina she ran off with timber wolves and we thought she was killed. But she came back and had a litter of three puppies. Two were white, the other black. I think she killed the black one. And she neglected the others. One died, and Mescal raised the other. We called him Wolf. He loves Mescal, and loves the sheep, and hates a wolf. Mescal puts a bell on him when she is driving, and the sheep know the bell. I think it would be a good plan for her to tie something red round his neck—a scarf, so as to keep you from shooting him for a wolf."

Nimble, alert, the big white dog was not still a moment. His duty was to keep the flock compact, to head the stragglers and turn them back; and he knew his part perfectly. There was dash and fire in his work. He never barked. As he circled the flock the small Navajo sheep, edging ever toward forbidden ground, bleated their way back to the fold, the larger ones wheeled reluctantly, and the old belled rams squared themselves, lowering their massive horns as if to butt him. Never, however, did they stand their ground when he reached them, for there was a decision about Wolf which brooked no opposition. At times when he was working on one side a crafty sheep on the other would steal out into the thicket. Then Mescal called and Wolf flashed back to her, lifting his proud head, eager, spirited, ready to take her order. A word, a wave of her whip sufficed for the dog to rout out the recalcitrant sheep and send him bleating to his fellows.

"He manages them easily now," said Naab, "but when the lambs come they can't be kept in. The coyotes and wolves hang out in the thickets and pick up the stragglers. The worst enemy of sheep, though, is the old grizzly bear. Usually he is grouchy, and dangerous to hunt. He comes into the herd, kills the mother sheep, and eats the milk-bag—no more! He will kill forty sheep in a night. Piute saw the tracks of one up on the high range, and believes this bear is following the flock. Let's get off into the woods some little way, into the edge of the thickets—for Piute always keeps to the glades—and see if we can pick off a few coyotes."

August cautioned Jack to step stealthily, and slip from cedar to cedar, to use every bunch of sage and juniper to hide his advance.

"Watch sharp, Jack. I've seen two already. Look for moving things. Don't try to see one quiet, for you can't till after your eye catches him moving. They are gray, gray as the cedars, the grass, the ground. Good! Yes, I see him, but don't shoot. That's too far. Wait. They sneak away, but they return. You can afford to make sure. Here now, by that stone—aim low and be quick."

In the course of a mile, without keeping the sheep near at hand, they saw upward of twenty coyotes, five of which Jack killed in as many shots.

"You've got the hang of it," said Naab, rubbing his hands. "You'll kill the varmints. Piute will skin and salt the pelts. Now I'm going up on the high range to look for bear sign. Go ahead, on your own hook."

Hare was regardless of time while he stole under the cedars and through the thickets, spying out the cunning coyotes. Then Naab's yell pealing out claimed his attention; he answered and returned. When they met he recounted his adventures in mingled excitement and disappointment.

"Are you tired?" asked Naab.

"Tired? No," replied Jack.

"Well, you mustn't overdo the very first day. I've news for you. There are some wild horses on the high range. I didn't see them, but found tracks everywhere. If they come down here you send Piute to close the trail at the upper end of the bench, and you close the one where we came up. There are only two trails where even a deer can get off this plateau, and both are narrow splits in the wall, which can be barred by the gates. We made the gates to keep the sheep in, and they'll serve a turn. If you get the wild horses on the bench send Piute for me at once."

They passed the Indian herding the sheep into a corral built against an uprising ridge of stone. Naab dispatched him to look for the dead coyotes. The three burros were in camp, two wearing empty pack-saddles, and Noddle, for once not asleep, was eating from Mescal's hand.

"Mescal, hadn't I better take Black Bolly home?" asked August.

"Mayn't I keep her?"

"She's yours. But you run a risk. There are wild horses on the range. Will you keep her hobbled?"

"Yes," replied Mescal, reluctantly. "Though I don't believe Bolly would run off from me."

"Look out she doesn't go, hobbles and all. Jack, here's the other bit of news I have for you. There's a big grizzly camping on the trail of our sheep. Now what I want to know is—shall I leave him to you, or put off work and come up here to wait for him myself?"

"Why—" said Jack, slowly, "whatever you say. If you think you can safely leave him to me—I'm willing."

"A grizzly won't be pleasant to face. I never knew one of those sheep-killers that wouldn't run at a man, if wounded."

"Tell me what to do."

"If he comes down it's more than likely to be after dark. Don't risk hunting him then. Wait till morning, and put Wolf on his trail. He'll be up in the rocks, and by holding in the dog you may find him asleep in a cave. However, if you happen to meet him by day do this. Don't waste any shots. Climb a ledge or tree if one be handy. If not, stand your ground. Get down on your knee and shoot and let him come. Mind you, he'll grunt when he's hit, and start for you, and keep coming till he's dead. Have confidence in yourself and your gun, for you can kill him. Aim low, and shoot steady. If he keeps on coming there's always a fatal shot, and that is when he rises. You'll see a bare spot on his breast. Put a forty-four into that, and he'll go down."

August had spoken so easily, quite as if he were explaining how to shear a yearling sheep, that Jack's feelings fluctuated between amazement and laughter. Verily this desert man was stripped of all the false fears of civilization.

"Now, Jack, I'm off. Good-bye and good luck. Mescal, look out for him. . . . So-ho! Noddle! Getup! Biscuit!" And with many a cheery word and slap he urged the burros into the forest, where they and his tall form soon disappeared among the trees.

Piute came stooping toward camp so burdened with coyotes that he could scarcely be seen under the gray pile. With a fervent "damn" he tumbled them under a cedar, and trotted back into the forest for another load. Jack insisted on assuming his share of the duties about camp; and Mescal assigned him to the task of gathering firewood, breaking red-hot sticks of wood into small pieces, and raking them into piles of live coals. Then they ate, these two alone. Jack did not do justice to the supper; excitement had robbed him of appetite. He told Mescal how he had crept upon the coyotes, how so many had eluded him, how he had missed a gray wolf. He plied her with questions about the sheep, and wanted to know if there would be more wolves, and if she thought the "silvertip" would come. He was quite carried away by the events of the day.

The sunset drew him to the rim. Dark clouds were mantling the desert like rolling smoke from a prairie-fire. He almost stumbled over Mescal, who sat with her back to a stone. Wolf lay with his head in her lap, and he growled.

"There's a storm on the desert," she said. "Those smoky streaks are flying sand. We may have snow to-night. It's colder, and the wind is north. See, I've a blanket. You had better get one."

He thanked her and went for it. Piute was eating his supper, and the peon had just come in. The bright camp-fire was agreeable, yet Hare did not feel cold. But he wrapped himself in a blanket and returned to Mescal and sat beside her. The desert lay indistinct in the foreground, inscrutable beyond;

the Cañon lost its line in gloom. The solemnity of the scene stilled his unrest, the strange freedom of longings unleashed that day. What had come over him? He shook his head; but with the consciousness of self returned a feeling of fatigue, the burning pain in his chest, the bitter-sweet smell of black sage and juniper.

"You love this outlook?" he asked.

"Yes."

"Do you sit here often?"

"Every evening."

"Is it the sunset that you care for, the roar of the river, just being here high above it all?"

"It's that last, perhaps; I don't know."

"Haven't you been lonely?"

"No."

"You'd rather be here with the sheep than be in Lund or Salt Lake City, as Esther and Judith want to be?"

"Yes."

Any other reply from her would not have been consistent with the impression she was making on him. As yet he had hardly regarded her as a young girl; she had been part of this beautiful desert-land. But he began to see in her a responsive being, influenced by his presence. If the situation was wonderful to him what must it be for her? Like a shy, elusive creature, unused to men, she was troubled by questions, fearful of the sound of her own voice. Yet in repose, as she watched the lights and shadows, she was serene, unconscious; her dark, quiet glance was dreamy and sad, and in it was the sombre, brooding strength of the desert.

Twilight and falling dew sent them back to the camp. Piute and Peon were skinning coyotes by the blaze of the fire. The night wind had not yet risen; the sheep were quiet; there was no sound save the crackle of burning cedar sticks. Jack began to talk;

he had to talk, so addressing Piute and the dumb peon, he struck at random into speech, and words flowed with a rush. Piute approved, for he said "damn" whenever his intelligence grasped a meaning, and the peon twisted his lips and fixed his diamond eyes upon Hare in rapt gaze. The sound of a voice was welcome to the sentinels of that lonely sheep-range. Jack talked of cities, of ships, of people, of simple things in the life he had left, and he discovered that Mescal listened. Not only did she listen; she became absorbed; it was romance to her, fulfilment of her vague dreams. Nor did she seek her tent till he ceased; then with a startled "goodnight" she was gone.

From under the snugness of his warm blankets Jack watched out the last wakeful moments of that day of days. A star peeped through the fringe of cedar foliage. The wind sighed, and rose steadily, to sweep over him with breath of ice, with the fragrance of juniper and black sage and a tang of cedar.

But that day was only the beginning of eventful days, of increasing charm, of forgetfulness of self, of time that passed unnoted. Every succeeding day was like its predecessor, only richer. Every day the hoar-frost silvered the dawn; the sheep browsed; the coyotes skulked in the thickets; the rifle spoke truer and truer. Every sunset Mescal's changing eyes mirrored the desert. Every twilight Jack sat beside her in the silence; every night, in the camp-fire flare, he talked to Piute and the peon.

The Indians were appreciative listeners, whether they understood Jack or not, but his talk with them was only a pretence. He wished to reveal the outside world to Mescal, and he saw with pleasure that every day she grew more interested.

One evening he was telling of New York City, of the monster buildings where men worked, and of the elevated railways, for the time was the late 'seventies and they were still a novelty. Then something unprecedented occurred, inasmuch as Piute earnestly and vigorously interrupted Jack, demanding to have this last strange story made more clear. Jack did his best in gesture and speech, but he had to appeal to Mescal to translate his meaning to the Indian. This Mescal did with surprising fluency. The result, however, was that Piute took exception to the story of trains carrying people through the air. He lost his grin and regarded Jack with much disfavor. Evidently he was experiencing the bitterness of misplaced trust.

"Heap damn lie!" he exclaimed with a growl, and stalked off into the gloom.

Piute's expressive doubt discomfited Hare, but only momentarily, for Mescal's silvery peal of laughter told him that the incident had brought them closer together. He laughed with her and discovered a well of joyousness behind her reserve. Thereafter he talked directly to Mescal. The ice being broken, she began to ask questions, shyly at first, yet more and more eagerly, until she forgot herself in the desire to learn of cities and people; of women especially, what they wore and how they lived, and all that life meant to them.

The sweetest thing which had ever come to Hare was the teaching of this desert girl. How naïve in her questions and how quick to grasp she was! The reaching out of her mind was like the unfolding of a rose. Evidently the Mormon restrictions had limited her opportunities to learn. But her thought had striven to escape its narrow confines, and now, liberated by sympathy and intelligence, it leaped forth.

Lambing-time came late in May, and Mescal, Wolf, Piute, and Jack knew no rest. Night-time was safer for the sheep than the day, though the howling of a thousand coyotes made it hideous for the shepherds. All in a day, seemingly, the little fleecy lambs came, as if by magic, and filled the forest with piping bleats. Then they were tottering after their mothers, gamboling at a day's growth, wilful as youth—and the carnage began. Boldly the coyotes darted out of thicket and bush, and many lambs never returned to their mothers. Gaunt shadows hovered always near; the great timber-wolves waited in covert for prey. Piute slept not at all, and the dog's jaws were flecked with blood morning and night. Jack hung up fifty-four coyotes the second day; the third he let them lie, seventy in number. Many times the rifle-barrel burned his hands. His aim grew unerring, so that running brutes in range dropped in their tracks. Many a gray coyote fell with a lamb in his teeth.

One night when sheep and lambs were in the corral, and the shepherds rested round the campfire, the dog rose quivering, sniffed the cold wind, and suddenly bristled with every hair standing erect.

"Wolf!" called Mescal.

The sheep began to bleat. A rippling crash, a splintering of wood, told of an irresistible onslaught on the corral fence.

"Chus—chus!" exclaimed Piute.

Wolf, not heeding Mescal's cry, flashed like lightning under the cedars. The rush of the sheep pattering across the corral was succeeded by an uproar.

"Bear! Bear!" cried Mescal, with dark eyes on Jack. He seized his rifle.

"Don't go," she implored, her hand on his arm. "Not at night—remember Father Naab said not."

"Listen! I won't stand that. I'll go. Here, get in the tree—quick!"

"No—no—"

"Do as I say!" It was a command. The girl wavered. He dropped the rifle and swung her up. "Climb!"

"No—don't go—Jack!"

With Piute at his heels he ran out into the darkness.

CHAPTER VI

The Wind in the Cedars

PIUTE'S INDIAN sense of the advantage of position in attack stood Jack in good stead; he led him up the ledge which overhung one end of the corral. In the pale starlight the sheep could be seen running in bands, massing together, crowding the fence; their cries made a deafening din.

The Indian shouted, but Jack could not understand him. A large black object was visible in the shade of the ledge. Piute fired his carbine. Before Jack could bring his rifle up the black thing moved into startlingly rapid flight. Then spouts of red flames illumined the corral. As he shot, Jack got fleeting glimpses of the bear moving like a dark streak against a blur of white. For all he could tell, no bullet took effect.

When certain that the visitor had departed, Jack descended into the corral. He and Piute searched for dead sheep, but, much to their surprise, found none. If the grizzly had killed one he must have taken it with him; and estimating his strength from the gap he had broken in the fence, he could easily have carried off a sheep. They repaired the break and returned to camp.

"He's gone, Mescal. Come down," called Jack into the cedar. "Let me help you—there! Wasn't it lucky? He wasn't so brave. Either the flashes from the guns or the dog scared him. I was amazed to see how fast he could run."

Piute found woolly brown fur hanging from Wolf's jaws.

"He's nipped the brute, that's sure," said Jack. "Good dog! Maybe he kept the bear from— Why, Mescal! you're white—you're shaking. There's no danger. Piute and I'll take turns watching with Wolf."

Mescal went silently into her tent.

The sheep quieted down and made no further disturbance that night. The dawn broke gray, with a cold north wind. Dun-colored clouds rolled up, hiding the tips of the crags on the upper range, and a flurry of snow whitened the cedars. After breakfast Jack tried to get Wolf to take the track of the grizzly, but the scent had cooled.

Next day Mescal drove the sheep eastward toward the crags, and about the middle of the afternoon reached the edge of the slope. Grass grew luxuriantly and it was easy to keep the sheep in. Moreover, that part of the forest had fewer trees and scarcely any sage or thickets, so that the lambs were safer, barring danger which might lurk in the seamed and cracked cliffs overshadowing the open grassy plots. Piute's task at the moment was to drag dead coyotes to the rim, near at hand, and throw them over. Mescal rested on a stone, and Wolf reclined at her feet.

Jack presently found a fresh deer track, and trailed it into the cedars, then up the slope to where the huge rocks massed.

Suddenly a cry from Mescal halted him; another, a piercing scream of mortal fright, sent him flying down the slope. He bounded out of the cedars into the open.

The white, well-bunched flock had spread, and streams of jumping sheep fled frantically from an enormous silver-backed bear.

As the bear struck right and left, a brute-engine of destruction, Jack sent a bullet into him at long range. Stung, the grizzly whirled, bit at his side, and then reared with a roar of fury.

But he did not see Jack. He dropped down and launched his huge bulk for Mescal. The blood rushed back to Jack's heart and his empty veins seemed to freeze.

The grizzly hurdled the streams of sheep. Terror for Mescal dominated Jack; if he had possessed wings he could not have flown quickly enough to head the bear. Checking himself with a suddenness that fetched him to his knees, he levelled the rifle. It waved as if it were a stick of willow. The bead-sight described a blurred curve round the bear. Yet he shot—in vain—again—in vain.

Above the bleat of sheep and trample of many hoofs rang out Mescal's cry, despairing.

She had turned, her hands over her breast. Wolf spread his legs before her and crouched to spring, mane erect, jaws wide.

By some lightning flash of memory, August Naab's words steadied Jack's shaken nerves. He aimed low and ahead of the running bear. Down the beast went in a sliding sprawl with a muffled roar of rage. Up he sprang, dangling a useless leg, yet leaping swiftly forward. One blow sent the attacking dog aside. Jack fired again. The bear became a wrestling, fiery demon, death-stricken, but full of savage fury. Jack aimed low and shot again.

Slowly now the grizzly reared, his frosted coat

blood flecked, his great head swaying. Another shot. There was one wide sweep of the huge paw, and then the bear sank forward, drooping slowly, and stretched all his length as if to rest.

Mescal, recalled to life, staggered backward. Between her and the outstretched paw was the distance of one short stride.

Jack, bounding up, made sure the bear was dead before he looked at Mescal. She was faint. Wolf whined about her. Piute came running from the cedars. Her eyes were still fixed in a look of fear.

"I couldn't run—I couldn't move," she said, shuddering. A blush drove the white from her cheeks as she raised her face to Jack. "He'd soon have reached me."

Piute added his encomium: "Damn—heap big bear—Jack kill um—big chief!"

Hare laughed away his own fear and turned their attention to the stampeded sheep. It was dark before they got the flock together again, and they never knew whether they had found them all. Supper-time was unusually quiet that night. Piute was jovial, but no one appeared willing to talk save the peon, and he could only grimace. The reaction of feeling following Mescal's escape had robbed Jack of strength of voice; he could scarcely whisper. Mescal spoke no word; her black lashes hid her eyes; she was silent, but there was that in her silence which was eloquent. Wolf, always indifferent save to Mescal, reacted to the subtle change, and as if to make amends laid his head on Jack's knees. The quiet hour round the camp-fire passed, and sleep claimed them. Another day dawned, awakening them fresh, faithful to their duties, regardless of what had gone before.

So the days slipped by. June came, with more leisure for the shepherds, better grazing for the sheep, heavier dews, lighter frosts, snow-squalls half rain, and bursting blossoms on the prickly thorns, wild-primrose patches in every shady spot, and bluebells lifting wan azure faces to the sun.

The last snow-storm of June threatened all one morning, hung menacing over the yellow crags, in dull lead clouds waiting for the wind. Then like ships heaving anchor to a single command they sailed down off the heights; and the cedar forest became the centre of a blinding, eddying storm. The flakes were as large as feathers, moist, almost warm. The low cedars changed to mounds of white; the sheep became drooping curves of snow; the little lambs were lost in the color of their own pure fleece. Though the storm had been long in coming, it was brief in passing. Wind-driven toward the desert, it moaned its last in the cedars, and swept away, a sheeted pall. Out over the cañon it floated, trailing long veils of white that thinned out, darkened, and failed far above the golden desert. The winding columns of snow merged into straight lines of leaden rain; the rain flowed into vapory mist, and the mist cleared in the gold-red glare of endless level and slope. No moisture reached the parched desert.

Jack marched into camp with a snowy burden over his shoulder. He flung it down, disclosing a small deer; then he shook the white mantle from his coat, and, whistling, kicked the fire-logs, and looked abroad at the silver cedars, now dripping under the sun, at the rainbows in the settling mists, at the rapidly melting snow on the ground.

"Got lost in that squall. Fine! Fine!" he exclaimed and threw wide his arms.

"Jack!" said Mescal. "Jack!" Memory had revived some forgotten thing. The dark olive of her skin crimsoned; her eyes dilated and shadowed with a rare change of emotion.

"Jack," she repeated.

"Well?" he replied, in surprise.

"To look at you!—I never dreamed—I'd forgotten—"

"What's the matter with me?" demanded Jack.

Wonderingly, her mind on the past, she replied: "You were dying when we found you at White Sage."

He drew himself up with a sharp catch in his breath, and stared at her as if he saw a ghost.

"Oh—Jack! You're going to get well!"

Her lips curved in a smile.

For an instant Jack Hare spent his soul in searching her face for truth. While waiting for death he had utterly forgotten it; he remembered now, when life gleamed in the girl's dark eyes. Passionate joy flooded his heart.

"Mescal—Mescal!" he cried, brokenly. The eyes were true that shed this sudden light on him; glad and sweet were the lips that bade him hope and live again. Blindly, instinctively he kissed them—a kiss unutterably grateful; then he fled into the forest, running without aim.

That flight ended in sheer exhaustion on the far rim of the plateau. The spreading cedars seemed to have eyes; and he shunned eyes in this hour. "God! to think I cared so much," he whispered. "What has happened?" With time relief came to limbs, to labored breast and lungs, but not to mind. In doubt that would not die, he looked at himself. The leanness of arms, the flat chest, the hollows were gone. He did not recognize his own body. He breathed to the depth of his lungs. No pain—only exhilaration! He pounded his chest—no pain! He dug his trembling fingers into the firm flesh over the apex of his right lung—the place of his torture—no pain!

"I wanted to live!" he cried. He buried his face in the fragrant juniper; he rolled on the soft brown mat of earth and hugged it close; he cooled his hot cheeks in the primrose clusters. He opened his eyes

to new bright green of cedar, to sky of a richer blue,
to a desert, strange, beckoning, enthralling as life itself. He counted backward a month, two months,
and marvelled at the swiftness of time. He counted
time forward, he looked into the future, and all was
beautiful—long days, long hunts, long rides, service
to his friend, freedom on the wild steppes, blue-
white dawns upon the eastern crags, red-gold sun-
sets over the lilac mountains of the desert. He saw
himself in triumphant health and strength, earning
day by day the spirit of this wilderness, coming to
fight for it, to live for it, and in far-off time, when he
had won his victory, to die for it.

Suddenly his mind was illumined. The lofty plateau with its healing breath of sage and juniper had
given back strength to him; the silence and solitude
and strife of his surroundings had called to something deep within him; but it was Mescal who made
this wild life sweet and significant. It was Mescal,
the embodiment of the desert spirit. Like a man facing a great light Hare divined his love. Through all
the days on the plateau, living with her the natural
free life of Indians, close to the earth, his unconscious love had ripened. He understood now her
charm for him; he knew now the lure of her wonderful eyes, flashing fire, desert-trained, like the falcon
eyes of her Indian grandfather. The knowledge of
what she had become to him dawned with a mounting desire that thrilled all his blood.

Twilight had enfolded the plateau when Hare
traced his way back to camp. Mescal was not there.
His supper awaited him; Piute hummed a song; the
peon sat grimacing at the fire. Hare told them to
eat, and moved away toward the rim.

Mescal was at her favorite seat, with the white
dog beside her; and she watched the desert where
the last glow of sunset gilded the mesas. How cold

and calm was her face! How strange to him in this new character!

"Mescal, I didn't know I loved you—then—but I know it now."

Her face dropped quickly from its level poise, hiding the brooding eyes; her hand trembled on Wolf's head.

"You spoke the truth. I'll get well. I'd rather have had it from your lips than from any in the world. I mean to live my life here where these wonderful things have come to me. The friendship of the good man who saved me, this wild, free desert, the glory of new hope, strength, life—and love."

He took her hand in his and whispered, "For I love you. Do you care for me? Mescal! It must be complete. Do you care—a little?"

The wind blew her dusky hair; he could not see her face; he tried gently to turn her to him. The hand he had taken lay warm and trembling in his, but it was not withdrawn. As he waited, in fear, in hope, it became still. Her slender form, rigid within his arm, gradually relaxed and yielded to him; her face sank on his breast, and her dark hair loosened from its band, covered her and blew across his lips. That was his answer.

The wind sang in the cedars. No longer a sigh, sad as thoughts of a past forever flown, but a song of what had come to him, of hope, of life, of Mescal's love, of the things to be!

CHAPTER VII

Silvermane

LITTLE DEW fell on the night of July 1st; the dawn brightened without mists; a hot sun rose; the short summer of the plateau had begun.

As Hare rose, refreshed and happy, from his breakfast, his whistle was cut short by the Indian.

"Ugh!" exclaimed Piute, lifting a dark finger. Black Bolly had thrown her nose-bag and slipped her halter, and she moved toward the opening in the cedars, her head high, her black ears straight up.

"Bolly!" called Mescal. The mare did not stop.

"What the deuce?" Hare ran forward to catch her.

"I never knew Bolly to act that way," said Mescal. "See—she didn't eat half the oats. Well, Bolly—Jack, look at Wolf!"

The white dog had risen and stood warily shifting his nose. He sniffed the wind, turned round and round, and slowly stiffened with his head pointed toward the eastern rise of the plateau.

"Hold, Wolf, hold!" called Mescal, as the dog appeared to be about to dash away.

"Ugh!" grunted Piute.

"Listen, Jack! Did you hear?" whispered the girl.

"Hear what?"

"Listen."

The warm breeze came down in puffs from the crags; it rustled in the cedars and blew fragrant whiffs of camp-fire smoke into his face; and presently it bore a low, prolonged whistle. He had never before heard its like. The sound broke the silence again, clearer, a keen, sharp whistle.

"What is it?" he queried, reaching for his rifle.

"Wild mustangs," said Mescal.

"No," corrected Piute, vehemently shaking his head. "Clea, clea."

"Jack, he says 'horse, horse.' It's a wild horse."

A third time the whistle rang down from the ridge, splitting the air, strong and trenchant, the fiery, shrill challenge of a stallion.

Black Bolly reared straight up.

Jack ran to the rise of ground above the camp, and looked over the cedars. "Oh!" he cried, and beckoned for Mescal. She ran to him, and Piute, tying Black Bolly, hurried after. "Look! look!" cried Jack. He pointed to a ridge rising to the left of the yellow crags. On the bare summit stood a splendid stallion clearly silhouetted against the ruddy morning sky. He was an iron-gray, wild and proud, with long silver-white mane waving in the wind.

"Silvermane! Silvermane!" exclaimed Mescal.

"What a magnificent animal!" Jack stared at the splendid picture for the moment before the horse moved back along the ridge and disappeared. Other horses, blacks and bays, showed above the sage for a moment, and they, too, passed out of sight.

"He's got some of his band with him," said Jack, thrilled with excitement. "Mescal, they're down off the upper range, and grazing along easy. The wind favors us. That whistle was just plain fight, judging from what Naab told me of wild stallions. He came to the hilltop, and whistled down defiance to any horse, wild or tame, that might be below. I'll slip round through the cedars, and block the trail leading up to the other range, and you and Piute close the gate of our trail at this end. Then send Piute down to tell Naab we've got Silvermane."

Jack chose the lowest edge of the plateau rim where the cedars were thickest for his detour to get behind the wild band; he ran from tree to tree, avoiding the open places, taking advantage of the thickets, keeping away from the ridge. He had never gone so far as the gate, but, knowing where the trail led into a split in the crags, he climbed the slope, and threaded a way over masses of fallen cliff, until he reached the base of the wall. The tracks of the wild-horse band were very fresh and plain in the yellow trail. Four stout posts guarded the opening, and a number of bars lay ready to be pushed into place. He put them up, making a gate ten feet high, an impregnable barrier. This done, he hurried back to camp.

"Jack, Bolly will need more watching to-day than the sheep, unless I let her loose. Why, she pulls and strains so she'll break that halter."

"She wants to go with the band. Isn't that it?"

"I don't like to think so. But Father Naab doesn't trust Bolly, though she's the best mustang he ever broke."

"Better keep her in," replied Jack, remembering Naab's warning. "I'll hobble her, so if she does break loose she can't go far."

When Mescal and Jack drove in the sheep that afternoon, rather earlier than usual, Piute had returned with August Naab, Dave, and Billy, a string of mustangs and a pack-train of burros.

"Hello, Mescal," cheerily called August, as they came into camp. "Well Jack—bless me! Why, my lad, how fine and brown—and yes, how you've filled out!" He crushed Jack's hand in his broad palm, and his gray eyes beamed. "I've not the gift of revelation—but, Jack, you're going to get well."

"Yes, I—" He had difficulty with his enunciation, but he thumped his breast significantly and smiled.

"Black sage and juniper!" exclaimed August. "In this air if a man doesn't go off quickly with pneumonia, he'll get well. I never had a doubt for you, Jack—and thank God!"

He questioned Piute and Mescal about the sheep, and was greatly pleased with their report. He shook his head when Jack spread out the grizzly-pelt, and asked for the story of the killing. Jack made a poor showing with the tale and slighted his share in it, but Mescal told it as it actually happened. And Naab's great hand resounded from Jack's shoulder. Then, catching sight of the pile of coyote-skins under the stone shelf, he gave vent to his surprise and delight. Then he came back to the object of his trip upon the plateau.

"So you've corralled Silvermane? Well, Jack, if he doesn't jump over the cliff he's ours. He can't get off any other way. How many horses with him?"

"We had no chance to count. I saw at least twelve."

"Good! He's out with his picked band. Weren't they all blacks and bays?"

"Yes."

"Jack, the history of that stallion wouldn't make you proud of him. We've corralled him by a lucky chance. If I don't miss my guess he's after Bolly. He has been a lot of trouble to ranchers all the way from the Nevada line across Utah. The stallions he's killed, the mares he's led off! Well, Dave, shall we thirst him out, or line up a long corral?"

"Better have a look around to-morrow," replied Dave. "It'll take a lot of chasing to run him down, but there's not a spring on the bench where we can throw up a trap-corral. We'll have to chase him."

"Mescal, has Bolly been good since Silvermane came down?"

"No, she hasn't," declared Mescal, and told of the circumstance.

"Bolly's all right," said Billy Naab. "Any mustang will do that. Keep her belled and hobbled."

"Silvermane would care a lot about that, if he wanted Bolly, wouldn't he?" queried Dave in quiet scorn. "Keep her roped and haltered, I say."

"Dave's right," said August. "You can't trust a wild mustang any more than a wild horse."

August was right. Black Bolly broke her halter about midnight and escaped into the forest; hobbled as she was. The Indian heard her first, and he awoke August, who aroused the others.

"Don't make any noise," he said, as Jack came up, throwing on his coat. "There's likely to be some fun here presently. Bolly's loose, broke her rope, and I think Silvermane is close. Listen sharp now."

The slight breeze favored them, the camp-fire was dead, and the night was clear and starlit. They had not been quiet many moments when the shrill neigh of a mustang rang out. The Naabs raised themselves and looked at one another in the starlight.

"Now what do you think of that?" whispered Billy.

"No more than I expected. It was Bolly," replied Dave.

"Bolly it was, confound her black hide!" added August. "Now, boys, did she whistle for Silvermane, or to warn him, which?"

"No telling," answered Billy. "Let's lie low and take a chance on him coming close. It proves one thing—you can't break a wild mare. That spirit may sleep in her blood, maybe for years, but some time it'll answer to—"

"Shut up—listen," interrupted Dave.

Jack strained his hearing, yet caught no sound except the distant yelp of a coyote. Moments went by.

"There!" whispered Dave.

From the direction of the ridge came the faint rattling of stones.

"They're coming," put in Billy.

Presently sharp clicks preceded the rattles, and the sounds began to merge into a regular rhythmic tramp. It softened at intervals, probably when the horses were under the cedars, and strengthened as they came out on the harder ground of the open.

"I see them," whispered Dave.

A black, undulating line wound out of the cedars, a line of horses approaching with drooping heads, hurrying a little as they neared the spring.

"Twenty-odd, all blacks and bays," said August, "and some of them are mustangs. But where's Silvermane?—Hark!"

Out among the cedars rose the peculiar halting thump of a hobbled horse trying to cover ground, followed by snorts and crashings of brush and the pound of plunging hoofs. The long black line stopped short and began to stamp. Then into the starlit glade below moved two shadows, the first a great gray horse with snowy mane; the second, a small, shiny, black mustang.

"Silvermane and Bolly!" exclaimed August, "and now she's broken her hobbles."

The stallion, in the fulfillment of a conquest such as had made him king of the wild ranges, was magnificent in action. Wheeling about her, neighing, and plunging, he arched his splendid neck and pushed his head against her. His action was that of a master. Suddenly Black Bolly snorted and whirled down the glade. Silvermane whistled one blast of anger or

terror and thundered after her. They vanished in
the gloom of the cedars, and the band of frightened
horses and mustangs clattered after them.

"It's one on me," remarked Billy. "That little mare
played us at the finish. Caught when she was a yearling, broken better than any mustang we ever had,
she has helped us run down many a stallion, and
now she runs off with that big white-maned brute!"

"They'll make a team, and if they get out of here
we'll have to chase them to the Great Salt Basin,"
replied Dave.

"Mescal, that's a well-behaved mustang of yours,"
said August; "not only did she break loose, but she
whistled an alarm to Silvermane and his band. Well,
roll in now everybody, and sleep."

At breakfast the following day the Naabs fell into
a discussion upon the possibility of there being
other means of exit from the plateau than the two
trails already closed. They had never run any mustangs on the plateau, and in the case of a wild horse
like Silvermane, who would take desperate chances,
it was advisable to know the ground exactly. Billy
and Dave, taking their mounts from the sheep-
corral, where they had put them up for the night,
rode in opposite directions around the rim of the
plateau. It was triangular in shape and some six or
seven miles in circumference; and the brothers rode
around it in less than an hour.

"Corralled," said Dave, laconically.

"Good! Did you see him? What kind of a bunch
has he with him?" asked his father.

"If we get the pick of the lot it will be worth two
weeks' work," replied Dave. "I saw him, and Bolly,
too. I believe we can catch her easily. She was off
from the bunch, and it looks as though the mares
were jealous. I think we can run her into a cove
under the wall and get her. Then Mescal can help us
run down the stallion. And you can look out on this

end for the best level stretch to drop the line of cedars and make our trap."

The brothers, at their father's nod, rode off into the forest. Naab had detained the peon, and now gave him orders and sent him off.

"To-night you can stand on the rim here, and watch him signal across to the top of Echo Cliffs to the Navajos," explained August to Jack. "I've sent for the best breaker of wild mustangs on the desert. Dave can break mustangs, and Piute is very good; but I want the best man in the country, because this is a grand horse and I intend to give him to you."

"To me!" exclaimed Hare.

"Yes, and if he's broken right at the start, he'll serve you faithfully and not try to bite your arm off every day, or kick your brains out. No white man can break a wild mustang to the best advantage."

"Why is that?"

"I don't know. To be truthful, I have an idea it's bad temper and lack of patience. Just wait till you see this Navajo go at Silvermane!"

After Mescal and Piute drove down the sheep, Jack accompanied Naab to the corral.

"I've brought up your saddle," said Naab, "and you can put it on any mustang here."

What a pleasure it was to be in the saddle again, and to feel strength to remain there! He rode with August all over the western end of the plateau. They came at length to a strip of ground, higher than the bordering forest, which was comparatively free of cedars and brush, and when August had surveyed it once he slapped his knee with satisfaction.

"Fine! better than I hoped for! This stretch is about a mile long, and narrow at this end. Now, Jack, you see the other side faces the rim, this side the forest, and at the end here is a wall of rock; luckily it curves in a half circle, which will save us work. We'll cut cedars, drag them in line, and make a big corral against the rock. From the opening in the corral we'll build two fences of trees; then we'll chase Silvermane till he's done, run him down into his level, and turn him inside the fence. No horse can break through a close line of cedars. He'll run till he's in the corral, and then we'll rope him."

"Great!" said Jack, all enthusiasm. "But isn't it going to take a lot of work?"

"Rather," said August, dryly. "It'll take a week to cut and drag the cedars, let alone to tire out that wild stallion. When the finish comes you want to be on that ledge where we'll have the corral."

They returned to camp and prepared supper. Mescal and Piute soon arrived, and, later, Dave and Billy on jaded mustangs. Black Bolly limped behind, stretching a long halter, an unhappy mustang with dusty, foam-stained coat and hanging head.

"Not bad," said August, examining the lame leg. "She'll be fit in a few days, long before we need her to help run down Silvermane. Bring the liniment and a cloth, one of you, and put her in the sheep-corral to-night."

Mescal's love for the mustang shone in her eyes while she smoothed out the crumpled mane and petted the slender neck.

"Bolly, to think you'd do it!" And Bolly dropped her head as though really ashamed.

When darkness fell they gathered on the rim to watch the signals. A fire blazed out of the black void below, and as they waited it brightened and flamed higher.

"Ugh!" said Piute, pointing across to the dark line of cliffs.

"Of course he'd see it first," laughed Naab. "Dave, have you caught it yet? Jack, see if you can make out a fire over on Echo Cliffs."

"No, I don't see any light except that white star. Have you seen it?"

"Long ago," replied Naab. "Here, sight along my finger and narrow your eyes down."

"I believe I see it—yes, I'm sure."

"Good. How about you, Mescal?"

"Yes," she replied.

Jack was amused, for Dave insisted that he had been next to the Indian, and Billy claimed priority to all of them. To these men bred on the desert keen sight was preeminently the chief of gifts.

"Jack, look sharp!" said August. "Peon is blanketing his fire. See the flicker? One, two—one, two—one. Now for the answer."

Jack peered out into the shadowy space, star-studded above, ebony below. Far across the depths shone a pin-point of steady light. The Indian grunted again, August vented his "Ha!" and then Jack saw the light blink like a star, go out for a second, and blink again.

"That's what I like to see," said August. "We're answered. Now all's over but the work."

Work it certainly was, as Jack discovered next day. He helped the brothers cut down cedars while August hauled them into line with his roan. What with this labor and the necessary camp duties nearly a week passed, and in the mean time Black Bolly recovered from her lameness. Twice the workers saw Silvermane standing on open high ridges, restive and suspicious, with his silver mane flying, and his head turned over his shoulder, watching, always watching.

"It'd be worth something to find out how long that stallion could go without water," commented Dave. "But we'll make his tongue hang out tomorrow. It'd serve him right to break him with Black Bolly."

Daylight came warm and misty; veils unrolled from the desert; a purple curtain lifted from the eastern crags; then the red sun burned.

Dave and Billy Naab mounted their mustangs, and each led another mount by a halter.

"We'll go to the ridge, cut Silvermane out of his band, and warm him up; then we'll drive him down to this end."

Hare, in his eagerness, found the time very tedious while August delayed about camp, punching new holes in his saddle-girth, shortening his stirrups, and smoothing kinks out of his lasso. At last he saddled the roan, and also Black Bolly. Mescal came out of her tent ready for the chase; she wore a short skirt of buckskin, and leggings of the same material. Her hair, braided, and fastened at the back, was bound by a double band closely fitting her black head. Hare walked, leading two mustangs by the halters, and Naab and Mescal rode, each of them followed by two other spare mounts. August tied three mustangs at one point along the level stretch, and three at another. Then he led Mescal and Jack to the top of the stone wall above the corral, where they had good view of a considerable part of the plateau.

The eastern rise of ground, a sage and juniper slope, was in plain sight. Hare saw a white flash; then Silvermane broke out of the cedars into the sage. One of the brothers raced him half the length of the slope, and then the other coming out headed him off down toward the forest. Soon the pounding of hoofs sounded through the trees nearer and nearer. Silvermane came out straight ahead on the open level. He was running easily.

"He hasn't opened up yet," said August.

Hare watched the stallion with sheer fascination. He ran seemingly without effort. What a stride he had; how beautifully his silver mane waved in the wind! He veered off to the left, out of sight in the brush, while Dave and Billy galloped up to the spot where August had tied the first three mustangs. Here they dismounted, changed saddles to fresh horses, and were off again.

The chase now was close and all down-hill for the watchers. Silvermane twinkled in and out among the cedars, and suddenly stopped short on the rim. He wheeled and coursed away toward the crags, and vanished. But soon he reappeared, for Billy had cut across and faced him about. Again he struck the level stretch. Dave was there in front of him. He shot away to the left and flashed through the glades beyond. The brothers saved their steeds, content to keep him cornered in that end of the plateau. Then August spurred his roan into the scene of action. Silvermane came out on the one piece of rising ground beyond the level, and stood looking backward toward the brothers. When the great roan crashed through the thickets into his sight he leaped as if he had been stung, and plunged away.

The Naabs had hemmed him in a triangle, Dave and Billy at the broad end, August at the apex, and now the real race began. August chased him up and down, along the rim, across to the long line of cedars, always in the end heading him for the open stretch. Down this he fled with flying mane, only to be checked by the relentless brothers. To cover this broad end of the open required riding the like of which Hare had never dreamed of. The brothers, taking advantage of the brief periods when the stallion was going toward August, changed their tired mustangs for fresh ones.

"Ho! Mescal!" rolled out August's voice. That was the call for Mescal to put Black Bolly after Silvermane. Her fleetness made the other mustangs seem slow. All in a flash she was round the corral, with Silvermane between her and the long fence of cedars. Uttering a piercing snort of terror the gray stallion lunged out, for the first time panic-stricken, and lengthened his stride in a wonderful way. He

raced down the stretch with his head over his
shoulder, watching the little black. Seeing her gaining, he burst into desperate headlong flight. He
saved nothing; he had found his match; he won that
first race down the level, but it had cost him his
best. If he had been fresh he might have left Black
Bolly far behind, but now he could not elude her.

August Naab let him run this time, and Silvermane, keeping close to the fence, passed the gate,
ran down to the rim, and wheeled. The black mustang was on him again, holding him in close to the
fence, driving him back down the stretch.

The brothers remorselessly turned him, and now
Mescal, forcing the running, caught him, lashed his
haunches with her whip, and drove him into the
gate of the corral.

August and his two sons were close behind, and
blocked the gate. Silvermane's race was nearly run.

"Hold here, boys," said August. "I'll go in and
drive him round and round till he's done, then,
when I yell, you stand aside and rope him as he
comes out."

Silvermane ran round the corral, tore at the steep
scaly walls, fell back and began his weary round
again and yet again. Then as sense and courage
yielded gradually to unreasoning terror, he ran
blindly; every time he passed the guarded gateway
his eyes were wilder, and his stride more labored.

"Now!" yelled August Naab.

Mescal drew out of the opening, and Dave and
Billy pulled away, one on each side, their lassoes
swinging loosely.

Silvermane sprang for the opening with something
of his old speed. As he went through, yellow loops
flashed in the sun, circling, narrowing, and he
seemed to run straight into them. One loop whipped
close round his glossy neck; the other caught his
head. Dave's mustang staggered under the violent

shock, went to his knees, struggled up and held firmly. Bill's mount slid on his haunches and spilled his rider from the saddle. Silvermane seemed to be climbing into the air. Then August Naab, darting through the gate in a cloud of dust, shot his lasso, catching the right foreleg. Silvermane landed hard, his hoofs striking fire from the stones; and for an instant strained in convulsive struggle; then fell heaving and groaning. In a twinkling Billy loosened his lasso over a knot, making of it a halter, and tied the end to a cedar stump.

The Naabs stood back and gazed at their prize.

Silvermane was badly spent; he was wet with foam, but no fleck of blood marred his mane; his superb coat showed scratches, but none cut into the flesh. After a while he rose, panting heavily, and trembling in every muscle. He was a beaten horse; the noble head was bowed; yet he showed no viciousness, only the fear of a trapped animal. He eyed Black Bolly and then the halter, as though he had divined the fatal connection between them.

CHAPTER VIII

The Breaker of Wild Mustangs

FOR A few days after the capture of Silvermane, a time full to the brim of excitement for Hare, he had no word with Mescal, save for morning and evening greetings. When he did come to seek her, with a purpose which had grown more impelling since August Naab's arrival, he learned to his bewilderment that she avoided him. She gave him no chance to speak to her alone; her accustomed resting-place on the rim knew her no more; early after supper she retired to her tent.

Hare nursed a grievance for forty-eight hours, and then, taking advantage of Piute's absence on an errand down to the farm, and of the Naabs' strenuous day with four vicious wild horses in the corral at one time, he walked out to the pasture where Mescal shepherded the flock.

"Mescal, why are you avoiding me?" he asked. "What has happened?"

She looked tired and unhappy, and her gaze, instead of meeting his, wandered to the crags.

"Nothing," she replied.

"But there must be something. You have given me no chance to talk to you, and I wanted to know if you'd let me speak to Father Naab."

"To Father Naab? Why—what about?"

"About you, of course—and me—that I love you and want to marry you."

She turned white. "No—no!"

Hare paused blankly, not so much at her refusal as at the unmistakable fear in her face.

"Why—not?" he asked presently, with an odd sense of trouble. There was more here than Mescal's habitual shyness.

"Because he'll be terribly angry."

"Angry—I don't understand. Why angry?"

The girl did not answer, and looked so forlorn that Hare attempted to take her in his arms. She resisted and broke from him.

"You must never—never do that again."

Hare drew back sharply.

"Why not? What's wrong? You must tell me, Mescal."

"I remembered." She hung her head.

"Remembered—what?"

"I am pledged to marry Father Naab's eldest son."

For a moment Hare did not understand. He stared at her unbelievingly.

"What did you say?" he asked, slowly.

Mescal repeated her words in a whisper.

"But—but Mescal—I love you. You let me kiss you," said Hare stupidly, as if he did not grasp her meaning. "You let me kiss you," he repeated.

"Oh, Jack, I forgot," she wailed. "It was so new, so strange, to have you up here. It was like a kind of dream. And after—after you kissed me I—I found out—"

"What, Mescal?"

Her silence answered him.

"But, Mescal, if you really love me you can't marry any one else," said Hare. It was the simple persistence of a simple swain.

"Oh, you don't know, you don't know. It's impossible!"

"Impossible!" Hare's anger flared up. "You let me believe I had won you. What kind of a girl are you? You were not true. Your actions were lies."

"Not lies," she faltered, and turned her face from him.

With no gentle hand he grasped her arm and forced her to look at him. But the misery in her eyes overcame him, and he roughly threw his arms around her and held her close.

"It can't be a lie. You do care for me—love me. Look at me." He drew her head back from his breast. Her face was pale and drawn; her eyes closed tight, with tears forcing a way out under the long lashes; her lips were parted. He bowed to their sweet nearness; he kissed them again and again, while the shade of the cedars seemed to whirl about him. "I love you, Mescal. You are mine—I will have you—I will keep you—I will not let him have you!"

She vibrated to that like a keen strung wire under a strong touch. All in a flash the trembling, shame-stricken girl was transformed. She leaned back in his arms, supple, pliant with quivering life, and for the first time gave him wide-open level eyes, in which there were now no tears, no shyness, no fear, but a dark smouldering fire.

"You do love me, Mescal?"

"I—I couldn't help it."

There was a pause, tense with feeling.

"Mescal, tell me—about your being pledged," he said, at last.

"I gave him my promise because there was nothing else to do. I was pledged to—to him in the church at White Sage. It can't be changed. I've got to marry—Father Naab's eldest son."

"Eldest son?" echoed Jack, suddenly mindful of the implication. "Why! that's Snap Naab. Ah! I begin to see light. That—Mescal—"

"I hate him."

"You hate him and you're pledged to marry him! ... God! Mescal, I'd utterly forgotten Snap Naab already has a wife."

"You've also forgotten that we're Mormons."

"Are you a Mormon?" he queried bluntly.

"I've been raised as one."

"That's not an answer. Are you one? Do you believe any man under God's sky ought to have more than one wife at a time?"

"No. But I've been taught that it gave woman greater glory in heaven. There have been men here before you, men who talked to me, and I doubted before I ever saw you. And afterward—I knew."

"Would not Father Naab release you?"

"Release me? Why, he would have taken me as a wife for himself but for Mother Mary. She hates me. So he pledged me to Snap."

"Does August Naab love you?"

"Love me? No. Not in the way you mean— perhaps as a daughter. But Mormons teach duty to church first, and say such love comes—to the wives—afterward. But it doesn't—not in the women I've seen. There's Mother Ruth—her heart is broken. She loves me, and I can tell."

"When was this—this marriage to be?"

"I don't know. Father Naab promised me to his son when he came home from the Navajo range. It would be soon if they found out that you and I—Jack, Snap Naab would kill you!"

The sudden thought startled the girl. Her eyes betrayed her terror.

"I mightn't be so easy to kill," said Hare, darkly. The words came unbidden, his first answer to the wild influences about him. "Mescal, I'm sorry— maybe I've brought you unhappiness."

"No. No. To be with you has been like sitting there on the rim watching the desert, the greatest happiness I have ever known. I used to love to be with the children, but Mother Mary forbade. When I am down there, which is seldom, I'm not allowed to play with the children any more."

"What can I do?" asked Hare, passionately.

"Don't speak to Father Naab. Don't let him guess. Don't leave me here alone," she answered low. It was not the Navajo speaking in her now. Love had sounded depths hitherto unplumbed; a quick, soft impulsiveness made the contrast sharp and vivid.

"How can I help but leave you if he wants me on the cattle ranges?"

"I don't know. You must think. He has been so pleased with what you've done. He's had Mormons up here, and two men not of his Church, and they did nothing. You've been ill, besides you're different. He will keep me with the sheep as long as he can, for two reasons—because I drive them best, he says, and because Snap Naab's wife must be persuaded to welcome me in her home."

"I'll stay, if I have to get a relapse and go down on my back again," declared Jack. "I hate to deceive him, but, Mescal, pledged or not—I love you, and I won't give up hope."

Her hands flew to her face again and tried to hide the dark blush.

"Mescal, there's one question I wish you'd answer. Does August Naab think he'll make a Mormon of me? Is that the secret of his wonderful kindness?"

"Of course he believes he'll make a Mormon of

you. That's his religion. He's felt that way over all the strangers who ever came out here. But he'd be the same to them without his hopes. I don't know the secret of his kindness, but I think he loves everybody and everything. And Jack, he's so good. I owe him all my life. He would not let the Navajos take me; he raised me, kept me, taught me. I can't break my promise to him. He's been a father to me, and I love him."

"I think I love him, too," replied Hare, simply.

With an effort he left her at last and mounted the grassy slope and climbed high up among the tottering yellow crags; and there he battled with himself. Whatever the charm of Mescal's surrender, and the insistence of his love, stern hammer-strokes of fairness, duty, honor, beat into his brain his debt to the man who had saved him. It was a long-drawn-out battle not to be won merely by saying right was right. He loved Mescal, she loved him; and something born in him with his new health, with the breath of this sage and juniper forest, with the sight of purple cañons and silent beckoning desert, made him fiercely tenacious of all that life had come to mean for him. He could not give her up—and yet—

Twilight forced Hare from his lofty retreat, and he trod his way campward, weary and jaded, but victorious over himself. He thought he had renounced his hope of Mescal; he returned with a resolve to be true to August, and to himself; bitterness he would not allow himself to feel. And yet he feared the rising in him of a new spirit akin to that of the desert itself, intractable and free.

"Well, Jack, we rode down the last of Silvermane's band," said August, at supper. "The Navajos came up and helped us out. To-morrow you'll see some fun, when we start to break Silvermane. As soon as that's done I'll go, leaving the Indians to bring the horses down when they're broken."

"Are you going to leave Silvermane with me?" asked Jack.

"Surely. Why, in three days, if I don't lose my guess, he'll be like a lamb. Those desert stallions can be made into the finest kind of saddle-horses. I've seen one or two. I want you to stay up here with the sheep. You're getting well, you'll soon be a strapping big fellow. Then when we drive the sheep down in the fall you can begin life on the cattle ranges, driving wild steers. There's where you'll grow lean and hard, like an iron bar. You'll need that horse, too, my lad."

"Why—because he's fast?" queried Jack, quickly answering to the implied suggestion.

August nodded gloomily. "I haven't the gift of revelation, but I've come to believe Martin Cole. Holderness's building an outpost for his riders close to Seeping Springs. He has no water. If he tries to pipe my water—" The pause was not a threat; it implied the Mormon's doubt of himself. "Then Dene is on the march this way. He's driven some of Marshall's cattle from the range next to mine. Dene got away with about a hundred head. The barefaced robber sold them in Lund to a buying company from Salt Lake."

"Is he openly an outlaw, a rustler?" inquired Hare.

"Everybody knows it, and he's finding White Sage and vicinity warmer than it was. Every time he comes in he and his band shoot up things pretty lively. Now the Mormons are slow to wrath. But they are awakening. All the way from Salt Lake to the border outlaws have come in. They'll never get the power on this desert that they had in the places from which they've been driven. Men of the Holderness type are more to be dreaded. He's a rancher, greedy, unscrupulous, but hard to corner in dishonesty. Dene is only a bad man, a gun-fighter. He and all his ilk will get run out of Utah. Did you ever hear of Plummer, John Slade, Boone Helm, any of those bad men?"

"No."

"Well, they were men to fear. Plummer was a sheriff in Idaho, a man high in the estimation of his townspeople, but he was the leader of the most desperate band of criminals ever known in the West; and he instigated the murder of, or killed outright, more than one hundred men. Slade was a bad man, fatal on the draw. Helm was a killing-machine. These men all tried Utah, and had to get out. So will Dene have to get out. But I'm afraid there'll be warm times before that happens. When you get in the thick of it you'll appreciate Silvermane."

"I surely will. But I can't see that wild stallion with a saddle and bridle, eating oats like any common horse, and being led to water."

"Well, he'll come to your whistle, presently, if I'm not greatly mistaken. You must make him love you, Jack. It can be done with any wild creature. Be gentle, but firm. Teach him to obey the slightest touch of rein, to stand when you throw your bridle on the ground, to come at your whistle. Always remember this. He's a desert-bred horse; he can live on scant browse and little water. Never break him of those best virtues in a horse. Never feed him grain if you can find a little patch of browse; never give him a drink till he needs it. That's one-tenth as often as a tame horse. Some day you'll be caught in the desert, and with these qualities of endurance Silvermane will carry you out."

Silvermane snorted defiance from the cedar corral next morning when the Naabs, and Indians, and Hare appeared. A half-naked sinewy Navajo with a face as changeless as a bronze mask sat astride August's blindfolded roan, Charger. He rode bareback except for a blanket strapped upon the horse; he carried only a long, thick halter, with a loop and a knot. When August opened the improvised gate, with its sharp bayonet-like branches of cedar, the Indian rode into the corral. The watchers climbed to the knoll. Silvermane snorted a blast of fear and anger. August's huge roan showed uneasiness; he stamped, and shook his head, as if to rid himself of the blinders.

Into the farthest corner of densely packed cedar boughs Silvermane pressed himself and watched. The Indian rode around the corral, circling closer and closer, yet appearing not to see the stallion. Many rounds he made; closer he got, and always with the same steady gait. Silvermane left his corner and tried another. The old unwearying round brought Charger and the Navajo close by him. Silvermane pranced out of his thicket of boughs; he whistled, he wheeled with his shiny hoofs lifting. In an hour the Indian was edging the outer circle of the corral, with the stallion pivoting in the centre, ears laid back, eyes shooting sparks, fight in every line of him. And the circle narrowed inward.

Suddenly the Navajo sent the roan at Silvermane and threw his halter. It spread out like a lasso, and the loop went over the head of the stallion, slipped to the knot and held fast, while the rope tightened. Silvermane leaped up, forehoofs pawing the air, and his long shrill cry was neither whistle, snort, nor screech, but all combined. He came down, missing Charger with his hoofs, sliding off his haunches. The Indian, his bronze muscles rippling, close-hauled on the rope, making half stitches round his bony wrist.

In a whirl of dust the roan drew closer to the gray, and Silvermane began a mad race around the corral. The roan ran with him nose to nose. When Silvermane saw he could not shake him, he opened his jaws, rolled back his lip in an ugly snarl, his white teeth glistening, and tried to bite. But the Indian's moccasined foot shot up under the stallion's ear and pressed him back. Then the roan hugged Silvermane so close that half the time the Navajo virtually rode two horses. But for the rigidity of his arms, and the play and sudden tension of his leg-muscles, the Indian's work would have appeared commonplace, so dexterous was he, so perfectly at home in his dangerous seat. Suddenly he whooped and August Naab hauled back the gate, and the two horses, neck and neck, thundered out upon the level stretch.

"Good!" cried August. "Let him rip now, Navvy. All over but the work, Jack. I feared Silvermane would spear himself on some of those dead cedar spikes in the corral. He's safe now."

Jack watched the horses plunge at breakneck speed down the stretch, circle at the forest edge, and come tearing back. Silvermane was pulling the roan faster than he had ever gone in his life, but the dark Indian kept his graceful seat. The speed slackened on the second turn, and decreased as, mile after mile, the imperturbable Indian held roan and gray side to side and let them run.

The time passed, but Hare's interest in the breaking of the stallion never flagged. He began to understand the Indian, and to feel what the restraint and drag must be to the horse. Never for a moment could Silvermane elude the huge roan, the tight halter, the relentless Navajo. Gallop fell to trot, and trot to jog, and jog to walk; and hour by hour, without whip or spur or word, the breaker of desert mustangs drove the wild stallion. If there were cruelty it was in his implacable slow patience, his far-sighted purpose. Silvermane would have killed himself in an hour; he would have cut himself to pieces in one headlong dash, but that steel arm suffered him only to wear himself out. Late that afternoon the Navajo led a dripping, drooping, foam-lashed stallion into the corral, tied him with the halter, and left him.

Later Silvermane drank of the water poured into the corral trough, and had not the strength or spirit to resent the Navajo's caressing hand on his mane.

Next morning the Indian rode again into the corral on blindfolded Charger. Again he dragged Silvermane out on the level and drove him up and down with remorseless, machine-like persistence. At noon he took him back, tied him up, and roped him fast. Silvermane tried to rear and kick, but the saddle went on, strapped with a flash of the dark-skinned hands. Then again Silvermane ran the level stretch beside the giant roan, only he carried a saddle now. At the first, he broke out with free wild stride as if to run forever from under the hateful thing. But as the afternoon waned he crept wea-riedly back to the corral.

On the morning of the third day the Navajo went into the corral without Charger, and roped the gray, tied him fast, and saddled him. Then he loosed the lassoes except the one around Silvermane's neck, which he whipped under his foreleg to draw him down. Silvermane heaved a groan which plainly said he never wanted to rise again. Swiftly the Indian knelt on the stallion's head; his hands flashed; there was a scream, a click of steel on bone; and proud Silvermane jumped to his feet with a bit between his teeth.

The Navajo, firmly in the saddle, rose with him, and Silvermane leaped through the corral gate, and out upon the stretch, lengthening out with every stride, and settling into a wild, despairing burst of speed. The white mane waved in the wind; the half-naked Navajo swayed to the motion. Horse and rider disappeared in the cedars.

They were gone all day. Toward night they appeared on the stretch. The Indian rode into camp and, dismounting, handed the bridle-rein to Naab. He spoke no word; his dark impassiveness invited no comment. Silvermane was dust-covered and sweat-stained. His silver crest had the same proud beauty, his neck still the splendid arch, his head the noble outline, but his was a broken spirit.

"Here, my lad," said August Naab, throwing the bridle-rein over Hare's arm. "What did I say once about seeing you on a great gray horse? Ah! Well, take him and know this: you've the swiftest horse in this desert country."

CHAPTER IX

The Scent of Desert-Water

SOON THE shepherds were left to a quiet unbroken by the whistle of wild mustangs, the whoop of hunters, the ring of iron-shod hoofs on the stones. The scream of an eagle, the bleating of sheep, the bark of a coyote were once more the only familiar sounds accentuating the silence of the plateau. For Hare, time seemed to stand still. He thought but little; his whole life was a matter of feeling from without. He rose at dawn, never failing to see the red sun tip the eastern crags; he glowed with the touch of cold spring-water and the morning air; he trailed Silvermane under the cedars and thrilled when the stallion, answering his call, thumped the ground with hobbled feet and came his way, learning day by day to be glad at sight of his master. He rode with Mescal behind the flock; he hunted hour by hour, crawling over the fragrant brown mats of cedar, through the sage and juniper, up the grassy slopes. He rode back to camp beside Mescal, drove the sheep, and put Silvermane to his fleetest to be at Black Bolly down the level stretch where once the gray, even with freedom at stake, had lost to the black. Then back to camp and fire and curling blue smoke, a supper that testified to busy Piute's farmward trips, sunset on the rim, endless changing desert, the wind in the cedars, bright stars in the blue, and sleep—so time stood still.

Mescal and Hare were together, or never far apart, from dawn to night. Until the sheep were in the corral, every moment had its duty, from campwork and care of horses to the many problems of the flock, so that they earned the rest on the rimwall at sundown. Only a touch of hands bridged the chasm between them. They never spoke of their love, of Mescal's future, of Jack's return to health; a glance and a smile, scarcely sad yet not altogether happy, was the substance of their dream. Where Jack had once talked about the cañon and desert, he now seldom spoke at all. From watching Mescal he had learned that to see was enough. But there were moments when some association recalled the past and the strangeness of the present faced him. Then he was wont to question Mescal.

"What are you thinking of?" he asked, curiously, interrupting their silence. She leaned against the rocks and kept a changeless, tranquil, unseeing gaze on the desert. The level eyes were full of thought, of sadness, of mystery; they seemed to look afar.

Then she turned to him with puzzled questioning look and enigmatical reply. "Thinking?" asked her eyes. "I wasn't thinking," were her words.

"I fancied—I don't know exactly what," he went on. "You looked so earnest. Do you ever think of going to the Navajos?"

"No."

"Or across that Painted Desert to find some place you seem to know, or see?"

"No."

"I don't know why, but, Mescal, sometimes I have the queerest ideas when I catch your eyes watching, watching. You look at once happy and sad. You see something out there that I can't see. Your eyes are haunted. I've a feeling that if I'd look into them I'd see the sun setting, the clouds coloring, the twilight shadows changing; and then back of that the secret of it all—of you—Oh! I can't explain, but it seems so."

"I never had a secret, except the one you know," she answered. "You ask me so often what I think about, and you always ask me when we're here." She was silent for a pause. "I don't think at all till you make me. It's beautiful out there. But that's not what it is to me. I can't tell you. When I sit down here all within me is—is somehow stilled. I watch— and it's different from what it is now, since you've made me think. Then I watch, and I see, that's all."

It came to Hare afterward with a little start of surprise that Mescal's purposeless, yet all-satisfying, watchful gaze had come to be part of his own experience. It was inscrutable to him, but he got from it a fancy, which he tried in vain to dispel, that something would happen to them out there on the desert.

And then he realized that when they returned to the camp-fire they seemed freed from this spell of the desert. The blaze-lit circle was shut in by the darkness; and the immensity of their wild environment, because for the hour it could not be seen, lost its paralyzing effect. Hare fell naturally into a talkative mood. Mescal had developed a vivacity, an ambition which contrasted strongly with her silent moods; she became alive and curious, human like the girls he had known in the East, and she fascinated him the more for this complexity.

The July rains did not come; the mists failed; the dews no longer freshened the grass, and the hot sun began to tell on shepherds and sheep. Both sought the shade. The flowers withered first—all the blue-bells and lavender patches of primrose, and pale-yellow lilies, and white thistle-blossoms. Only the deep magenta of cactus and vermilion of Indian paint-brush, flowers of the sun, survived the heat. Day by day the shepherds scanned the sky for storm-clouds that did not appear. The spring ran lower and lower. At last the ditch that carried water to the corral went dry, and the margin of the pool began to retreat. Then Mescal sent Piute down for August Naab.

He arrived at the plateau the next day with Dave and at once ordered the breaking up of camp.

"It will rain some time," he said, "but we can't wait any longer. Dave, when did you last see the Blue Star water-hole?"

"On the trip in from Silver Cup, ten days ago. The water-hole was full then."

"Will there be water enough now?"

"We've got to chance it. There's no water here, and no springs on the upper range where we can drive sheep; we've got to go round under the Star."

"That's so," replied August. His fears needed confirmation, because his hopes always influenced his judgment till no hope was left. "I wish I had brought Zeke and George. It'll be a hard drive, though we've got Jack and Mescal to help."

Hot as it was August Naab lost no time in the start. Piute led the train on foot, and the flock, used to following him, got under way readily. Dave and Mescal rode along the sides, and August with Jack came behind, with the pack-burros bringing up the rear. Wolf circled them all, keeping the flanks close in, heading the lambs that strayed, and, ever vigilant, made the drive orderly and rapid.

The trail to the upper range was wide and easy of ascent, the first of it winding under crags, the latter part climbing long slopes. It forked before the summit, where dark pine-trees showed against the sky, one fork ascending, the other, which Piute took, beginning to go down. It admitted of no extended view, being shut in for the most part on the left, but there were times when Hare could see a curving stream of sheep on half a mile of descending trail. Once started down the flock could not be stopped, that was as plain as Piute's hard task. There were times when Hare could have tossed a pebble on the Indian just below him, yet there were more than three thousand sheep, strung out in line between them. Clouds of dust rolled up, sheets of gravel and shale rattled down the inclines, the clatter, clatter, clatter of little hoofs, the steady baa-baa-baa filled the air. Save for the crowding of lambs off the trail, and a jamming of sheep in the corners, the drive went on without mishap. Hare was glad to see the lambs scramble back bleating for their mothers, and to note that, though peril threatened at every steep turn, the steady downflow always made space for the sheep behind. He was glad, too, when through a wide break ahead his eye followed the face of a vast cliff down to the red ground below, and he knew the flock would soon be safe on the level.

A blast as from a furnace smote Hare from this open break in the wall. The air was dust-laden, and carried besides the smell of dust and the warm breath of desert growths, a dank odor that was unpleasant.

The sheep massed in a flock on the level, and the drivers spread to their places. The route lay under projecting red cliffs, between the base and enor-

mous sections of wall that had broken off and fallen
far out. There was no weathering slope; the wind
had carried away the smaller stones and particles,
and had cut the huge pieces of pinnacle and tower
into hollowed forms. This zone of rim merged into
another of strange contrast, the sloping red stream
of sand which flowed from the wall of the cañon.

Piute swung the flock up to the left into an
amphitheatre, and there halted. The sheep formed a
densely packed mass in the curve of the wall. Dave
Naab galloped back toward August and Hare, and
before he reached them shouted out: "The water-
hole's plugged!"

"What?" yelled his father.

"Plugged, filled with stone and sand."

"Was it a cave-in?"

"I reckon not. There's been no rain."

August spurred his roan after Dave, and Hare
kept close behind them, till they reined in on a
muddy bank. What had once been a water-hole was
a red and yellow heap of shale, fragments of stones,
gravel, and sand. There was no water, and the
sheep were bleating. August dismounted and
climbed high above the hole to examine the slope;
soon he strode down with giant steps, his huge fists
clinched, shaking his gray mane like a lion.

"I've found the tracks! Somebody climbed up and
rolled the stones, started the cave-in. Who?"

"Holderness's men. They did the same for Martin
Cole's water-hole at Rocky Point. How old are the
tracks?"

"Two days, perhaps. We can't follow them. What
can be done?"

"Some of Holderness's men are Mormons, and
others are square fellows. They wouldn't stand for
such work as this, and somebody ought to ride in
there and tell them."

"And get shot up by the men paid to do the dirty

work. No. I won't hear of it. This amounts to nothing; we seldom use this hole, only twice a year when driving the flock. But it makes me fear for Silver Cup and Seeping Springs."

"It makes me fear for the sheep, if this wind doesn't change."

"Ah! I had forgotten the river scent. It's not strong to-night. We might venture if it wasn't for the strip of sand. We'll camp here and start the drive at dawn."

The sun went down under a crimson veil; a dull glow spread, fan-shaped, upward; twilight faded to darkness with the going down of the wind. August Naab paced to and fro before his tired and thirsty flock.

"I'd like to know," said Hare to Dave, "why those men filled up this water-hole."

"Holderness wants to cut us off from Silver Cup Spring, and this was a half-way water-hole. Probably he didn't know we had the sheep upland, but he wouldn't have cared. He's set himself to get our cattle range and he'll stop at nothing. Prospects look black for us. Father never gives up. He doesn't believe yet that we can lose our water. He prays and hopes, and sees good and mercy in his worst enemies."

"If Holderness works as far as Silver Cup, how will he go to work to steal another man's range and water?"

"He'll throw up a cabin, send in his men, drive in ten thousand steers."

"Well, will his men try to keep you away from your own water, or your cattle?"

"Not openly. They'll pretend to welcome us, and drive our cattle away in our absence. You see there are only five of us to ride the ranges, and we'd need five times five to watch all the stock."

"Then you can't stop this outrage?"

"There's only one way," said Dave, significantly tapping the black handle of his Colt. "Holderness thinks he pulls the wool over our eyes by talking of the cattle company that employs him. He's the company himself, and he's hand and glove with Dene."

"And I suppose, if your father and you boys were to ride over to Holderness's newest stand, and tell him to get off, there would be a fight."

"We'd never reach him now, that is, if we went together. One of us alone might get to see him, especially in White Sage. If we all rode over to his ranch we'd have to fight his men before we reached the corrals. You yourself will find it pretty warm when you go out with us on the ranges, and if you make White Sage you'll find it hot. You're called 'Dene's spy' there, and the rustlers are still looking for you. I wouldn't worry about it, though."

"Why not, I'd like to know?" inquired Hare, with a short laugh.

"Well, if you're like the other Gentiles who have come into Utah you won't have scruples about drawing on a man. Father says the draw comes natural to you, and you're as quick as he is. Then he says you can beat any rifle shot he ever saw, and that long-barrelled gun you've got will shoot a mile. So if it comes to shooting—why, you can shoot. If you want to run—who's going to catch you on that white-maned stallion? We talked about you, George and I; we're might glad you're well and can ride with us."

Long into the night Jack Hare thought over this talk. It opened up a vista of the range-life into which he was soon to enter. He tried to silence the voice within that cried out, eager and reckless, for the long rides on the windy open. The years of his illness returned in fancy, the narrow room with the lamp and the book, and the tears over stories and dreams of adventure never to be for such as he.

And now how wonderful was life! It was, after all, to
be full for him. It was already full. Already he slept
on the ground, open to the sky. He looked up at a
wild black cliff, mountain-high, with its windworn
star of blue; he felt himself on the threshold of the
desert, with that subtle mystery waiting; he knew
himself to be close to strenuous action on the
ranges, companion of those sombre Mormons, ex-
posed to their peril, making their cause his cause,
their life his life. What of their friendship, their confidence? Was he worthy? Would he fail at the pinch?
What a man he must become to approach their simple estimate of him! Because he had found health
and strength, because he could shoot, because he
had the fleetest horse on the desert, were these reasons for their friendship? No, these were only
reasons for their trust. August Naab loved him. Mescal loved him; Dave and George made of him a
brother. "They shall have my life," he muttered.

The bleating of the sheep heralded another day.
With the brightening light began the drive over the
sand. Under the cliff the shade was cool and fresh;
there was no wind; the sheep made good progress.
But the broken line of shade crept inward toward
the flock, and passed it. The sun beat down, and the
wind arose. A red haze of fine sand eddied about
the toiling sheep and shepherds. Piute trudged
ahead leading the king-ram, old Socker, the leader
of the flock; Mescal and Hare rode at the right, turning their faces from the sand-filled puffs of wind; August and Dave drove behind; Wolf, as always, took
care of the stragglers. An hour went by without
signs of distress; and with half the five-mile trip at
his back August Naab's voice gathered cheer. The
sun beat hotter. Another hour told a different
story—the sheep labored; they had to be forced by
urge of whip, by knees of horses, by Wolf's threaten-
ing bark. They stopped altogether during the fre-

quent hot sand-blasts, and could not be driven. So
time dragged. The flock straggled out to a long irregular line; rams refused to budge till they were
ready; sheep lay down to rest; lambs fell. But there
was an end to the belt of sand, and August Naab at
last drove the lagging trailers out upon the stony
bench.

The sun was about two hours past the meridian;
the red walls of the desert were closing in; the
V-shaped split where the Colorado cut through was
in sight. The trail now was wide and unobstructed
and the distance short, yet August Naab ever and
anon turned to face the cañon and shook his head
in anxious foreboding.

It quickly dawned upon Hare that the sheep were
behaving in a way new and singular to him. They
packed densely now, crowding forward, many raising their heads over the haunches of others and
bleating. They were not in their usual calm pattering hurry, but nervous, excited, and continually facing west toward the cañon, noses up. On the top of
the next little ridge Hare heard Silvermane snort as
he did when led to drink. There was a scent of water on the wind. Hare caught it, a damp, muggy
smell. The sheep had noticed it long before, and
now under its nearer, stronger influence, began to
bleat wildly, to run faster, to crowd without aim.

"There's work ahead. Keep them packed and going. Turn the wheelers," ordered August.

What had been a drive became a flight. And it
was well so long as the sheep headed straight up
the trail. Piute had to go to the right to avoid being
run down. Mescal rode up to fill his place. Hare
took his cue from Dave, and rode along the flank,
crowding the sheep inward. August cracked his
whip behind. For half a mile the flock kept to the
trail, then, as if by common consent, they sheered
off to the right. With this move August and Dave

were transformed from quiet almost to frenzy. They galloped to the fore, and into the very faces of the turning sheep, and drove them back. Then the rearguard of the flock curved outward.

"Drive them in!" roared August.

Hare sent Silvermane at the deflecting sheep and frightened them into line.

Wolf no longer had power to chase the stragglers; they had to be turned by a horse. All along the flank noses pointed outward; here and there sheep wilder than the others leaped forward to lead a widening wave of bobbing woolly backs. Mescal engaged one point, Hare another, Dave another, and August Naab's roan thundered up and down the constantly broken line. All this while as the shepherds fought back the sheep, the flight continued faster eastward, farther cañonward. Each side gained, but the flock gained more toward the cañon than the drivers gained toward the oasis.

By August's hoarse yells, by Dave's stern face and ceaseless swift action, by the increasing din, Hare knew terrible danger hung over the flock; what it was he could not tell. He heard the roar of the river rapids, and it seemed that the sheep heard it with him. They plunged madly; they had gone wild from the scent and sound of water. Their eyes gleamed red; their tongues flew out. There was no aim to the rush of the great body of sheep, but they followed the leaders and the leaders followed the scent. And the drivers headed them off, rode them down, ceaselessly, riding forward to check one outbreak, wheeling backward to check another.

The flight became a rout. Hare was in the thick of dust and din, of the terror-stricken jumping mob, of the ever-starting, ever-widening streams of sheep; he rode and yelled and fired his Colt. The dust choked him, the sun burned him, the flying pebbles cut his cheek. Once he had a glimpse of Black Bolly in a mêlée of dust and sheep; Dave's mustang blurred in his sight; August's roan seemed to be double. Then Silvermane, of his own accord, was out before them all.

The sheep had almost gained the victory, their keen noses were pointed toward the water, nothing could stop their flight, but still the drivers dashed at them, ever fighting, never wearying, never ceasing.

At the last incline, where a gentle slope led down to a dark break in the desert, the rout became a stampede. Left and right flanks swung round, the line lengthened, and round the struggling horses, knee-deep in woolly backs, split the streams to flow together beyond in one resistless river of sheep. Mescal forced Bolly out of danger; Dave escaped the right flank, August and Hare swept on with the flood, till the horses, sighting the dark cañon, halted to stand like rocks.

"Will they run over the rim?" yelled Hare, horrified. His voice came to him as a whisper. August Naab, sweat-stained in red dust, haggard, gray locks streaming in the wind, raised his arms above his head, hopeless.

The long nodding line of woolly forms, lifting like the crest of a yellow wave, plunged out and down in rounded billow over the cañon rim. With din of hoofs and bleats the sheep spilled themselves over the precipice, and an awful deafening roar boomed up from the river, like the spreading thunderous crash of an avalanche.

How endless seemed that fatal plunge! The last line of sheep, pressing close to those gone before, and yet impelled by the strange instinct of life, turned their eyes too late on the brink, carried over by their own momentum.

The sliding roar ceased; its echo, muffled and hollow, pealed from the cliffs, then rumbled down the cañon to merge at length in the sullen, dull, continuous sound of the rapids.

Hare turned at last from that narrow iron-walled cleft, the depth of which he had not seen, and now had no wish to see; and his eyes fell upon a little Navajo lamb limping in the trail of the flock, headed for the cañon, as sure as its mother in purpose. He dismounted and seized it to find, to his infinite wonder and gladness, that it wore a string and bell round its neck.

It was Mescal's pet.

CHAPTER X

Riding the Ranges

THE SHEPHERDS were home in the oasis that evening, and next day the tragedy of the sheep was a thing of the past. No other circumstances of Hare's four months with the Naabs had so affected him as this swift inevitable sweeping away of the flock; nothing else had so vividly told him the nature of this country of abrupt heights and depths. He remembered August Naab's magnificent gesture of despair; and now the man was cheerful again; he showed no sign of his great loss. His tasks were many, and when one was done, he went on to the next. If Hare had not had many proofs of this Mormon's feeling he would have thought him callous. August Naab trusted God and men, loved animals, did what he had to do with all his force, and accepted fate. The tragedy of the sheep had been only an incident in a tragical life—that Hare divined with awe.

Mescal sorrowed, and Wolf mourned in sympathy with her, for their occupation was gone, but both brightened when August made known his intention to cross the river to the Navajo range, to trade with the Indians for another flock. He began his preparations immediately. The snow freshets had long run out of the river, the water was low, and he wanted to fetch the sheep down before the summer rains. He also wanted to find out what kept his son Snap so long among the Navajos.

"I'll take Billy and go at once. Dave, you join George and Zeke out on the Silver Cup range. Take Jack with you. Brand all the cattle you can before the snow flies. Get out of Dene's way if he rides over, and avoid Holderness's men. I'll have no fights. But keep your eyes sharp for their doings."

It was a relief to Hare that Snap Naab had not yet returned to the oasis, for he felt a sense of freedom which otherwise would have been lacking. He spent the whole of a long calm summer day in the orchard and the vineyard. The fruit season was at its height. Grapes, plums, pears, melons were ripe and luscious. Midsummer was vacation-time for the children, and they flocked into the trees like birds. The girls were picking grapes; Mother Ruth enlisted Jack in her service at the pear-trees; Mescal came, too, and caught the golden pears he threw down, and smiled up at him; Wolf was there, and Noddle; Black Bolly pushed her black nose over the fence, and whinnied for apples; the turkeys strutted, the peafowls preened their beautiful plumage, the guinea-hens ran like quail. Save for those frowning red cliffs Hare would have forgotten where he was; the warm sun, the yellow fruit, the merry screams of children, the joyous laughter of girls, were pleasant reminders of autumn picnic days long gone. But, in the face of those dominating wind-scarred walls, he could not forget.

That night Hare endeavored to see Mescal alone for a few moments, to see her once more with unguarded eyes, to whisper a few words, to say good-bye; but it was impossible.

On the morrow he rode out of the red cliff gate with Dave and the pack-horses, a dull ache in his heart; for amid the cheering crowd of children and women who bade them good-bye he had caught the wave of Mescal's hand and a look of her eyes that would be with him always. What might happen before he returned, if he ever did return! For he knew now, as well as he could feel Silvermane's easy stride, that out there under the white glare of desert, the white gleam of the slopes of Coconina, was wild life awaiting him. And he shut his teeth, and narrowed his eyes, and faced it with an eager joy that was in strange contrast to the pang in his breast.

That morning the wind dipped down off the Vermillion Cliffs and whipped west; there was no scent of river-water, and Hare thought of the fatality of the sheep-drive, when, for one day out of the year, a moistened dank breeze had met the flock on the narrow bench. Soon the bench lay far behind them, and the strip of treacherous sand, and the maze of sculptured cliff under the Blue Star, and the hummocky low ridges beyond, with their dry white washes. Silvermane kept on in front. Already Hare had learned that the gray would have no horse before him. His pace was swift, steady, tireless. Dave was astride his Navajo mount, an Indian-bred horse, half mustang, which had to be held in with a firm rein. The pack-train strung out far behind, trotting faithfully along, with the white packs, like the humps of camels, nodding up and down. Jack and Dave slackened their gait at the foot of the stony divide. It was an ascent of miles, so long that it did not appear steep. Here the pack-train caught up, and thereafter hung at the heels of the riders.

From the broad bare summit Jack saw the Silver

Cup valley-range with eyes which seemed to magnify the winding trail, the long red wall, the green slopes, the dots of sage and cattle. Then he made allowance for months of unobstructed vision; he had learned to see; his eyes had adjusted themselves to distance and dimensions.

Silver Cup Spring lay in a bright green spot close under a break in the rocky slope that soon lost its gray cliff in the shaggy cedared side of Coconina.

The camp of the brothers was situated upon this cliff in a split between two sections of wall. Well sheltered from the north and west winds was a grassy plot which afforded a good survey of the valley and the trails. Dave and Jack received glad greetings from Zeke and George, and Silvermane was an object of wonder and admiration. Zeke, who had often seen the gray and chased him too, walked round and round him, stroking the silver mane, feeling the great chest muscles, slapping his flanks.

"Well, well, Silvermane, to think I'd live to see you wearing a saddle and bridle! He's even bigger than I thought. There's a horse, Hare! Never will be another like him in this desert. If Dene ever sees that horse he'll chase him to the Great Salt Basin. Dene's crazy about fast horses. He's from Kentucky, somebody said, and knows a horse when he sees one."

"How are things?" queried Dave.

"We can't complain much," replied Zeke, "though we've wasted some time on old Whitefoot. He's been chasing our horses. It's been pretty hot and dry. Most of the cattle are on the slopes; fair browse yet. There's a bunch of steers gone up on the mountain, and some more round toward the Saddle or the cañon."

"Been over Seeping Springs way?"

"Yes. No change since your trip. Holderness's cattle are ranging in the upper valley. George found tracks near the spring. We believe somebody was watching there and made off when we came up."

"We'll see Holderness's men when we get to riding out," put in George. "And some of Dene's too. Zeke met Two-Spot Chance and Culver below at the spring one day, sort of surprised them."

"What day was that?"

"Let's see, this's Friday. It was last Monday."

"What were they doing over here?"

"Said they were tracking a horse that had broken his hobbles. But they seemed uneasy, and soon rode off."

"Did either of them ride a horse with one shoe shy?"

"Now I think of it, yes. Zeke noticed the track at the spring."

"Well, Chance and Culver had been out our way," declared Dave. "I saw their tracks, and they filled up the Blue Star water-hole—and cost us three thousand sheep."

Then he related the story of the drive of the sheep, the finding of the plugged water-hole, the scent of the Colorado, and the plunge of the sheep into the cañon.

"We've saved one, Mescal's belled lamb," he concluded.

Neither Zeke nor George had a word in reply. Hare thought their silence unnatural. Neither did the mask-like stillness of their faces change. But Hare saw in their eyes a pointed clear flame, vibrating like a compass-needle, a mere glimmering spark.

"I'd like to know," continued Dave, calmly poking the fire, "who hired Dene's men to plug the water-hole. Dene couldn't do that. He loves a horse, and any man who loves a horse couldn't fill a water-hole in this desert."

Hare entered upon his new duties as a range-rider with a zeal that almost made up for his lack of experience; he bade fair to develop into a right-hand man for Dave, under whose watchful eye he worked. His natural qualifications were soon shown; he could ride, though his seat was awkward and clumsy compared to that of the desert rangers, a fault that Dave said would correct itself as time fitted him close to the saddle and to the swing of his horse. His sight had become extraordinarily keen for a new-comer on the ranges, and when experience had taught him the landmarks, the trails, the distances, the difference between smoke and dust and haze, when he could distinguish a band of mustangs from cattle, and range-riders from outlaws or Indians; in a word, when he had learned to know what it was that he saw, to trust his judgment, he would have acquired the basic feature of a rider's training. But he showed no gift for the lasso, that other essential requirement of his new calling.

"It's funny," said Dave, patiently, "you can't get the hang of it. Maybe it's born in a fellow. Now handling a gun seems to come natural for some fellows, and you're one of them. If only you could get the rope away as quick as you can throw your gun!"

Jack kept faithfully at it, unmindful of defeats, often chagrined when he missed some easy opportunity. Not improbably he might have failed altogether if he had been riding an ordinary horse, or if he had to try roping from a fiery mustang. But Silvermane was as intelligent as he was beautiful and fleet. The horse learned rapidly the agile turns and sudden stops necessary, and as for free running he never got enough. Out on the range Silvermane always had his head up and watched; his life had been spent in watching; he saw cattle, riders, mustangs, deer, coyotes, every moving thing. So that Hare, in the chasing of a cow, had but to start Silvermane, and then he could devote himself to the handling of his rope. It took him ten times longer to lasso the

cow than it took Silvermane to head the animal.
Dave laughed at some of Jack's exploits, encour-
aged him often, praised his intent if not his deed;
and always after a run nodded at Silvermane in
mute admiration.

Branding the cows and yearlings and tame steers
which watered at Silver Cup, and never wandered
far away, was play according to Dave's version.
"Wait till we get after the wild steers up on the
mountain and in the cañons," he would say when
Jack dropped like a log at supper. Work it certainly
was for him. At night he was so tired that he could
scarcely crawl into bed; his back felt as if it were
broken; his legs were raw, and his bones ached.
Many mornings he thought it impossible to arise,
but always he crawled out, grim and haggard, and
hobbled round the camp-fire to warm his sore and
bruised muscles. Then when Zeke and George rode
in with the horses the day's work began. During
these weeks of his "hardening up," as Dave called it,
Hare bore much pain, but he continued well and
never missed a day. At the most trying time when
for a few days he had to be helped on and off
Silvermane—for he insisted that he would not stay
in camp—the brothers made his work as light as
possible. They gave him the branding outfit to
carry, a running-iron and a little pot with charcoal
and bellows; and with these he followed the riders
at a convenient distance and leisurely pace.

Some days they branded one hundred cattle. By
October they had August Naab's crudely fashioned
cross on thousands of cows and steers. Still the
stock kept coming down from the mountain, driven
to the valley by cold weather and snow-covered
grass. It was well into November before the riders
finished at Silver Cup, and then arose a question as
to whether it would be advisable to go to Seeping
Springs or to the cañons farther west along the

slope of Coconina. George favored the former, but Dave overruled him.

"Father's orders," he said. "He wants us to ride Seeping Springs last because he'll be with us then, and Snap too. We're going to have trouble over there."

"How's this branding stock going to help the matter any, I'd like to know?" inquired George. "We Mormons never needed it."

"Father says we'll all have to come to it. Holderness's stock is branded. Perhaps he's marked a good many steers of ours. We can't tell. But if we have our own branded we'll know what's ours. If he drives our stock we'll know it; if Dene steals, it can be proved that he steals."

"Well, what then? Do you think he'll care for that, or Holderness either?"

"No, only it makes this difference: both things will then be barefaced robbery. We've never been able to prove anything, though we boys know; we don't need any proof. Father gives these men the benefit of a doubt. We've got to stand by him. I know, George, your hand's begun to itch for your gun. So does mine. But we've orders to obey."

Many gullies and cañons headed up on the slope of Coconina west of Silver Cup, and ran down to open wide on the flat desert. They contained plots of white sage and bunches of rich grass and cold springs. The steers that ranged these ravines were wild as wolves, and in the tangled thickets of juniper and manzanita and jumbles of weathered cliff they were exceedingly difficult to catch.

Well it was that Hare had received his initiation and had become inured to rough incessant work, for now he came to know the real stuff of which these Mormons were made. No obstacle barred them. They penetrated the gullies to the last step; they rode weathered slopes that were difficult for deer to stick upon; they thrashed the bayonet-guarded manzanita copses; they climbed into labyrinthine fastnesses, penetrating to every nook where a steer could hide. Miles of sliding slope and marble-bottomed streambeds were ascended on foot, for cattle could climb where a horse could not. Climbing was arduous enough, yet the hardest and most perilous toil began when a wild steer was cornered. They roped the animals on moving slopes of weathered stone, and branded them on the edges of precipices.

The days and weeks passed, how many no one counted or cared. The circle of the sun daily lowered over the south end of Coconina; and the black snow-clouds crept down the slopes. Frost whitened the ground at dawn, and held half the day in the shade. Winter was close at the heels of the long autumn.

As for Hare, true to August Naab's assertion, he had lost flesh and suffered, and though the process was heart-breaking in its severity, he hung on till he hardened into a leather-lunged, wire-muscled man, capable of keeping pace with his companions.

He began his day with the dawn when he threw off the frost-coated tarpaulin; the icy water brought him a glow of exhilaration; he drank in the spiced cold air, and there was the spring of the deer-hunter in his step as he went down the slope for his horse. He no longer feared that Silvermane would run away. The gray's bell could always be heard near camp in the mornings, and when Hare whistled there came always the answering thump of hobbled feet. When Silvermane saw him striding through the cedars or across the grassy belt of the valley he would neigh his gladness. Hare had come to love Silvermane and talked to him and treated him as if he were human.

When the mustangs were brought into camp the day's work began, the same work as that of yesterday, and yet with endless variety, with ever-changing situations that called for quick wits, steel arms, stout hearts, and unflagging energies. The darkening blue sky and the sun-tipped crags of Vermillion Cliffs were signals to start for camp. They ate like wolves, sat for a while around the camp-fire, a ragged, weary, silent group; and soon lay down, their dark faces in the shadow of the cedars.

In the beginning of this toil-filled time Hare had resolutely set himself to forget Mescal, and he had succeeded at least for a time, when he was so sore and weary that he scarcely thought at all. But she came back to him, and then there was seldom an hour that was not hers. The long months which seemed years since he had seen her, the change in him wrought by labor and peril, the deepening friendship between him and Dave, even the love he bore Silvermane—these, instead of making dim the memory of the dark-eyed girl, only made him tenderer in his thought of her.

Snow drove the riders from the cañon-camp down to Silver Cup, where they found August Naab and Snap, who had ridden in the day before.

"Now you couldn't guess how many cattle are back there in the cañons," said Dave to his father.

"I haven't any idea," answered August, dubiously.

"Five thousand head."

"Dave!" His father's tone was incredulous.

"Yes. You know we haven't been back in there for years. The stock has multiplied rapidly in spite of the lions and wolves. Not only that, but they're safe from the winter, and are not likely to be found by Dene or anybody else."

"How do you make that out?"

"The first cattle we drove in used to come back here to Silver Cup to winter. Then they stopped coming, and we almost forgot them. Well, they've got a trail round under the Saddle, and they go down and winter in the cañon. In summer they head up those rocky gullies, but they can't get up on the mountain. So it isn't likely any one will ever discover them. They are wild as deer and fatter than any stock on the ranges."

"Good! That's the best news I've had in many a day. Now, boys, we'll ride the mountain slope toward Seeping Springs, drive the cattle down, and finish up this branding. Somebody ought to go to White Sage. I'd like to know what's going on, what Holderness is up to, what Dene is doing, if there's any stock being driven to Lund."

"I told you I'd go," said Snap Naab.

"I don't want you to," replied his father. "I guess it can wait till spring, then we'll all go in. I might have thought to bring you boys out some clothes and boots. You're pretty ragged. Jack there, especially, looks like a scarecrow. Has he worked as hard as he looks?"

"Father, he never lost a day," replied Dave, warmly, "and you know what riding is in these cañons."

August Naab looked at Hare and laughed. "It'd be funny, wouldn't it, if Holderness tried to slap you now? I always knew you'd do, Jack, and now you're one of us, and you'll have a share with my sons in the cattle."

But the generous promise failed to offset the feeling aroused by the presence of Snap Naab. With the first sight of Snap's sharp face and strange eyes Hare became conscious of an inward heat, which he had felt before, but never as now, when there seemed to be an actual flame within his breast. Yet Snap seemed greatly changed; the red flush, the swollen lines no longer showed in his face; evidently in his absence on the Navajo desert he had had no liquor; he was good-natured, lively, much inclined to joking, and he seemed to have entirely forgotten his animosity toward Hare. It was easy for

Hare to see that the man's evil nature was in the ascendancy only when he was under the dominance of drink. But he could not forgive; he could not forget. Mescal's dark, beautiful eyes haunted him. Even now she might be married to this man. Perhaps that was why Snap appeared to be in such cheerful spirits. Suspense added its burdensome insistent question, but he could not bring himself to ask August if the marriage had taken place. For a day he fought to resign himself to the inevitability of the Mormon custom, to forget Mescal, and then he gave up trying. This surrender he felt to be something crucial in his life, though he could not wholly understand it. It was the darkening of his spirit; the death of boyish gentleness; the concluding step from youth into a forced manhood. The desert regeneration had not stopped at turning weak lungs, vitiated blood, and flaccid muscles into a powerful man; it was at work on his mind, his heart, his soul. They answered more and more to the call of some outside, ever-present, fiercely subtle thing.

Thenceforth he no longer vexed himself by trying to forget Mescal; if she came to mind he told himself the truth, that the weeks and months had only added to his love. And though it was bitter-sweet there was relief in speaking the truth to himself. He no longer blinded himself by hoping, striving to have generous feelings toward Snap Naab; he called the inward fire by its real name—jealousy—and knew that in the end it would become hatred.

On the third morning after leaving Silver Cup the riders were working slowly along the slope of Coconina; and Hare having driven down a bunch of cattle, found himself on an open ridge near the temporary camp. Happening to glance up the valley he saw what appeared to be smoke hanging over Seeping Springs.

"That can't be dust," he soliloquized. "Looks blue to me."

He studied the hazy bluish cloud for some time, but it was so many miles away that he could not be certain whether it was smoke or not, so he decided to ride over and make sure. None of the Naabs was in camp, and there was no telling when they would return, so he set off alone. He expected to get back before dark, but it was of little consequence whether he did or not, for he had his blanket under the saddle, and grain for Silvermane and food for himself in the saddle-bags.

Long before Silvermane's easy trot had covered half the distance Hare recognized the cloud that had made him curious. It was smoke. He thought that range-riders were camping at the springs, and he meant to see what they were about. After three hours of brisk travel he reached the top of a low rolling knoll that hid Seeping Springs. He remembered the springs were up under the red wall, and that the pool where the cattle drank was lower down in a clump of cedars. He saw smoke rising in a column from the cedars, and he heard the lowing of cattle.

"Something wrong here," he muttered. Following the trail, he rode through the cedars to come upon the dry hole where the pool had once been. There was no water in the flume. The bellowing cattle came from beyond the cedars, down the other side of the ridge. He was not long in reaching the open, and then one glance made all clear.

A new pool, large as a little lake, shone in the twilight, and round it a jostling horned mass of cattle were pressing against a high corral. The flume that fed water to the pool was fenced all the way up to the springs.

Jack slowly rode down the ridge with eyes roving

under the cedars and up to the wall. Not a man was in sight.

When he got to the fire he saw that it was not many hours old and was surrounded by fresh boot and horse tracks in the dust. Piles of slender pine logs, trimmed flat on one side, were proof of somebody's intention to erect a cabin. In a rage he flung himself from the saddle. It was not many moments' work for him to push part of the fire under the fence, and part of it against the pile of logs. The pitch-pines went off like rockets, driving the thirsty cattle back.

"I'm going to trail those horse-tracks," said Hare.

He tore down a portion of the fence enclosing the flume, and gave Silvermane a drink, then put him to a fast trot on the white trail. The tracks he had resolved to follow were clean-cut. A few inches of snow had fallen in the valley, and melting, had softened the hard ground. Silvermane kept to his gait with the tirelessness of a desert horse. August Naab had once said fifty miles a day would be play for the stallion. All the afternoon Hare watched the trail speed toward him and the end of Coconina rise above him. Long before sunset he had reached the slope of the mountain and had begun the ascent. Half-way up he came to the snow and counted the tracks of three horses. At twilight he rode into the glade where August Naab had waited for his Navajo friends. There, in a sheltered nook among the rocks, he unsaddled Silvermane, covered and fed him, built a fire, ate sparingly of his meat and bread, and rolling up in his blanket, was soon asleep.

He was up and off before sunrise, and he came out on the western slope of Coconina just as the shadowy valley awakened from its misty sleep into daylight. Soon the Pink Cliffs leaned out, glimmering and vast, to change from gloomy gray to rosy glow, and then to brighten and to redden in the morning sun.

The snow thinned and failed, but the iron-cut horse-tracks showed plainly in the trail. At the foot of the mountain the tracks left the White Sage trail and led off to the north toward the cliffs. Hare searched the red sage-spotted waste for Holderness's ranch. He located it, a black patch on the rising edge of the valley under the wall, and turned Silvermane into the tracks that pointed straight toward it.

The sun cleared Coconina and shone warm on his back; the Pink Cliffs lifted higher and higher before him. From the ridge-tops he saw the black patch grow into cabins and corrals. As he neared the ranch he came into rolling pasture-land where the bleached grass shone white and the cattle were ranging in the thousands. This range had once belonged to Martin Cole, and Hare thought of the bitter Mormon as he noted the snug cabins for the riders, the rambling, picturesque ranch-house, the large corrals, and the long flume that ran down from the cliff. There was a corral full of shaggy horses, and another full of steers, and two lines of cattle, one going into a pond-corral, and one coming out. The air was gray with dust. A bunch of yearlings were licking at huge lumps of brown rock-salt. A wagonful of cowhides stood before the ranchhouse.

Hare reined in at the door and halloed.

A red-faced ranger with sandy hair and twinkling eyes appeared.

"Hello, stranger, get down an' come in," he said.

"Is Holderness here?" asked Hare.

"No. He's been to Lund with a bunch of steers. I reckon he'll be in White Sage by now. I'm Snood, the foreman. Is it a job ridin' you want?"

"No."

"Say! thet hoss—" he exclaimed. His gaze of friendly curiosity had moved from Hare to Silvermane. "You can corral me if it ain't thet Sevier range stallion!"

"Yes," said Hare.

Snood's whoop brought three riders to the door, and when he pointed to the horse, they stepped out with good-natured grins and admiring eyes.

"I never seen him but onc't," said one.

"Lordy, what a hoss!" Snood walked round Silvermane. "If I owned this ranch I'd trade it for that stallion. I know Silvermane. He an' I hed some chases over in Nevada. An', stranger, who might you be?"

"I'm one of August Naab's riders."

"Dene's spy!" Snood looked Hare over carefully, with much interest, and without any show of ill-will. "I've heerd of you. An' what might one of Naab's riders want of Holderness?"

"I rode in to Seeping Springs yesterday," said Hare, eyeing the foreman. "There was a new pond, fenced in. Our cattle couldn't drink. There were a lot of trimmed logs. Somebody was going to build a cabin. I burned the corrals and logs—and I trailed fresh tracks from Seeping Springs to this ranch."

"The hell you did!" shouted Snood, and his face flamed. "See here, stranger, you're the second man to accuse some of my riders of such dirty tricks. That's enough for me. I was foreman of this ranch till this minute. I was foreman, but there were things goin' on thet I didn't know of. I kicked on thet deal with Martin Cole. I quit. I steal no man's water. Is thet good with you?"

Snood's query was as much a challenge as a question. He bit savagely at his pipe. Hare offered his hand.

"Your word goes. Dave Naab said you might be Holderness's foreman, but you weren't a liar or a thief. I'd believe it even if Dave hadn't told me."

"Them fellers you tracked rode in here yesterday. They're gone now. I've no more to say, except I never hired them."

"I'm glad to hear it. Good-day, Snood, I'm in something of a hurry."

With that Hare faced about in the direction of White Sage. Once clear of the corrals he saw the village closer than he had expected to find it. He walked Silvermane most of the way, and jogged along the rest, so that he reached the village in the twilight. Memory served him well. He rode in as August Naab had ridden out, and arrived at the Bishop's barn-yard, where he put up his horse. Then he went to the house. It was necessary to introduce himself, for none of the Bishop's family recognized in him the young man they had once befriended. The old Bishop prayed and reminded him of the laying on of hands. The women served him with food, the young men brought him new boots and garments to replace those that had been worn to tatters. Then they plied him with questions about the Naabs, whom they had not seen for nearly a year. They rejoiced at his recovered health; they welcomed him with warm words.

Later Hare sought an interview alone with the Bishop's sons, and he told them of the loss of the sheep, of the burning of the new corrals, of the tracks leading to Holderness's ranch. In turn they warned him of his danger, and gave him information desired by August Naab. Holderness's grasp on the outlying ranges and water-rights had slowly and surely tightened; every month he acquired new territory; he drove cattle regularly to Lund, and it was no secret that much of the stock came from the eastern slope of Coconina. He could not hire enough riders to do his work. A suspicion that he was not a cattle-man but a rustler had slowly gained ground; it was scarcely hinted, but it was believed.

His friendship with Dene had become offensive to the Mormons, who had formerly been on good footing with him. Dene's killing of Martin Cole was believed to have been at Holderness's instigation. Cole had threatened Holderness. Then Dene and Cole had met in the main street of White Sage. Cole's death ushered in the bloody time that he had prophesied. Dene's band had grown; no man could say how many men he had or who they were. Chance and Culver were openly his lieutenants, and whenever they came into the village there was shooting. There were ugly rumors afloat in regard to their treatment of Mormon women. The wives and daughters of once peaceful White Sage dared no longer venture out-of-doors after nightfall. There was more money in coin and more whiskey than ever before in the village. Lund and the few villages northward were terrorized as well as White Sage. It was a bitter story.

The Bishop and his sons tried to persuade Hare next morning to leave the village without seeing Holderness, urging the futility of such a meeting.

"I will see him," said Hare. He spent the morning at the cottage, and when it came time to take his leave he smiled into the anxious faces. "If I weren't able to take care of myself August Naab would never have said so."

Had Hare asked himself what he intended to do when he faced Holderness he could not have told. His feelings were pent-in, bound, but at the bottom something rankled. His mind seemed steeped in still thunderous atmosphere.

How well he remembered the quaint wide street, the gray church! As he rode many persons stopped to gaze at Silvermane. He turned the corner into the main thoroughfare. A new building had been added to the several stores. Mustangs stood, bridles down, before the doors; men lounged along the railings.

As he dismounted he heard the loungers speak of his horse, and he saw their leisurely manner quicken. He stepped into the store to meet more men, among them August Naab's friend Abe. Hare might never have been in White Sage for all the recognition he found, but he excited something keener than curiosity. He asked for spurs, a clasp-knife and some other necessaries, and he contrived, when momentarily out of sight behind a pile of boxes, to whisper his identity to Abe. The Mormon was dumbfounded. When he came out of his trance he showed his gladness, and at a question of Hare's he silently pointed toward the saloon.

Hare faced the open door. The room had been enlarged; it was now on a level with the store floor, and was blue with smoke, foul with the fumes of rum, and noisy with the voices of dark, rugged men.

A man in the middle of the room was dancing a jig.

"Hello, who's this?" he said, straightening up.

It might have been the stopping of the dance or the quick spark in Hare's eyes that suddenly quieted the room. Hare had once vowed to himself that he would never forget the scarred face; it belonged to the outlaw Chance.

The sight of it flashed into the gulf of Hare's mind like a meteor into black night. A sudden madness raced through his veins.

"Hello! Don't you know me?" he said, with a long step that brought him close to Chance.

The outlaw stood irresolute. Was this an old friend or an enemy? His beady eyes scintillated and twitched as if they sought to look him over, yet dared not because it was only in the face that intention could be read.

The stillness of the room broke to a hoarse whisper from some one.

"Look how he packs his gun."

Another man answering whispered: "There's not six men in Utah who pack a gun thet way."

Chance heard these whispers, for his eye shifted downward the merest fraction of a second. The brick color of his face turned a dirty white.

"Do you know me?" demanded Hare.

Chance's answer was a spasmodic jerking of his hand toward his hip. Hare's arm moved quicker, and Chance's Colt went spinning to the floor.

"Too slow," said Hare. Then he flung Chance backward and struck him blows that sent his head with sodden thuds against the log wall. Chance sank to the floor in a heap.

Hare kicked the outlaw's gun out of the way, and wheeled to the crowd. Holderness stood foremost, his tall form leaning against the bar, his clear eyes shining like light on ice.

"Do you know me?" asked Hare, curtly.

Holderness started slightly. "I certainly don't," he replied.

"You slapped my face once." Hare leaned close to the rancher. "Slap it now—you rustler!"

In the slow, guarded instant when Hare's gaze held Holderness and the other men, a low murmuring ran through the room.

"Dene's spy!" suddenly burst out Holderness.

Hare slapped his face. Then he backed a few paces with his right arm held before him almost as high as his shoulder, the wrist rigid, the fingers quivering.

"Don't try to draw, Holderness. Thet's August Naab's trick with a gun," whispered a man, hurriedly.

"Holderness, I made a bonfire over at Seeping Springs," said Hare. "I burned the new corrals your men built, and I tracked them to your ranch. Snood threw up his job when he heard it. He's an honest man, and no honest man will work for a water-thief, a cattle-rustler, a sheep-killer. You're shown up, Holderness. Leave the country before some one kills you—understand, before some one kills you!"

Holderness stood motionless against the bar, his eyes fierce with passionate hate.

Hare backed step by step to the outside door, his right hand still high, his look holding the crowd bound to the last instant. Then he slipped out, scattered the group round Silvermane, and struck hard with the spurs.

The gray, never before spurred, broke down the road into his old wild speed.

Men were crossing from the corner of the green square. One, a compact little fellow, swarthy, his dark hair long and flowing, with jaunty and alert air, was Dene, the outlaw leader. He stopped, with his companions, to let the horse cross.

Hare guided the thundering stallion slightly to the left. Silvermane swerved and in two mighty leaps bore down on the outlaw. Dene saved himself by quickly leaping aside, but even as he moved Silvermane struck him with his left fore-leg, sending him into the dust.

At the street corner Hare glanced back. Yelling men were rushing from the saloon and some of them fired after him. The bullets whistled harmlessly behind Hare. Then the corner house shut off his view.

Silvermane lengthened out and stretched lower with his white mane flying and his nose pointed level for the desert.

CHAPTER XI

The Desert-Hawk

TOWARD THE close of the next day Jack Hare arrived at Seeping Springs. A pile of gray ashes marked the spot where the trimmed logs had lain. Round the pool ran a black circle hard packed into the ground by many hoofs. Even the board flume had been burned to a level with the glancing sheet of water. Hare was slipping Silvermane's bit to let him drink when he heard a halloo. Dave Naab galloped out of the cedars, and presently August Naab and his other sons appeared with a pack-train.

"Now you've played hob!" exclaimed Dave. He swung out of his saddle and gripped Hare with both hands. "I know what you've done; I know where you've been. Father will be furious, but don't you care."

The other Naabs trotted down the slope and lined their horses before the pool. The sons stared in blank astonishment; the father surveyed the scene slowly, and then fixed wrathful eyes on Hare.

"What does this mean?" he demanded, with the sonorous roll of his angry voice.

Hare told all that had happened.

August Naab's gloomy face worked, and his eagle-gaze had in it a strange far-seeing light; his mind was dwelling upon his mystic power of revelation.

"I see—I see," he said haltingly.

"Ki—yi-i-i!" yelled Dave Naab with all the power of his lungs. His head was back, his mouth wide open, his face red, his neck corded and swollen with the intensity of his passion.

"Be still—boy!" ordered his father. "Hare, this was madness—but tell me what you learned."

Briefly Hare repeated all that he had been told at the Bishop's, and concluded with the killing of Martin Cole by Dene.

August Naab bowed his head and his giant frame shook under the force of his emotion. Martin Cole was the last of his life-long friends.

"This—this outlaw—you say you ran him down?" asked Naab, rising haggard and shaken out of his grief.

"Yes. He didn't recognize me or know what was coming till Silvermane was on him. But he was quick, and fell sidewise. Silvermane's knees sent him sprawling."

"What will it all lead to?" asked August Naab, and in his extremity he appealed to his eldest son.

"The bars are down," said Snap Naab, with a click of his long teeth.

"Father," began Dave Naab earnestly, "Jack has done a splendid thing. The news will fly over Utah like wild-fire. Mormons are slow. They need a leader. But they can follow and they will. We can't cure these evils by hoping and praying. We've got to fight!"

"Dave's right, Dad, it means fight," cried George, with his fist clinched high.

"You've been wrong, Father, in holding back," said Zeke Naab, his lean jaw bulging. "This Holderness will steal the water and meat out of our children's mouths. We've got to fight!"

"Let's ride to White Sage," put in Snap Naab, and the little flecks in his eyes were dancing. "I'll throw a gun on Dene. I can get to him. We've been tolerable friends. He's wanted me to join his band. I'll kill him."

He laughed as he raised his right hand and swept it down to his left side; the blue Colt lay on his outstretched palm. Dene's life and Holderness's, too, hung in the balance between two deadly snaps of this desert-wolf's teeth. He was one of the Naabs, and yet apart from them, for neither religion, nor friendship, nor life itself mattered to him.

August Naab's huge bulk shook again, not this time with grief, but in wrestling effort to withstand the fiery influence of this unholy fighting spirit among his sons.

"I am forbidden."

His answer was gentle, but its very gentleness breathed of his battle over himself, of allegiance to something beyond earthly duty. "We'll drive the cattle to Silver Cup," he decided, "and then go home. I give up Seeping Springs. Perhaps this valley and water will content Holderness."

When they reached the oasis Hare was surprised to find that it was the day before Christmas. The welcome given the long-absent riders was like a celebration. Much to Hare's disappointment Mescal did not appear; the home-coming was not joyful to him because it lacked her welcoming smile.

Christmas Day ushered in the short desert winter; ice formed in the ditches and snow fell, but neither long resisted the reflection of the sun from the walls. The early morning hours were devoted to religious services. At midday dinner was served in

the big room of August Naab's cabin. At one end
was a stone fireplace where logs blazed and crackled.

In all his days Hare had never seen such a boun-
tiful board. Yet he was unable to appreciate it, to
share in the general thanksgiving. Dominating all
other feeling was the fear that Mescal would come
in and take a seat by Snap Naab's side. When Snap
seated himself opposite with his pale little wife Hare
found himself waiting for Mescal with an intensity
that made him dead to all else. The girls, Judith, Esther, Rebecca, came running gayly in, clad in their
best dresses, with bright ribbons to honor the occa-
sion. Rebecca took the seat beside Snap, and Hare
gulped with a hard contraction of his throat. Mescal
was not yet a Mormon's wife! He seemed to be lifted
upward, to grow light-headed with the blessed assurance. Then Mescal entered and took the seat
next to him. She smiled and spoke, and the blood
beat thick in his ears.

That moment was happy, but it was as nothing to
its successor. Under the table-cover Mescal's hand
found his, and pressed it daringly and gladly. Her
hand lingered in his all the time August Naab spent
in carving the turkey—lingered there even though
Snap Naab's hawk eyes were never far away. In the
warm touch of her hand, in some subtle thing that
radiated from her Hare felt a change in the girl he
loved. A few months had wrought in her some indefinable difference, even as they had increased his
love to its full volume and depth. Had his absence
brought her to the realization of her woman's
heart?

In the afternoon Hare left the house and spent a
little while with Silvermane; then he wandered
along the wall to the head of the oasis, and found
a seat on the fence. The next few weeks presented

to him a situation that would be difficult to endure. He would be near Mescal, but only to have the truth forced cruelly home to him every sane moment—that she was not for him. Out on the ranges he had abandoned himself to dreams of her; they had been beautiful; they had made the long hours seems like minutes; but they had forged chains that could not be broken, and now he was hopelessly fettered.

The clatter of hoofs roused him from a reverie which was half sad, half sweet. Mescal came tearing down the level on Black Bolly. She pulled in the mustang and halted beside Hare to hold out shyly a red scarf embroidered with Navajo symbols in white and red beads.

"I've wanted a chance to give you this," she said, "a little Christmas present."

For a few seconds Hare could find no words.

"Did you make it for me, Mescal?" he finally asked. "How good of you! I'll keep it always."

"Put it on now—let me tie it—there!"

"But, child. Suppose he—they saw it?"

"I don't care who sees it."

She met him with clear, level eyes. Her curt, crisp speech was full of meaning. He looked long at her, with a yearning denied for many a day. Her face was the same, yet wonderfully changed; the same in line and color, but different in soul and spirit. The old sombre shadow lay deep in the eyes, but to it had been added gleam of will and reflection of thought. The whole face had been refined and transformed.

"Mescal! What's happened? You're not the same. You seem almost happy. Have you—has he—given you up?"

"Don't you know Mormons better than that? The thing is the same—so far as they're concerned."

"But Mescal—*are* you going to marry him? For God's sake, tell me."

"Never." It was a woman's word, instant, inflexible, desperate. With a deep breath Hare realized where the girl had changed.

"Still you're promised, pledged to him! How'll you get out of it?"

"I don't know how. But I'll cut out my tongue, and be dumb as my poor peon before I'll speak the word that'll make me Snap Naab's wife."

There was a long silence. Mescal smoothed out Bolly's mane, and Hare gazed up at the walls with eyes that did not see them.

Presently he spoke. "I'm afraid for you. Snap watched us to-day at dinner."

"He's jealous."

"Suppose he sees this scarf?"

Mescal laughed defiantly. It was bewildering for Hare to hear her.

"He'll—Mescal, I may yet come to this." Hare's laugh echoed Mescal's as he pointed to the enclosure under the wall, where the graves showed bare and rough.

Her warm color fled, but it flooded back, rich, mantling brow and cheek and neck.

"Snap Naab will never kill you," she said impulsively.

"Mescal."

She swiftly turned her face away as his hand closed on hers.

"Mescal, do you love me?"

The trembling of her fingers and the heaving of her bosom lent his hope conviction. "Mescal," he went on, "these past months have been years, years of toiling, thinking, changing, but always loving. I'm not the man you knew. I'm wild—I'm starved for a sight of you. I love you! Mescal, my desert flower!"

She raised her free hand to his shoulder and

swayed toward him. He held her a moment, clasped tight, and then released her.

"I'm quite mad!" he exclaimed, in a passion of self-reproach. "What a risk I'm putting on you! But I couldn't help it. Look at me— Just once—please— Mescal, just one look. . . . Now go."

The drama of the succeeding days was of absorbing interest. Hare had liberty; there was little work for him to do save to care for Silvermane. He tried to hunt foxes in the caves and clefts; he rode up and down the broad space under the walls; he sought the open desert only to be driven in by the bitter, biting winds. Then he would return to the big living-room of the Naabs and sit before the burning logs. This spacious room was warm, light, pleasant, and was used by every one in leisure hours. Mescal spent most of her time there. She was engaged upon a new frock of buckskin, and over this she bent with her needle and beads. When there was a chance Hare talked with her, speaking one language with his tongue, a far different one with his eyes. When she was not present he looked into the glowing red fire and dreamed of her.

In the evenings when Snap came in to his wooing and drew Mescal into a corner, Hare watched with covert glance and smouldering jealousy. Somehow he had come to see all things and all people in the desert glass, and his symbol for Snap Naab was the desert-hawk. Snap's eyes were as wild and piercing as those of a hawk; his nose and mouth were as the beak of a hawk; his hands resembled the claws of a hawk and the spurs he wore, always bloody, were still more significant of his ruthless nature. Then Snap's courting of the girl, the cool assurance, the unhastening ease, were like the slow rise, the sail, and the poise of a desert-hawk before the downward lightning-swift swoop on his quarry.

It was intolerable for Hare to sit there in the evenings, to try to play with the children who loved
him, to talk to August Naab when his eye seemed
ever drawn to the quiet couple in the corner, and
his ear was unconsciously strained to catch a passing word. That hour was a miserable one for him,
yet he could not bring himself to leave the room. He
never saw Snap touch her; he never heard Mescal's
voice; he believed that she spoke very little. When
the hour was over and Mescal rose to pass to her
room, then his doubt, his fear, his misery, were as
though they had never been, for as Mescal said
good-night she would give him one look, swift as a
flash, and in it were womanliness and purity, and
something beyond his comprehension. Her Indian
serenity and mysticism veiled yet suggested some
secret, some power by which she might yet escape
the iron band of this Mormon rule. Hare could not
fathom it. In that good-night glance was a meaning
for him alone, if meaning ever shone in woman's
eyes, and it said: "I will be true to you and to myself!"

Once the idea struck him that as soon as spring returned it would be an easy matter, and probably
wise, for him to leave the oasis and go up into Utah,
far from the desert-cañon country. But the thought
refused to stay before his consciousness a moment.
New life had flushed his veins here. He loved the
dreamy, sleepy oasis with its mellow sunshine always
at rest on the glistening walls; he loved the cedar-
scented plateau where hope had dawned, and the
wind-swept sand-strips where hard out-of-door life
and work had renewed his wasting youth; he loved
the cañon winding away toward Coconina, opening
into wide abyss; and always, more than all, he loved
the Painted Desert, with its ever-changing pictures,
printed in sweeping dust and bare peaks and purple
haze. He loved the beauty of these places, and the

wildness in them had an affinity with something strange and untamed in him. He would never leave them. When his blood had cooled, when this tumultuous thrill and swell had worn themselves out, happiness would come again.

Early in the winter Snap Naab had forced his wife to visit his father's house with him; and she had remained in the room, white-faced, passionately jealous, while he wooed Mescal. Then had come a scene. Hare had not been present, but he knew its result. Snap had been furious, his father grave, Mescal tearful and ashamed. The wife found many ways to interrupt her husband's love-making. She sent the children for him; she was taken suddenly ill; she discovered that the corral gate was open and his cream-colored pinto, dearest to his heart, was running loose; she even set her cottage on fire.

One Sunday evening just before twilight Hare was sitting on the porch with August Naab and Dave, when their talk was interrupted by Snap's loud calling for his wife. At first the sounds came from inside his cabin. Then he put his head out of a window and yelled. Plainly he was both impatient and angry. It was nearly time for him to make his Sunday call upon Mescal.

"Something's wrong," muttered Dave.

"Hester! Hester!" yelled Snap.

Mother Ruth came out and said that Hester was not there.

"Where is she?" Snap banged on the window-sill with his fists. "Find her, somebody—Hester!"

"Son, this is the Sabbath," called Father Naab, gravely. "Lower your voice. Now what's the matter?"

"Matter!" bawled Snap, giving way to rage. "When I was asleep Hester stole all my clothes. She's hid them—she's run off—there's not a damn thing for me to put on! I'll—"

The roar of laughter from August and Dave drowned the rest of the speech. Hare managed to stifle his own mouth. Snap pulled in his head and slammed the window shut.

"Jack," said August, "even among Mormons the course of true love never runs smooth."

Hare finally forgot his bitter humor in pity for the wife. Snap came to care not at all for her messages and tricks, and he let nothing interfere with his evening beside Mescal. It was plain that he had gone far on the road of love. Whatever he had been in the beginning of the betrothal, he was now a lover, eager, importunate. His hawk's eyes were softer than Hare had ever seen them; he was obliging, kind, gay, an altogether different Snap Naab. He groomed himself often, and wore clean scarfs, and left off his bloody spurs. For eight months he had not touched the bottle. When spring approached he was madly in love with Mescal. And the marriage was delayed because his wife would not have another woman in her home.

Once Hare heard Snap remonstrating with his father.

"If she don't come to time soon I'll keep the kids and send her back to her father."

"Don't be hasty, son. Let her have time," replied August. "Women must be humored. I'll wager she'll give in before the cottonwood blows, and that's not long."

It was Hare's habit, as the days grew warmer, to walk a good deal, and one evening, as twilight shadowed the oasis and grew black under the towering walls, he strolled out toward the fields. While passing Snap's cottage Hare heard a woman's voice in passionate protest and a man's in strident anger. Later as he stood with his arm on Silvermane, a woman's scream, at first high-pitched, then suddenly faint and smothered, caused him to grow rigid, and his hand clinched tight. When he went back by the cottage a low moaning confirmed his suspicion.

That evening Snap appeared unusually bright and happy; and he asked his father to name the day for the wedding. August did so in a loud voice and with evident relief. Then the quaint Mormon congratulations were offered to Mescal. To Hare, watching the strange girl with the distressingly keen intuition of an unfortunate lover, she appeared as pleased as any of them that the marriage was settled. But there was no shyness, no blushing confusion. When Snap bent to kiss her—his first kiss—she slightly turned her face, so that his lips brushed her cheek, yet even then her self-command did not break for an instant. It was a task for Hare to pretend to congratulate her; nevertheless he mumbled something. She lifted her long lashes, and there, deep beneath the shadows, was unutterable anguish. It gave him a shock. He went to his room, convinced that she had yielded; and though he could not blame her, and he knew she was helpless, he cried out in reproach and resentment. She had failed him, as he had known she must fail. He tossed on his bed and thought; he lay quiet, wide-open eyes staring into the darkness, and his mind burned and seethed. Through the hours of that long night he learned what love had cost him.

With the morning light came some degree of resignation. Several days went slowly by, bringing the first of April, which was to be the wedding-day. August Naab had said it would come before the cottonwoods shed their white floss; and their buds had just commenced to open. The day was not a holiday, and George and Zeke and Dave began to pack for the ranges, yet there was an air of jollity and festivity. Snap Naab had a springy step and jaunty mien. Once he regarded Hare with a slow smile.

Piute prepared to drive his new flock up on the plateau. The women of the household were busy and excited; the children romped.

The afternoon waned into twilight, and Hare sought the quiet shadows under the wall near the river trail. He meant to stay there until August Naab had pronounced his son and Mescal man and wife. The dull roar of the rapids borne on a faint puff of westerly breeze was lulled into a soothing murmur. A radiant white star peeped over the black rim of the wall. The solitude and silence were speaking to Hare's heart, easing his pain, when a soft patter of moccasined feet brought him bolt upright.

A slender form rounded the corner wall. It was Mescal. The white dog Wolf hung close by her side. Swiftly she reached Hare.

"Mescal!" he exclaimed.

"Hush! Speak softly," she whispered fearfully. Her hands were clinging to his.

"Jack, do you love me still?"

More than woman's sweetness was in the whisper; the portent of indefinable motive made Hare tremble like a shaking leaf.

"Good heavens! You are to be married in a few minutes—What do you mean? Where are you going? this buckskin suit—and Wolf with you—Mescal!"

"There's no time—only a word—hurry—do you love me still?" she panted, with great shining eyes close to his.

"Love you? With all my soul!"

"Listen," she whispered, and leaned against him. A fresh breeze bore the boom of the river. She caught her breath quickly: "I love you!—I love you!—Good-bye!"

She kissed him and broke from his clasp. Then silently, like a shadow, with the white dog close beside her, she disappeared in the darkness of the river trail.

She was gone before he came out of his bewilderment. He rushed down the trail; he called her name. The gloom had swallowed her, and only the echo of his voice made answer.

CHAPTER XII

Echo Cliffs

WHEN THOUGHT came clearly to him he halted irresolute. For Mescal's sake he must not appear to have had any part in her headlong flight, or any knowledge of it.

With stealthy footsteps he reached the cottonwoods, stole under the gloomy shade, and felt his way to a point beyond the twinkling lights. Then, peering through the gloom until assured he was safe from observation, and taking the dark side of the house, he gained the hall, and his room. He threw himself on his bed, and endeavored to compose himself, to quiet his vibrating nerves, to still the triumphant bell-beat of his heart. For a while all his being swung to the palpitating consciousness of joy—Mescal had taken her freedom. She had escaped the swoop of the hawk.

While Hare lay there, trying to gather his shattered senses, the merry sound of voices and the music of an accordion hummed from the big living-room next to his. Presently heavy boots thumped on the floor of the hall; then a hand rapped on his door.

"Jack, are you there?" called August Naab.

"Yes."

"Come along then."

Hare rose, opened the door and followed August. The room was bright with lights; the table was set, and the Naabs, large and small, were standing expectantly. As Hare found a place behind them Snap Naab entered with his wife. She was as pale as if she were in her shroud. Hare caught Mother Ruth's pitying subdued glance as she drew the frail little woman to her side. When August Naab began fingering his Bible the whispering ceased.

"Why don't they fetch her?" he questioned.

"Judith, Esther, bring her in," said Mother Mary, calling into the hallway.

Quick footsteps, and the girls burst in impetuously, exclaiming: "Mescal's not there!"

"Where is she, then?" demanded August Naab, going to the door. *"Mescal!"* he called.

Succeeding his authoritative summons only the cheery sputter of the wood-fire broke the silence.

"She hadn't put on her white frock," went on Judith.

"Her buckskins aren't hanging where they always are," continued Esther.

August Naab laid his Bible on the table. "I always feared it," he said simply.

"She's gone!" cried Snap Naab. He ran into the hall, into Mescal's room, and returned trailing the white wedding-dress. "The time we thought she spent to put this on she's been—"

He choked over the words, and sank into a chair, face convulsed, hands shaking, weak in the grip of a grief that he had never before known. Suddenly he flung the dress into the fire. His wife fell to the floor in a dead faint. Then the desert-hawk showed his claws. His hands tore at the close scarf round his throat as if to liberate a fury that was stifling him; his face lost all semblance to anything human. He began to howl, to rave, to curse; and his father circled him with iron arm and dragged him from the room.

The children were whimpering, the wives lamenting. The quiet men searched the house and yard and corrals and fields. But they found no sign of Mescal. After long hours the excitement subsided and all sought their beds.

Morning disclosed the facts of Mescal's flight. She had dressed for the trail; a knapsack was missing and food enough to fill it; Wolf was gone; Noddle was not in his corral; the peon slave had not slept in his shack; there were moccasin-tracks and burro-tracks and dog-tracks in the sand at the river crossing, and one of the boats was gone. This boat was not moored to the opposite shore. Questions arose. Had the boat sunk? Had the fugitives crossed safely or had they drifted into the cañon? Dave Naab rode out along the river and saw the boat, a mile below the rapids, bottom side up and lodged on a sand-bar.

"She got across, and then set the boat loose," said August. "That's the Indian of her. If she went up on the cliffs to the Navajos maybe we'll find her. If she went into the Painted Desert—" a grave shake of his shaggy head completed his sentence.

Morning also disclosed Snap Naab once more in the clutch of his demon, drunk and unconscious, lying like a log on the porch of his cottage.

"This means ruin to him," said his father. "He had one chance; he was mad over Mescal, and if he had got her, he might have conquered his thirst for rum."

He gave orders for the sheep to be driven up on

the plateau, and for his sons to ride out to the cattle ranges. He bade Hare pack and get in readiness to accompany him to the Navajo cliffs, there to search for Mescal.

The river was low, as the spring thaws had not yet set in, and the crossing promised none of the hazard so menacing at a later period. Billy Naab rowed across with the saddle and packs. Then August had to crowd the lazy burros into the water. Silvermane went in with a rush, and Charger took to the river like an old duck. August and Jack sat in the stern of the boat, while Billy handled the oars. They crossed swiftly and safely. The three burros were then loaded, two with packs, the other with a heavy water-bag.

"See there," said August, pointing to tracks in the sand. The imprints of little moccasins reassured Hare, for he had feared the possibility suggested by the upturned boat. "Perhaps it'll be better if I never find her," continued Naab. "If I bring her back Snap's as likely to kill her as to marry her. But I must try to find her. Only what to do with her—"

"Give her to me," interrupted Jack.

"Hare!"

"I love her!"

Naab's stern face relaxed. "Well, I'm beat! Though I don't see why you should be different from all the others. It was that time you spent with her on the plateau. I thought you too sick to think of a woman!"

"Mescal cares for me," said Hare.

"Ah! That accounts. Hare, did you play me fair?"

"We tried to, though we couldn't help loving."

"She would have married Snap but for you."

"Yes. But I couldn't help that. You brought me out here, and saved my life. I know what I owe you. Mescal meant to marry your son when I left for the range last fall. But she's a true woman and couldn't.

August Naab, if we ever find her will you marry her
to him—now?"

"That depends. Did you know she intended to
run?"

"I never dreamed of it. I learned it only at the last
moment. I met her on the river trail."

"You should have stopped her."

Hare maintained silence.

"You should have told me," went on Naab.

"I couldn't. I'm only human."

"Well, well, I'm not blaming you, Hare. I had hot
blood once. But I'm afraid the desert will not be
large enough for you and Snap. She's pledged to
him. You can't change the Mormon Church. For the
sake of peace I'd give you Mescal, if I could. Snap
will either have her or kill her. I'm going to hunt this
desert in advance of him, because he'll trail her like
a hound. It would be better to marry her to him
than to see her dead."

"I'm not so sure of that."

"Hare, your nose is on a blood scent, like a wolf's.
I can see—I've always seen—well, remember, it's
man to man between you now."

During this talk they were winding under Echo
Cliffs, gradually climbing, and working up to a level
with the desert, which they presently attained at a
point near the head of the cañon. The trail swerved
to the left, following the base of the cliffs. The
tracks of Noddle and Wolf were plainly visible in the
dust. Hare felt that if they ever led out into the immense airy space of the desert all hope of finding
Mescal must be abandoned.

They trailed the tracks of the dog and burro to
Bitter Seeps, a shallow spring of alkali, and there
lost all track of them. The path up the cliffs to the
Navajo ranges was bare, time-worn in solid rock,
and showed only the imprint of age. Desertward the
ridges of shale, the washes of copper earth, baked

in the sun, gave no sign of the fugitives' course. August Naab shrugged his broad shoulders and pointed his horse to the cliff. It was dusk when they surmounted it.

They camped in the lee of an uplifting crag. When the wind died down the night was no longer unpleasantly cool; and Hare, finding August Naab uncommunicative and sleepy, strolled along the rim of the cliff, as he had been wont to do in the sheep-herding days. He could scarcely dissociate them from the present, for the bitter-sweet smell of tree and bush, the almost inaudible sigh of breeze, the opening and shutting of the great white stars in the blue dome, the silence, the sense of the invisible void beneath him—all were thought-provoking parts of that past of which nothing could ever be forgotten. And it was a silence which brought much to the ear that could hear. It was a silence penetrated by faint and distant sounds, by mourning wolf, or moan of wind in a splintered crag. Weird and low, an inarticulate voice, it wailed up from the desert, winding along the hollow trail, freeing itself in the wide air, and dying away. He had often heard the scream of lion and cry of wildcat, but this was the strange sound of which August Naab had told him, the mysterious call of cañon and desert night.

Daylight showed Echo Cliffs to be of vastly greater range than the sister plateau across the river. The roll of cedar level, the heave of craggy ridge, the dip of white-sage valley gave this side a diversity widely differing from the two steps of the Vermillion tableland. August Naab followed a trail leading back toward the river. For the most part thick cedars hid the surroundings from Hare's view; occasionally, however, he had a backward glimpse from a high point, or a wide prospect below, where the trail overlooked an oval hemmed-in valley.

About midday August Naab brushed through a

thicket, and came abruptly on a declivity. He turned
to his companion with a wave of his hand.

"The Navajo camp," he said. "Eschtah has lived
there for many years. It's the only permanent Navajo camp I know. These Indians are nomads. Most
of them live wherever the sheep lead them. This
plateau ranges for a hundred miles, farther than any
white man knows, and everywhere, in the valleys
and green nooks, will be found Navajo hogans.
That's why we may never find Mescal."

Hare's gaze travelled down over the tips of cedar
and crag to a pleasant vale, dotted with round
mound-like white-streaked hogans, from which lazy
floating columns of blue smoke curled upward. Mustangs and burros and sheep browsed on the white
patches of grass. Bright-red blankets blazed on the
cedar branches. There was slow colorful movement
of Indians, passing in and out of their homes. The
scene brought irresistibly to Hare the thought of
summer, of long warm afternoons, of leisure that
took no stock of time.

On the way down the trail they encountered a
flock of sheep driven by a little Navajo boy on a
brown burro. It was difficult to tell which was the
more surprised, the long-eared burro, which stood
stock-still, or the boy, who first kicked and pounded
his shaggy steed, and then jumped off and ran with
black locks flying. Farther down Indian girls started
up from their tasks, and darted silently into the
shade of the cedars. August Naab whooped when
he reached the valley, and Indian braves appeared,
to cluster round him, shake his hand and Hare's,
and lead them toward the centre of the encampment.

The hogans where these desert savages dwelt
were all alike; only the chief's was larger. From without it resembled a mound of clay with a few white
logs, half imbedded, shining against the brick red.

August Naab drew aside a blanket hanging over a
door, and entered, beckoning his companion to follow. Inured as Hare had become to the smell and
smart of wood-smoke, for a moment he could not
see, or scarcely breathe, so thick was the atmosphere. A fire, the size of which attested the desert
Indian's love of warmth, blazed in the middle of the
hogan, and sent part of its smoke upward through a
round hole in the roof. Eschtah, with blanket over
his shoulders, his lean black head bent, sat near the
fire. He noted the entrance of his visitors, but immediately resumed his meditative posture, and appeared to be unaware of their presence.

Hare followed August's example, sitting down and
speaking no word. His eyes, however, roved dis-
creetly to and fro. Eschtah's three wives presented
great differences in age and appearance. The eldest
was a wrinkled, parchment-skinned old hag who sat
sightless before the fire; the next was a solid square
squaw, employed in the task of combing a naked
boy's hair with a comb made of stiff thin roots tied
tightly in a round bunch. Judging from the young-
ster's actions and grimaces, this combing process
was not a pleasant one. The third wife, much younger, had a comely face, and long braids of black
hair, of which, evidently, she was proud. She leaned
on her knees over a flat slab of rock, and holding in
her hands a long oval stone, she rolled and mashed
corn into meal. There were young braves, handsome in their bronze-skinned way, with bands binding their straight thick hair, silver rings in their
ears, silver bracelets on their wrists, silver buttons
on their moccasins. There were girls who looked up
from their blanket-weaving with shy curiosity, and
then turned to their frames strung with long
threads. Under their nimble fingers the wool-
carrying needles slipped in and out, and the colored stripes grew apace. Then there were younger

boys and girls, all bright-eyed and curious; and babies sleeping on blankets. Where the walls and ceiling were not covered with buckskin garments, weapons and blankets, Hare saw the white wood-ribs of the hogan structure. It was a work of art, this circular house of forked logs and branches, interwoven into a dome, arched and strong, and all covered and cemented with clay.

At a touch of August's hand Hare turned to the old chief; and awaited his speech. It came with the uplifting of Eschtah's head, and the offering of his hand in the white man's salute. August's replies were slow and labored; he could not speak the Navajo language fluently, but he understood it.

"The White Prophet is welcome," was the chief's greeting. "Does he come for sheep or braves or to honor the Navajo in his home?"

"Eschtah, he seeks the Flower of the Desert," replied August Naab. "Mescal has left him. Her trail leads to the bitter waters under the cliff, and then is as a bird's."

"Eschtah has waited, yet Mescal has not come to him."

"She has not been here?"

"Mescal's shadow has not gladdened the Navajo's door."

"She has climbed the crags or wandered into the cañons. The white father loves her; he must find her."

"Eschtah's braves and mustangs are for his friend's use. The Navajo will find her if she is not as the grain of drifting sand. But is the White Prophet wise in his years? Let the Flower of the Desert take root in the soil of her forefathers."

"Eschtah's wisdom is great, but he thinks only of Indian blood. Mescal is half white, and her ways have been the ways of the white man. Nor does Eschtah think of the white man's love."

"The desert has called. Where is the White Prophet's vision? White blood and red blood will not mix. The Indian's blood pales in the white man's stream; or it burns red for the sun and the waste and the wild. Eschtah's forefathers, sleeping here in the silence, have called the Desert Flower."

"It is true. But the white man is bound; he cannot be as the Indian; he does not content himself with life as it is; he hopes and prays for change; he believes in the progress of his race on earth. Therefore Eschtah's white friend seeks Mescal; he has brought her up as his own; he wants to take her home, to love her better, to trust to the future."

"The white man's ways are white man's ways. Eschtah understands. He remembers his daughter lying here. He closed her dead eyes and sent word to his white friend. He named this child for the flower that blows in the wind of silent places. Eschtah gave his granddaughter to his friend. She has been the bond between them. Now she is flown and the White Father seeks the Navajo. Let him command. Eschtah has spoken."

Eschtah pressed into Naab's service a band of young braves, under the guidance of several warriors who knew every trail of the range, every water-hole, every cranny where even a wolf might hide. They swept the river-end of the plateau, and working westward, scoured the levels, ridges, valleys, climbed to the peaks, and sent their Indian dogs into the thickets and caves. From Eschtah's encampment westward the hogans diminished in number till only one here and there was discovered, hidden under a yellow wall, or amid a clump of cedars. All the Indians met with were sternly questioned by the chiefs, their dwellings were searched, and the ground about their water-holes was closely examined. Mile after mile the plateau was covered by these Indians, who beat the brush and pene-

trated the fastnesses with a hunting instinct that
left scarcely a rabbit-burrow unrevealed. The days
sped by; the circle of the sun arched higher; the
patches of snow in high places disappeared; and
the search proceeded westward. They camped
where the night overtook them, sometimes near water and grass, sometimes in bare dry places. To the
westward the plateau widened. Rugged ridges rose
here and there, and seared crags split the sky like
sharp sawteeth. And after many miles of wild up-
ranging they reached a divide which marked the
line of Eschtah's domain.

Naab's dogged persistence and the Navajos' faith-
fulness carried them into the country of the Moki
Indians, a tribe classed as slaves by the proud race
of Eschtah. Here they searched the villages and an-
cient tombs and ruins, but of Mescal there was
never a trace.

Hare rode as diligently and searched as indefati-
gably as August, but he never had any real hope of
finding the girl. To hunt for her, however, despite its
hopelessness, was a melancholy satisfaction, for
never was she out of his mind.

Nor was the month's hard riding with the Navajos
without profit. He made friends with the Indians,
and learned to speak many of their words. Then a
whole host of desert tricks became part of his accu-
mulating knowledge. In climbing the crags, in looking for water and grass, in loosing Silvermane at
night and searching for him at dawn, in marking
tracks on hard ground, in all the sight and feeling
and smell of desert things he learned much from
the Navajos. The whole outward life of the Indian
was concerned with the material aspect of Nature—
dust, rock, air, wind, smoke, the cedars, the beasts
of the desert. These things made up the Indians'
day. The Navajos were worshippers of the physical;
the sun was their supreme god. In the mornings

when the gray of dawn flushed to rosy red they began their chant to the sun. At sunset the Navajos were watchful and silent with faces westward. The Moki Indians also, Hare observed, had their morning service to the great giver of light. In the gloom of early dawn, before the pink appeared in the east, and all was whitening gray, the Mokis emerged from their little mud and stone huts and sat upon the roofs with blanketed and drooping heads.

One day August Naab showed in few words how significant a factor the sun was in the lives of desert men.

"We've got to turn back," he said to Hare. "The sun's getting hot and the snow will melt in the mountains. If the Colorado rises too high we can't cross."

They were two days in riding back to the encampment. Eschtah received them in dignified silence, expressive of his regret. When their time of departure arrived he accompanied them to the head of the nearest trail, which started down from Saweep Peak, the highest point of Echo Cliffs. It was the Navajos' outlook over the Painted Desert.

"Mescal is there," said August Naab. "She's there with the slave Eschtah gave her. He leads Mescal. Who can follow him there?"

The old chieftain reined in his horse, beside the time-hollowed trail, and the same hand that waved his white friend downward swept up in slow stately gesture toward the illimitable expanse. It was a warrior's salute to an unconquered world. Hare saw in his falcon eyes the still gleam, the brooding fire, the mystical passion that haunted the eyes of Mescal.

"The slave without a tongue is a wolf. He scents the trails and the waters. Eschtah's eyes have grown old watching here, but he has seen no Indian who could follow Mescal's slave. Eschtah will lie there, but no Indian will know the path to the place of his sleep. Mescal's trail is lost in the sand. No man may find it. Eschtah's words are wisdom. Look!"

To search for any living creatures in that borderless domain of colored dune, of shifting cloud of sand, of purple curtain shrouding mesa and dome, appeared the vainest of all human endeavors. It seemed a veritable rainbow realm of the sun. At first only the beauty stirred Hare—he saw the copper belt close under the cliffs, the white beds of alkali and washes of silt farther out, the wind-ploughed cañons and dust-encumbered ridges ranging west and east, the scalloped slopes of the flat tableland rising low, the tips of volcanic peaks leading the eye beyond to veils and vapors hovering over blue clefts and dim line of level lanes, and so on, and on, out to the vast unknown. Then Hare grasped a little of its meaning. It was a sun-painted, sun-governed world. Here was deep and majestic Nature eternal and unchangeable. But it was only through Eschtah's eyes that he saw its parched slopes, its terrifying desolateness, its sleeping death.

When the old chieftain's lips opened Hare anticipated the austere speech, the import that meant only pain to him, and his whole inner being seemed to shrink.

"The White Prophet's child of red blood is lost to him," said Eschtah. "The Flower of the Desert is as a grain of drifting sand."

CHAPTER XIII

The Sombre Line

AUGUST NAAB hoped that Mescal might have returned in his absence; but to Hare such hope was vain. The women of the oasis met them with gloomy faces presaging bad news, and they were reluctant to tell it. Mescal's flight had been forgotten in the sterner and sadder misfortune that had followed.

Snap Naab's wife lay dangerously ill, the victim of his drunken frenzy. For days after the departure of August and Jack the man had kept himself in a stupor; then his store of drink failing, he had come out of his almost senseless state into an insane frenzy. He had tried to kill his wife and wreck his cottage, being prevented in the nick of time by Dave Naab, the only one of his brothers who dared approach him. Then he had ridden off on the White Sage trail and had not been heard from since.

The Mormon put forth all his skill in surgery and medicine to save the life of his son's wife, but he admitted that he had grave misgivings as to her recovery. But these in no manner affected his patience, gentleness, and cheer. While there was life there was hope, said August Naab. He bade Hare, after he had rested awhile, to pack and ride out to the range, and tell his sons that he would come later.

It was a relief to leave the oasis, and Hare started the same day, and made Silver Cup that night. As he rode under the low-branching cedars toward the bright camp-fire he looked about him sharply. But not one of the four faces ruddy in the glow belonged to Snap Naab.

"Hello, Jack," called Dave Naab, into the dark. "I knew that was you. Silvermane sure rings bells when he hoofs it down the stones. How're you and Dad? and did you find Mescal? I'll bet that desert child led you clear to the Little Colorado."

Hare told the story of the fruitless search.

"It's no more than we expected," said Dave. "The man doesn't live who can trail the peon. Mescal's like a captured wild mustang that's slipped her halter and gone free. She'll die out there on the desert or turn into a stalk of the Indian cactus for which she's named. It's a pity, for she's a good girl, too good for Snap."

"What's your news?" inquired Hare.

"Oh, nothing much," replied Dave, with a short laugh. "The cattle wintered well. We've had little to do but hang round and watch. Zeke and I chased old Whitefoot one day, and got pretty close to Seeping Springs. We met Joe Stube, a rider who was once a friend of Zeke's. He's with Holderness now, and he said that Holderness had rebuilt the corrals at the spring; also he has put up a big cabin, and he has a dozen riders there. Stube told us Snap had been shooting up White Sage. He finished up by killing Snood. They got into an argument about you."

"About me!"

"Yes, it seems that Snood took your part, and

Snap wouldn't stand for it. Too bad! Snood was a good fellow. There's no use talking, Snap's going too far—he is—" Dave did not conclude his remark, and the silence was more significant than any utterance.

"What will the Mormons in White Sage say about Snap's killing Snood?"

"They've said a lot. This even-break business goes all right among gun-fighters, but the Mormons call killing murder. They've outlawed Culver, and Snap will be outlawed next."

"Your father hinted that Snap would find the desert too small for him and me."

"Jack, you can't be too careful. I've wanted to speak to you about it. Snap will ride in here some day and then—" Dave's pause was not reassuring.

And it was only on the third day after Dave's remark that Hare, riding down the mountain with a deer he had shot, looked out from the trail and saw Snap's cream pinto trotting toward Silver Cup. Beside Snap rode a tall man on a big bay. When Hare reached camp he reported to George and Zeke what he had seen, and learned in reply that Dave had already caught sight of the horsemen, and had gone down to the edge of the cedars. While they were speaking Dave hurriedly ran up the trail.

"It's Snap and Holderness," he called out, sharply. "What's Snap doing with Holderness? What's he bringing him here for?"

"I don't like the looks of it," replied Zeke, deliberately.

"Jack, what'll you do?" asked Dave, suddenly.

"Do? What can I do? I'm not going to run out of camp because of a visit from men who don't like me."

"It might be wisest."

"Do you ask me to run to avoid a meeting with your brother?"

"No." The dull red came to Dave's cheek. "But will you draw on him?"

"Certainly not. He's August Naab's son and your brother."

"Yes, and you're my friend, which Snap won't think of. Will you draw on Holderness, then?"

"For the life of me, Dave, I can't tell you," replied Hare, pacing the trail. "Something must break loose in me before I can kill a man. I'd draw, I suppose, in self-defence. But what good would it do me to pull too late? Dave, this thing is what I've feared. I'm not afraid of Snap or Holderness, not that way. I mean I'm not ready. Look here, would either of them shoot an unarmed man?"

"Lord, I hope not; I don't think so. But you're packing your gun."

Hare unbuckled his cartridge-belt, which held his Colt, and hung it over the pommel of his saddle; then he sat down on one of the stone seats near the camp-fire.

"There they come," whispered Zeke, and he rose to his feet, followed by George.

"Steady, you fellows," said Dave, with a warning glance. "I'll do the talking."

Holderness and Snap appeared among the cedars, and trotting out into the glade reined in their mounts a few paces from the fire. Dave Naab stood directly before Hare, and George and Zeke stepped aside.

"Howdy, boys?" called out Holderness, with a smile, which was like a gleam of light playing on a frozen lake. His amber eyes were steady, their gaze contracted into piercing yellow points. Dave studied the cattle-man with cool scorn, but refusing to speak to him, addressed his brother.

"Snap, what do you mean by riding in here with this fellow?"

"I'm Holderness's new foreman. We're just looking

round," replied Snap. The hard lines, the sullen shade, the hawk-beak cruelty had returned tenfold to his face, and his glance was like a living, leaping flame.

"New foreman!" exclaimed Dave. His jaw dropped and he stared in amazement. "No—you can't mean that—you're drunk!"

"That's what I said," growled Snap.

"You're a liar!" shouted Dave, a crimson blot blurring with the brown on his cheeks. He jumped off the ground in his fury.

"It's true, Naab; he's my new foreman," put in Holderness, suavely. "A hundred a month—in gold— and I've got as good a place for you."

"Well, by God!" Dave's arms came down and his face blanched to his lips. "Holderness!"

"I know what you'd say," interrupted the ranchman. "But stop it. I know you're game. And what's the use of fighting? I'm talking business. I'll—"

"You can't talk business or anything else to me," said Dave Naab, and he veered sharply toward his brother. "Say it again, Snap Naab. You've hired out to ride for this man?"

"That's it."

"You're going against your father, your brothers, your own flesh and blood?"

"I can't see it that way."

"Then you're a drunken, easily-led fool. This man's no rancher. He's a rustler. He ruined Martin Cole, the father of your first wife. He's stolen our cattle; he's jumped our water-rights. He's trying to break us. For God's sake, ain't you a man?"

"Things have gone bad for me," replied Snap, sullenly, shifting in his saddle. "I reckon I'll do better to cut out alone for myself."

"You crooked cur! But you're only my half-brother, after all. I always knew you'd come to something bad, but I never thought you'd disgrace the Naabs and break your father's heart. Now then, what do you want here? Be quick. This's our range and you and your boss can't ride here. You can't even water your horses. Out with it!"

At this, Hare, who had been so absorbed as to forget himself, suddenly felt a cold tightening of the skin of his face, and a hard swell of his breast. The dance of Snap's eyes, the downward flit of his hand seemed instantaneous with a red flash and loud report. Instinctively Hare dodged, but the light impact of something like a puff of air gave place to a tearing hot agony. Then he slipped down, back to the stone, with a bloody hand fumbling at his breast.

Dave leaped with tigerish agility, and knocking up the levelled Colt, held Snap as in a vise. George Naab gave Holderness's horse a sharp kick which made the mettlesome beast jump so suddenly that his rider was nearly unseated. Zeke ran to Hare and laid him back against the stone.

"Cool down, there!" ordered Zeke. "He's done for."

"My God—my God!" cried Dave, in a broken voice. "Not—not dead?"

"Shot through the heart!"

Dave Naab flung Snap backward, almost off his horse. "Damn you! run, or I'll kill you. And you, Holderness! Remember! If we ever meet again—you draw!" He tore a branch from a cedar and slashed both horses. They plunged out of the glade, and clattering over the stones, brushing the cedars, disappeared. Dave groped blindly back toward his brothers.

"Zeke, this's awful. Another murder by Snap! And my friend! . . . Who's to tell Father?"

Then Hare sat up, leaning against the stone, his shirt open and his bare shoulder bloody; his face was pale, but his eyes were smiling. "Cheer up, Dave. I'm not dead yet."

"Sure. he's not," said Zeke. "He ducked none too soon, or too late, and caught the bullet high up in the shoulder."

Dave sat down very quietly without a word, and the hand he laid on Hare's knee shook a little.

"When I saw George go for his gun," went on Zeke, "I knew there'd be a lively time in a minute if it wasn't stopped, so I just said Jack was dead."

"Do you think they came over to get me?" asked Hare.

"No doubt," replied Dave, lifting his face and wiping the sweat from his brow. "I knew that from the first, but I was so dazed by Snap's going over to Holderness that I couldn't keep my wits, and I didn't mark Snap edging over till too late."

"Listen, I hear horses," said Zeke, looking up from his task over Hare's wound.

"It's Billy, up on the home trail," added George. "Yes, and there's Father with him. Good Lord, must we tell him about Snap?"

"Some one must tell him," answered Dave.

"That'll be you, then. You always do the talking."

August Naab galloped into the glade, and swung himself out of the saddle. "I heard a shot. What's this? Who's hurt?—Hare! Why—lad—how is it with you?"

"Not bad," rejoined Hare.

"Let me see," August thrust Zeke aside. "A bullet-hole—just missed the bone—not serious. Tie it up tight. I'll take him home to-morrow. . . . Hare, who's been here?"

"Snap rode in and left his respects."

"Snap! Already? Yet I knew it——I saw it. You had Providence with you, lad, for this wound is not bad. Snap surprised you, then?"

"No. I knew it was coming."

"Jack hung his belt and gun on Silvermane's saddle," said Dave. "He didn't feel as if he could draw on either Snap or Holderness—"

"Holderness!"

"Yes. Snap rode in with Holderness. Hare thought if he was unarmed they wouldn't draw. But Snap did."

"Was he drunk?"

"No. They came over to kill Hare." Dave went on to recount the incident in full. "And—and see here, Dad—that's not all. Snap's gone to the bad."

Dave Naab hid his face while he told of his brother's treachery; the others turned away, and Hare closed his eyes.

For long moments there was silence broken only by the tramp of the old man as he strode heavily to and fro. At last the footsteps ceased, and Hare opened his eyes to see Naab's tall form erect, his arms uplifted, his shaggy head rigid.

"Hare," began August, presently. "I'm responsible for this cowardly attack on you. I brought you out here. This is the second one. Beware of the third! I see—but tell me, do you remember that I said you must meet Snap as man to man?"

"Yes."

"Don't you want to live?"

"Of course."

"You hold to no Mormon creed?"

"Why, no," Hare replied, wonderingly.

"What was the reason I taught you my trick with a gun?"

"I suppose it was to help me to defend myself."

"Then why do you let yourself be shot down in cold blood? Why did you hang up your gun? Why didn't you draw on Snap? Was it because of his father, his brothers, his family?"

"Partly, but not altogether," replied Hare, slowly. "I didn't know before what I know now. My flesh sickened at the thought of killing a man, even to save my own life; and to kill—your son—"

"No son of mine!" thundered Naab. "Remember that when next you meet. I don't want your blood on my hands. Don't stand to be killed like a sheep! If you have felt duty to me, I release you."

Zeke finished bandaging the wound. Making a bed of blankets, he lifted Hare into it, and covered him, cautioning him to lie still. Hare had a sensation of extreme lassitude, a deep drowsiness which permeated even to his bones. There were intervals of oblivion, then a time when the stars blinked in his eyes; he heard the wind, Silvermane's bell, the murmur of voices, yet all seemed remote from him, intangible as things in a dream.

He rode home next day, drooping in the saddle and fainting at the end of the trail, with the strong arm of August Naab upholding him. His wound was dressed and he was put to bed, where he lay sleeping most of the time, brooding the rest.

In three weeks he was in the saddle again, riding out over the red strip of desert toward the range. During his convalescence he had learned that he had come to the sombre line of choice. Either he must deliberately back away, and show his unfitness to survive in the desert, or he must step across into its dark wilds. The stern question haunted him. Yet he knew a swift decision waited on the crucial moment.

He sought lonely rides more than ever, and, like Silvermane, he was always watching and listening. His duties carried him half-way to Seeping Springs, across the valley to the red wall, up the slope of Coconina far into the forest of stately pines. What with Silvermane's wonderful scent and sight, and his own constant watchfulness, there were never range-riders or wild horses nor even deer near him without his knowledge.

The days flew by; spring had long since given place to summer; the blaze of sun and blast of flying sand were succeeded by the cooling breezes from the mountain; October brought the flurries of snow and November the dark storm-clouds.

Hare was the last of the riders to be driven off the mountain. The brothers were waiting for him at Silver Cup, and they at once packed and started for home.

August Naab listened to the details of the range-riding since his absence, with silent surprise. Holderness and Snap had kept away from Silver Cup after the supposed killing of Hare. Occasionally a group of horsemen rode across the valley or up a trail within sight of Dave and his followers, but there was never a meeting. Not a steer had been driven off the range that summer and fall; and except for the menace always hanging in the blue smoke over Seeping Springs the range-riding had passed without unusual incident.

So for Hare the months had gone by swiftly; though when he looked back afterward they seemed years. The winter at the oasis he filled as best he could, with the children playing in the yard, with Silvermane under the sunny lee of the great red wall, with any work that offered itself. It was during the long evenings, when he could not be active, that time oppressed him, and the memories of the past hurt him. A glimpse of the red sunset through the cliff-gate toward the west would start the train of thought; he both loved and hated the Painted Desert. Mescal was there in the purple shadows. He dreamed of her in the glowing embers of the log-fire. He saw her on Black Bolly with hair flying free to the wind. And he could not shut out the picture of her sitting in the corner of the room, silent, with bowed head, while the man to whom she was pledged hung close over her. That memory had a sting. It was like a spark of fire dropped on the wound in his breast where the desert-hawk had struck him. It was like a light gleaming on the sombre line he was waiting to cross.

CHAPTER XIV

Wolf

ON THE anniversary of the night Mescal disappeared the mysterious voice which had called to Hare so often and so strangely again pierced his slumber, and brought him bolt upright in his bed shuddering and listening. The dark room was as quiet as a tomb. He fell back into his blankets trembling with emotion. Sleep did not close his eyes again that night; he lay in a fever waiting for the dawn, and when the gray gloom lightened he knew what he must do.

After breakfast he sought August Naab. "May I go across the river?" he asked.

The old man looked up from his carpenter's task and fastened his glance on Hare. "Mescal?"

"Yes."

"I saw it long ago." He shook his head and spread his great hands. "There's no use for me to say what the desert is. If you ever come back you'll bring her. Yes, you may go. It's a man's deed. God keep you!"

Hare spoke to no other person; he filled one saddle-bag with grain, another with meat, bread, and dried fruits, strapped a five-gallon leather water-sack back of Silvermane's saddle, and set out toward the river. At the crossing-bar he removed Silvermane's equipments and placed them in the boat. At that moment a long howl, as of a dog baying the moon, startled him from his musings, and his eyes sought the river-bank, up and down, and then the opposite side. An animal, which at first he took to be a gray timber-wolf, was running along the sand-bar of the landing.

"Pretty white for a wolf," he muttered. "Might be a Navajo dog."

The beast sat down on his haunches and, lifting a lean head, sent up a doleful howl. Then he began trotting along the bar, every few paces stepping to the edge of the water. Presently he spied Hare, and he began to bark furiously.

"It's a dog all right; wants to get across," said Hare. "Where have I seen him?"

Suddenly he sprang to his feet, almost upsetting the boat. "He's like Mescal's Wolf!" He looked closer, his heart beginning to thump, and then he yelled: "Ki-yi! Wolf! Hyer! Hyer!"

The dog leaped straight up in the air, and coming down, began to dash back and forth along the sand with piercing yelps.

"It's Wolf! Mescal must be near," cried Hare. A veil obscured his sight, and every vein was like a hot cord. "Wolf! Wolf! I'm coming!"

With trembling hands he tied Silvermane's bridle to the stern seat of the boat and pushed off. In his eagerness he rowed too hard, dragging Silvermane's nose under water, and he had to check himself. Time and again he turned to call to the dog. At length the bow grated on the sand, and Silvermane emerged with a splash and a snort.

"Wolf, old fellow!" cried Hare. "Where's Mescal? Wolf, where is she?" He threw his arms around the dog. Wolf whined, licked Hare's face, and breaking away, ran up the sandy trail, and back again. But he barked no more; he waited to see if Hare was following.

"All right, Wolf—coming." Never had Hare saddled so speedily, nor mounted so quickly. He sent Silvermane into the willow-skirted trail close behind the dog, up on the rocky bench, and then under the bulging wall. Wolf reached the level between the cañon and Echo Cliffs, and then started straight west toward the Painted Desert. He trotted a few rods and turned to see if the man was coming.

Doubt, fear, uncertainty ceased for Hare. With the first blast of dust-scented air in his face he knew Wolf was leading him to Mescal. He knew that the cry he had heard in his dream was hers, that the old mysterious promise of the desert had at last begun its fulfilment. He gave one sharp exultant answer to that call. The horizon, ever-widening, lay before him, and the treeless plains, the sun-scorched slopes, the sandy stretches, the massed blocks of black mesas, all seemed to welcome him; his soul sang within him.

For Mescal was there. Far away she must be, a mere grain of sand in all that world of drifting sands, perhaps ill, perhaps hurt, but alive, waiting for him, calling for him, crying out with a voice that no distance could silence. He did not see the sharp peaks as pitiless barriers, nor the mesas and domes as black-faced death, nor the moisture-drinking sands as life-sucking foes to plant and beast and man. That painted wonderland had sheltered Mescal for a year. He had loved it for its color, its change, its secrecy; he loved it now because it had not been a grave for Mescal, but a home. Therefore he laughed at the deceiving yellow distances in the foreground of glistening mesas, at the deceiving purple distances of the far-off horizon. The wind blew a song in his ears; the dry desert odors were fragrance in his nostrils; the sand tasted sweet between his teeth, and the quivering heat-waves, veiling the desert in transparent haze, framed beautiful pictures for his eyes.

Wolf kept to the fore for some thirty paces, and though he had ceased to stop, he still looked back to see if the horse and man were following. Hare had noted the dog occasionally in the first hours of travel, but he had given his eyes mostly to the broken line of sky and desert in the west, to the receding contour of Echo Cliffs, to the spread and break of the desert near at hand. Here and there life showed itself in a gaunt coyote sneaking into the cactus, or a horned toad huddling down in the dust, or a jewel-eyed lizard sunning himself upon a stone. It was only when his excited fancy had cooled that Hare came to look closely at Wolf. But for the dog's color he could not have been distinguished from a real wolf. His head and ears and tail dropped, and he was lame in his right front paw.

Hare halted in the shade of a stone, dismounted and called the dog to him. Wolf returned without quickness, without eagerness, without any of the old-time friendliness of shepherding days. His eyes were sad and strange. Hare felt a sudden foreboding, but rejected it with passionate force. Yet a chill remained. Lifting Wolf's paw he discovered that the ball of the foot was worn through; whereupon he called into service a piece of buckskin, and fashioning a rude moccasin he tied it round the foot. Wolf licked his hand, but there was no change in the sad light of his eyes. He turned toward the west as if anxious to be off.

"All right, old fellow," said Hare, "only go slow.

From the look of that foot I think you've turned back on a long trail."

Again they faced the west, dog leading, man following, and addressed themselves to a gradual ascent. When it had been surmounted Hare realized that his ride so far had brought him only through an anteroom; the real portal now stood open to the Painted Desert. The immensity of the thing seemed to reach up to him with a thousand lines, ridges, cañons, all ascending out of a purple gulf. The arms of the desert enveloped him, a chill beneath their warmth.

As he descended into the valley, keeping close to Wolf, he marked a straight course in line with a volcanic spur. He was surprised when the dog, though continually threading jumbles of rock, heading cañons, crossing deep washes, and going round obstructions, always veered back to this bearing as true as a compass-needle to its magnet.

Hare felt the air growing warmer and closer as he continued the descent. By mid-afternoon, when he had travelled perhaps thirty miles, he was moist from head to foot, and Silvermane's coat was wet. Looking backward Hare had a blank feeling of loss; the sweeping line of Echo Cliffs had retreated behind the horizon. There was no familiar landmark left.

Sunset brought him to a standstill, as much from its sudden glorious gathering of brilliant crimsons splashed with gold, as from its warning that the day was done. Hare made his camp beside a stone which would serve as a wind-break. He laid his saddle for a pillow and his blanket for a bed. He gave Silvermane a nose-bag full of water, and then one of grain; he fed the dog, and afterward attended to his own needs. When his task was done the desert brightness had faded to gray; the warm air had blown away on a cool breeze, and night ap-

proached. He scooped out a little hollow in the
sand for his hips, took a last look at Silvermane haltered to the rock, and calling Wolf to his side
stretched himself to rest. He was used to lying on
the ground, under the open sky, out where the wind
blew and the sand seeped in, yet all these were different on this night. He was in the Painted Desert;
Wolf crept close to him; Mescal lay somewhere
under the blue-white stars.

He awakened and arose before any color of dawn
hinted of the day. While he fed his four-footed companions the sky warmed and lightened. A tinge of
rose gathered in the east. The air was cool and
transparent. He tried to cheer Wolf out of his sad-
eyed forlornness, and failed.

Hare vaulted into the saddle. The day had its possibilities, and while he had sobered down from his
first unthinking exuberance, there was still a ring in
his voice as he called to the dog:

"On, Wolf, on, old boy!"

Out of the east burst the sun, and the gray curtain was lifted by shafts of pink and white and gold,
flashing westward long trails of color.

When they started the actions of the dog showed
Hare that Wolf was not tracking a back-trail, but travelling by instinct. There were draws which necessi-
tated a search for a crossing, and areas of broken
rock which had to be rounded, and steep flat mesas
rising in the path, and strips of deep sand and cañons
impassable for long distances. But the dog always
found a way and always came back to a line with the
black spur that Hare had marked. It still stood in
sharp relief, no nearer than before, receding with every step, an illusive landmark, which Hare began to
distrust.

Then quite suddenly it vanished in the ragged
blue mass of the Ghost Mountains. Hare had seen
them several times, though never so distinctly. The

purple tips, the bold rock-ribs, the shadowed
cañons, so sharp and clear in the morning light—
how impossible to believe that these were only the
deceit of the desert mirage! Yet so they were; even
for the Navajos they were spirit-mountains.

The splintered desert-floor merged into an area of
sand. Wolf slowed his trot, and Silvermane's hoofs
sunk deep. Dismounting Hare labored beside him,
and felt the heat steal through his boots and burn
the soles of his feet. Hare plodded onward, stopping
once to tie another moccasin on Wolf's worn paw,
this time the left one; and often he pulled the stop-
per from the water-bag and cooled his parching lips
and throat. The waves of the sand-dunes were as
the waves of the ocean. He did not look backward,
dreading to see what little progress he had made.
Ahead were miles on miles of graceful heaps, swelling mounds, crested ridges, all different, yet regular
and rhythmical, drift on drift, dune on dune, in endless waves. Wisps of sand were whipped from their
summits in white ribbons and wreaths, and pale
clouds of sand shrouded little hollows. The morning
breeze, rising out of the west, approached in a rippling line, like the crest of an inflowing tide.

Silvermane snorted, lifted his ears and looked
westward toward a yellow pall which swooped up
from the desert.

"Sand-storm," said Hare, and calling Wolf he made
for the nearest rock that was large enough to shelter
them. The whirling sand-cloud mushroomed into an
enormous desert covering, engulfing the dunes, ob-
scuring the light. The sunlight failed; the day turned
to gloom. Then an eddying fog of sand and dust enveloped Hare. His last glimpse before he covered his
face with a silk handkerchief was of sheets of sand
streaming past his shelter. The storm came with a
low, soft, hissing roar, like the sound in a seashell
magnified. Breathing through the handkerchief Hare

avoided inhaling the sand which beat against his face, but the finer dust particles filtered through and stifled him. At first he felt that he would suffocate, and he coughed and gasped; but presently, when the thicker sand-clouds had passed, he managed to get air enough to breathe. Then he waited patiently while the steady seeping rustle swept by, and the band of his hat sagged heavier, and the load on his shoulders had to be continually shaken off, and the weighty trap round his feet crept upward. When the light, fine touch ceased he removed the covering from his face to see himself standing nearly to his knees in sand, and Silvermane's back and the saddle burdened with it. The storm was moving eastward, a dull red now with the sun faintly showing through it like a ball of fire.

"Well, Wolf, old boy, how many storms like that will we have to weather?" asked Hare, in a cheery tone which he had to force. He knew these sand-storms were but vagaries of the desert-wind. Before the hour closed he had to seek the cover of a stone and wait for another to pass. Then he was caught in the open, with not a shelter in sight. He was compelled to turn his back to a third storm, the worst of all, and to bear as best he could the heavy impact of the first blow, and the succeeding rush and flow of sand. After that his head drooped and he wearily trudged beside Silvermane, dreading the interminable distance he must cover before once more gaining hard ground. But he discovered that it was useless to try to judge distance on the desert. What had appeared miles at his last look turned out to be only rods.

It was good to get into the saddle again and face clear air. Far away the black spur again loomed up, now surrounded by groups of mesas with sage-slopes tinged with green. That surely meant the end of this long trail; the faint spots of green lent suggestion of a desert water-hole; there Mescal must be, hidden in some shady cañon. Hare built his hopes anew.

So he pressed on down a plain of bare rock dotted by huge bowlders; and out upon a level floor of scant sage and grease-wood where a few living creatures, a desert-hawk sailing low, lizards darting into holes, and a swiftly running ground-bird, emphasized the lack of life in the waste. He entered a zone of clay-dunes of violet and heliotrope hues; and then a belt of lava and cactus. Reddish points studded the desert, and here and there were meagre patches of white grass. Far away myriads of cactus plants showed like a troop of distorted horsemen. As he went on the grass failed, and streams of jagged lava flowed downward. Beds of cinders told of the fury of a volcanic fire. Soon Hare had to dismount to make moccasins for Wolf's hind feet; and to lead Silvermane carefully over the cracked lava. For a while there were strips of ground bare of lava and harboring only an occasional bunch of cactus, but soon every foot free of the reddish iron bore a projecting mass of fierce spikes and thorns. The huge barrel-shaped cacti, and thickets of slender dark-green rods with bayonet points, and broad leaves with yellow spines, drove Hare and his sore-footed fellow-travellers to the lava.

Hare thought there must be an end to it some time, yet it seemed as though he were never to cross that black forbidding inferno. Blistered by the heat, pierced by the thorns, lame from long toil on the lava, he was sorely spent when once more he stepped out upon the bare desert. On pitching camp he made the grievous discovery that the water-bag had leaked or the water had evaporated, for there was only enough left for one more day. He ministered to thirsty dog and horse in silence, his mind revolving the grim fact of his situation.

His little fire of grease-wood threw a wan circle into the surrounding blackness. Not a sound hinted of life. He longed for even the bark of a coyote. Silvermane stooped motionless with tired head. Wolf stretched limply on the sand. Hare rolled into his blanket and stretched out with slow aching relief.

He dreamed he was a boy roaming over the green hills of the old farm, wading through dewy clover-fields, and fishing in the Connecticut River. It was the long vacation-time, an endless freedom. Then he was at the swimming-hole, and playmates tied his clothes in knots, and with shouts of glee ran up the bank leaving him there to shiver.

When he awakened the blazing globe of the sun had arisen over the eastern horizon, and the red of the desert swathed all the reach of valley.

Hare pondered whether he should use his water at once or dole it out. That ball of fire in the sky, a glazed circle, like iron at white heat, decided for him. The sun would be hot and would evaporate such water as leakage did not claim, and so he shared alike with Wolf, and gave the rest to Silvermane.

For an hour the mocking lilac mountains hung in the air and then paled in the intense light. The day was soundless and windless, and the heat-waves rose from the desert like smoke. For Hare the realities were the baked clay flats, where Silvermane broke through at every step; the beds of alkali, which sent aloft clouds of powdered dust; the deep gullies full of round bowlders; thickets of mesquite and prickly thorn which tore at his legs; the weary detour to head the cañons; the climb to get between two bridging mesas; and always the haunting presence of the sad-eyed dog. His unrealities were the shimmering sheets of water in every low place; the baseless mountains floating in the air; the green slopes rising at hand; beautiful buttes of dark blue riding the open sand, like monstrous barks at sea; the changing outlines of desert shapes in pink haze and veils of purple and white lustre—all illusions, all mysterious tricks of the mirage.

In the heat of midday Hare yielded to its influence and reined in his horse under a slate-bank where there was shade. His face was swollen and peeling, and his lips had begun to dry and crack and taste of alkali. Then Wolf pattered on; Silvermane kept at his heels; Hare dozed in the saddle. His eyes burned in their sockets from the glare, and it was a relief to shut out the barren reaches. So the afternoon waned.

Silvermane stumbled, jolting Hare out of his stupid lethargy. Before him spread a great field of bowlders with not a slope or a ridge or a mesa or an escarpment. Not even a tip of a spur rose in the background. He rubbed his sore eyes. Was this another illusion?

When Silvermane started onward Hare thought of the Navajos' custom to trust horse and dog in such an emergency. They were desert-bred; beyond human understanding were their sight and scent. He was at the mercy now of Wolf's instinct and Silvermane's endurance. Resignation brought him a certain calmness of soul, cold as the touch of an icy hand on fevered cheek. He remembered the desert secret in Mescal's eyes; he was about to solve it. He remembered August Naab's words: "It's a man's deed!" If so, he had achieved the spirit of it, if not the letter. He remembered Eschtah's tribute to the wilderness of painted wastes: "There is the grave of the Navajo, and no one knows the trail to the place of his sleep!" He remembered the something evermore about to be, the unknown always subtly calling; now it was revealed in the stone-fettering grip of the desert. It had opened wide to him, bright with its face of danger, beautiful with its painted windows, inscrutable with its alluring call. Bidding him enter, it had closed behind him; now he looked upon it in its iron order, its strange ruins racked by fire, its inevitable remorselessness.

CHAPTER XV

Desert Night

THE GRAY stallion, finding the rein loose on his neck, trotted forward and overtook the dog, and thereafter followed at his heels. With the setting of the sun a slight breeze stirred, and freshened as twilight fell, rolling away the sultry atmosphere. Then the black desert night mantled the plain.

For a while this blackness soothed the pain of Hare's sun-blinded eyes. It was a relief to have the unattainable horizon line blotted out. But by-and-by the opaque gloom brought home to him, as the day had never done, the reality of his solitude. He was alone in this immense place of barrenness, and his dumb companions were the world to him. Wolf pattered onward, a silent guide; and Silvermane followed, never lagging, sure-footed in the dark, faithful to his master. All the love Hare had borne the horse was as nothing to that which came to him on this desert night. In and out, round and round, ever winding, ever zigzagging, Silvermane hung close to Wolf, and the sandy lanes between the bowlders gave forth no sound. Dog and horse, free to choose their trail, trotted onward miles and miles into the night.

A pale light in the east turned to a glow, then to gold, and the round disc of the moon silhouetted the black bowlders on the horizon. It cleared the dotted line and rose, an oval orange-hued strange moon, not mellow nor silvery nor gloriously brilliant as Hare had known it in the past, but a vast dead-gold melancholy orb, rising sadly over the desert. To Hare it was the crowning reminder of lifelessness; it fitted this world of dull gleaming stones.

Silvermane went lame and slackened his trot, causing Hare to rein in and dismount. He lifted the right forefoot, the one the horse had favored, and found a stone imbedded tightly in the hoof. He pried it out with his knife and mounted again. Wolf shone faintly far ahead, and presently he uttered a mournful cry which sent a chill to the rider's heart. The silence had been oppressive before; now it was terrible. It was not a silence of life. It had been broken suddenly by Wolf's howl, and had closed sharply after it, without echo; it was a silence of death.

Hare took care not to fall behind Wolf again, he had no wish to hear that cry repeated. The dog moved onward with silent feet; the horse wound after him with hoofs padded in the sand; the moon lifted and the desert gleamed; the bowlders grew larger and the lanes wider. So the night wore on, and Hare's eyelids grew heavy, and his whole weary body cried out for rest and forgetfulness. He nodded until he swayed in the saddle; then righted himself, only to doze again. The east gave birth to the morning star. The whitening sky was the harbinger of day. Hare could not bring himself to face the light and heat, and he stopped at a wind-worn cave

under a shelving rock. He was asleep when he
rolled out on the sand-strewn floor. Once he awoke
and it was still day, for his eyes quickly shut upon
the glare. He lay sweltering till once more slumber
claimed him. The dog awakened him, with cold
nose and low whine. Another twilight had fallen.
Hare crawled out, stiff and sore, hungry and parching with thirst. He made an attempt to eat, but it
was a failure. There was a dry burning in his throat,
a dizzy feeling in his brain, and there were red
flashes before his eyes. Wolf refused meat, and
Silvermane turned from the grain, and lowered his
head to munch a few blades of desert grass.

Then the journey began, and the night fell black.
A cool wind blew from the west, the white stars
blinked, the weird moon rose with its ghastly glow.
Huge bowlders rose before him in grotesque
shapes, tombs and pillars and statues of Nature's
dead, carved by wind and sand. But some had life
in Hare's disordered fancy. They loomed and towered over him, and stalked abroad and peered at
him with deep-set eyes.

Hare fought with all his force against this mood of
gloom. Wolf was not a phantom; he trotted forward
with unerring instinct; and he would find water, and
that meant life. Silvermane, desert-steeled, would
travel to the furthermost corner of this hell of sand-
swept stone. Hare tried to collect all his spirit, all
his energies, but the battle seemed to be going
against him. All about him was silence, breathless
silence, insupportable silence of ages. Desert spec-
tres danced in the darkness. The worn-out moon
gleamed golden over the worn-out waste. Desola-
tion lurked under the sable shadows.

Hare rode on into the night, tumbled from his
saddle in the gray of dawn to sleep, and stumbled
in the twilight to his drooping horse. His eyes were
blind now to the desert shapes, his brain burned

and his tongue filled his mouth. Silvermane trod
ever upon Wolf's heels; he had come into the king-
dom of his desert-strength; he lifted his drooping
head and lengthened his stride; weariness had gone
and he snorted his welcome to something on the
wind. Then he passed the limping dog and led the
way.

Hare held to the pommel and bent dizzily forward
in the saddle. Silvermane was going down, step by
step, with metallic clicks upon flinty rock. Whether
he went down or up was all the same to Hare; he
held on with closed eyes and whispered to himself.
Down and down, step by step, cracking the stones
with iron-shod hoofs, the gray stallion worked his
perilous way, sure-footed as a mountain-sheep.
Then he stopped with a great slow heave and bent
his head.

The black bulge of a cañon rim blurred in Hare's
hot eyes. A trickling sound penetrated his tired
brain. His ears had grown like his eyes—false. Only
another delusion! As he had been tortured with the
sight of lake and stream now he was to be tortured
with the sound of running water. Yet he listened, for
it was sweet even in its mockery. What a clear mu-
sical tinkle, like silver bells tossing on the wind! He
listened. Soft murmuring flow, babble and gurgle, little hollow fall and splash!

Suddenly Silvermane, lifting his head, broke the
silence of the cañon with a great sigh of content. It
pierced the dull fantasy of Hare's mind; it burst the
gloomy spell. The sigh and the snort which followed were Silvermane's triumphant signals when
he had drunk his fill.

Hare fell from the saddle. The gray dog lay
stretched low in the darkness. Hare crawled beside
him and reached out with his hot hands. Smooth
cool marble rock, growing slippery, then wet, led
into running water. He slid forward on his face and

wonderful cold thrills quivered over his burning skin. He drank and drank until he could drink no more. Then he lay back upon the rock; the madness of his brain went out with the light of the stars, and he slept.

When he awoke red cañon walls leaned far above him to a gap spanned by blue sky. A song of rushing water murmured near his ears. He looked down; a spring gushed from a crack in the wall; Silvermane cropped green bushes, and Wolf sat on his haunches waiting, but no longer with sad eyes and strange mien. Hare raised himself, looking again and again, and slowly gathered his wits. The crimson blur had gone from his eyes and the burning from his skin, and the painful swelling from his tongue.

He drank long and deeply, and rising with clearing thoughts and thankful heart, he kissed Wolf's white head, and laid his arms round Silvermane's neck. He fed them, and ate himself, not without difficulty, for his lips were puffed and his tongue felt like a piece of rope. When he had eaten, his strength came back.

At a word Wolf, with a wag of his tail, splashed into the gravelly stream bed. Hare followed on foot, leading Silvermane. There were little beds of pebbles and beaches of sand and short steps down which the water babbled. The cañon was narrow and tortuous; Hare could not see ahead or below, for the projecting red cliffs, growing higher as he descended, walled out the view. The blue stream of sky above grew bluer and the light and shade less bright. For an hour he went down steadily without a check, and the farther down the rougher grew the way. Bowlders wedged in narrow places made foaming waterfalls. Silvermane clicked down confidently.

The slender stream of water, swelled by seeping springs and little rills, gained the dignity of a brook; it began to dash merrily and hurriedly downward.

The depth of the falls, the height of cliffs, and the size of the bowlders increased in the descent. Wolf splashed on unmindful; there was a new spirit in his movements; and when he looked back for his laboring companions there was friendly protest in his eyes. Silvermane's mien plainly showed that where a dog could go he could follow. Silvermane's blood was heated; the desert was an old story to him; it had only tired him and parched his throat; this cañon of downward steps and falls, with ever-deepening drops, was new to him, and roused his mettle; and from his long training in the wilds he had gained a marvellous sure-footedness.

The cañon narrowed as it deepened; the jutting walls leaned together, shutting out the light; the sky above was now a ribbon of blue, only to be seen when Hare threw back his head and stared straight up.

"It'll be easier climbing up, Silvermane," he panted—"if we ever get the chance."

The sand and gravel and shale had disappeared; all was bare clean-washed rock. In many places the brook failed as a trail, for it leaped down in white sheets over mossy cliffs. Hare faced these walls in despair. But wolf led on over the ledges and Silvermane followed, nothing daunted. At last Hare shrank back from a hole which defied him utterly. Even Wolf hesitated. The cañon was barely twenty feet wide; the floor ended in a precipice; the stream leaped out and fell into a dark cleft from which no sound arose. On the right there was a shelf of rock; it was scarce half a foot broad at the narrowest and then apparently vanished altogether. Hare stared helplessly up at the slanting shut-in walls.

While he hesitated Wolf pattered out upon the ledge and Silvermane stamped restlessly. With a desperate fear of losing his beloved horse Hare let go the bridle and stepped upon the ledge. He

walked rapidly, for a slow step meant uncertainty
and a false one meant death. He heard the sharp
ring of Silvermane's shoes, and he listened in agonized suspense for the slip, the snort, the crash
that he feared must come. But it did not come. Seeing nothing except the narrow ledge, yet feeling the
blue abyss beneath him, he bent all his mind to his
task, and finally walked out into lighter space upon
level rock. To his infinite relief Silvermane appeared
rounding a corner out of the dark passage, and was
soon beside him.

Hare cried aloud in welcome.

The cañon widened; there was a clear demarca-
tion where the red walls gave place to yellow; the
brook showed no outlet from its subterranean chan-
nel. Sheer exhaustion made Hare almost forget his
mission; the strength of his resolve had gone into
mechanical toil; he kept on, conscious only of the
smart of bruised hands and feet and the ache of laboring lungs.

Time went on and the sun hung in the midst of
the broadening belt of blue sky. A long slant of yellow slope led down to a sage-covered level, which
Hare crossed, pleased to see blooming cacti and
wondering at their slender lofty green stems shining
with gold flowers. He descended into a ravine which
became precipitous. Here he made only slow advance. At the bottom he found himself in a wonderful lane with an almost level floor; here flowed a
shallow stream bordered by green willows. Wolf
took the direction of the flowing water. Hare's
thoughts were all of Mescal, and his hopes began to
mount, his heart to beat high.

He gazed ahead with straining eyes. Presently
there was not a break in the walls. A drowsy hum of
falling water came to Hare, strange reminder of the
oasis, the dull roar of the Colorado, and of Mescal.

His flagging energies leaped into life with the

cañon suddenly opening to bright light and blue sky
and beautiful valley, white and gold in blossom,
green with grass and cottonwood. On a flower-
scented wind rushed that muffled roar again, like
distant thunder.

Wolf dashed into the cottonwoods. Silvermane
whistled with satisfaction and reached for the long
grass.

For Hare the light held something more than
beauty, the breeze something more than sweet
scent of water and blossom. Both were charged
with meaning—with suspense.

Wolf appeared in the open leaping upon a slender
brown-garbed form.

"Mescal!" cried Hare.

With a cry she ran to him, her arms outstretched,
her hair flying in the wind, her dark eyes wild with
joy.

CHAPTER XVI

Thunder River

FOR AN instant Hare's brain reeled, and Mescal's broken murmurings were meaningless. Then his faculties grew steady and acute; he held the girl as if he intended never to let her go. Mescal clung to him with a wildness that gave him anxiety for her reason; there was something almost fierce in the tension of her arms, in the blind groping for his face.

"Mescal! It's Jack, safe and well," he said. "Let me look at you."

At the sound of his voice all her rigid strength changed to a yielding weakness; she leaned back supported by his arms and looked at him. Hare trembled before the dusky level glance he remembered so well, and as tears began to flow he drew her head to his shoulder. He had forgotten to prepare himself for a different Mescal. Despite the quivering smile of happiness, her eyes were strained with pain. The oval contour, the rich bloom of her face had gone; beauty was there still, but it was the ghost of the old beauty.

"Jack—is it—really you?" she asked.

He answered with a kiss.

She slipped out of his arms breathless and scarlet. "Tell me all—"

"There's much to tell, but not before you kiss me. It has been more than a year."

"Only a year! Have I been gone only a year?"

"Yes, a year. But it's past now. Kiss me, Mescal. One kiss will pay for that long year, though it broke my heart."

Shyly she raised her hands to his shoulders and put her lips to his. "Yes, you've found me, Jack, thank God! just in time!"

"Mescal! What's wrong? Aren't you well?"

"Pretty well. But if you had not come soon I should have starved."

"Starved? Let me get my saddle-bags—I have bread and meat."

"Wait. I'm not so hungry now. I mean very soon I should not have had any food at all."

"But your peon—the dumb Indian? Surely he could find something to eat. What of him? Where is he?"

"My peon is dead. He has been dead for months, I don't know how many."

"Dead! What was the matter with him?"

"I never knew. I found him dead one morning and I buried him in the sand."

Mescal led Hare under the cottonwoods and pointed to the Indian's grave, now green with grass. Farther on in a circle of trees stood a little hogan skilfully constructed out of brush; the edge of a red blanket peeped from the door; a burnt-out fire smoked on a stone fireplace, and blackened earthen vessels lay near. The white seeds of the cottonwoods were flying light as feathers; plum-trees were pink in blossom; there were vines twining all about; through the openings in the foliage shone the blue of sky and red of cliff. Patches of blossoming flowers were here and there lit to brilliance by golden shafts of sunlight. The twitter of birds and hum of bees were almost drowned in the soft roar of water.

"Is that the Colorado I hear?" asked Hare.

"No, that's Thunder River. The Colorado is farther down in the Grand Cañon."

"Farther down! Mescal, I must have come a mile from the rim. Where are we?"

"We are almost at the Colorado, and directly under the head of Coconina. We can see the mountain from the break in the valley below."

"Come sit by me here under this tree. Tell me—how did you ever get here?"

Then Mescal told him how the peon had led her on a long trail from Bitter Seeps, how they had camped at desert water-holes, and on the fourth day descended to Thunder River.

"I was quite happy at first. It's always summer down here. There were rabbits, birds, beaver, and fruit—we had enough to eat. I explored the valley with Wolf or rode Noddle up and down the cañon. Then my peon died, and I had to shift for myself. There came a time when the beaver left the valley, and Wolf and I had to make a rabbit serve for days. I knew then I'd have to get across the desert to the Navajos or starve in the cañon. I hesitated about climbing out into the desert, for I wasn't sure of the trail to the water-holes. Noddle wandered off up the cañon and never came back. After he was gone and I knew I couldn't get out I grew homesick. The days weren't so bad because I was always hunting for something to eat, but the nights were lonely. I couldn't sleep. I lay awake listening to the river, and at last I could hear whispering and singing and music, and strange sounds, and low thunder, always low thunder. I wasn't really frightened, only lonely, and the cañon was so black and full of mutterings. Sometimes I'd dream I was back on the plateau with you, Jack, and Bolly and the sheep, and when I'd awake in the loneliness I'd cry right out—"

"Mescal, I heard those cries," said Hare.

"It was strange—the way I felt. I believe if I'd never known and—and loved you, Jack, I'd have forgotten home. After I'd been here a while, I seemed to be drifting, drifting. It was as if I had lived in the cañon long before, and was remembering. The feeling was strong, but always thoughts of you, and of the big world, brought me back to the present with its loneliness and fear of starvation. Then I wanted you, and I'd cry out. I knew I must send Wolf home. How hard it was to make him go! But at last he trotted off, looking backward, and I—waited and waited."

She leaned against him. The hand which had plucked at his sleeve dropped to his fingers and clung there. Hare knew how her story had slighted the perils and privations of that long year. She had grown lonely in the cañon darkness; she had sent Wolf away and had waited—all was said in that. But more than any speech, the look of her, and the story told in the thin brown hands touched his heart. Not for an instant since his arrival had she altogether let loose of his fingers, or coat, or arm. She had lived so long alone in this weird world of silence and moving shadows and murmuring water, that she needed to feel the substance of her hopes, to assure herself of the reality of the man she loved.

"My mustang—Bolly—tell me of her," said Mescal.

"Bolly's fine. Sleek and fat and lazy! She's been in the fields ever since you left. Not a bridle on her. Many times have I seen her poke her black muzzle over the fence and look down the lane. She'd never forget you, Mescal."

"Oh! how I want to see her! Tell me—everything."

"Wait a little. Let me fetch Silvermane and we'll make a fire and eat. Then—"

"Tell me now."

"Well, Mescal, it's soon told." Then came the story of events growing out of her flight. When he told of the shooting at Silver Cup, Mescal rose with heaving bosom and blazing eyes.

"It was nothing—I wasn't hurt much. Only the intention was bad. We saw no more of Snap or Holderness. The worst of it all was that Snap's wife died."

"Oh, I am sorry—sorry. Poor Father Naab! How he must hate me, the cause of it all! But I couldn't stay—I couldn't marry Snap."

"Don't blame yourself, Mescal. What Snap might have done if you had married him is guesswork. He might have left drink alone a while longer. But he was bad clean through. I heard Dave Naab tell him that. Snap would have gone over to Holderness sooner or later. And now he's a rustler, if not worse."

"Then those men think Snap killed you?"

"Yes."

"What's going to happen when you meet Snap, or any of them?"

"Somebody will be surprised," replied Hare, with a laugh.

"Jack, it's no laughing matter." She fastened her hands in the lapels of his coat and her eyes grew sad. "You can never hang up your gun again."

"No. But perhaps I can keep out of their way, especially Snap's. Mescal, you've forgotten Silvermane, and how he can run."

"I haven't forgotten. He can run, but he can't beat

Bolly." She said this with a hint of her old spirit. "Jack—you want to take me back home?"

"Of course. What did you expect when you sent Wolf?"

"I didn't expect. I just wanted to see you, or somebody, and I thought of the Navajos. Couldn't I live with them? Why can't we stay here or in a cañon across the Colorado where there's plenty of game?"

"I'm going to take you home and Father Naab shall marry you—to—to me."

Startled, Mescal fell back upon his shoulder and did not stir nor speak for a long time. "Did—did you tell him?"

"Yes."

"What did he say? Was he angry? Tell me."

"He was kind and good as he always is. He said if I found you, then the issue would be between Snap and me, as man to man. You are still pledged to Snap in the Mormon Church and that can't be changed. I don't suppose even if he's outlawed that it could be changed."

"Snap will not let any grass grow in the trails to the oasis," said Mescal. "Once he finds I've come back to life he'll have me. You don't know him, Jack. I'm afraid to go home."

"My dear, there's no other place for us to go. We can't live the life of Indians."

"But Jack, think of me watching you ride out from home! Think of me always looking for Snap! I couldn't endure it. I've grown weak in this year of absence."

"Mescal, look at me." His voice rang as he held her face to face. "We must decide everything. Now—say you love me!"

"Yes—yes."

"Say it."

"I—love you—Jack."

"Say you'll marry me!"

"I will marry you."

"Then listen. I'll get you out of this cañon and take you home. You are mine and I'll keep you." He held her tightly with strong arms; his face paled, his eyes darkened. "I don't want to meet Snap Naab. I shall try to keep out of his way. I hope I can. But Mescal, I'm yours now. Your happiness—perhaps your life—depends on me. That makes a difference. Understand!"

Silvermane walked into the glade with a saddle-girth so tight that his master unbuckled it only by dint of repeated effort. Evidently the rich grass of Thunder River Cañon appealed strongly to the desert stallion.

"Here, Silver, how do you expect to carry us out if you eat and drink like that?" Hare removed the saddle and tethered the gray to one of the cotton-woods. Wolf came trotting into camp proudly carrying a rabbit.

"Mescal, can we get across the Colorado and find a way up over Coconina?" asked Hare.

"Yes, I'm sure we can. My peon never made a mistake about directions. There's no trail, but Navajos have crossed the river at this season, and worked up a cañon."

The shadows had gathered under the cliffs, and the rosy light high up on the ramparts had chilled and waned when Hare and Mescal sat down to their meal. Wolf lay close to the girl and begged for morsels. Then in the twilight they sat together content to be silent, listening to the low thunder of the river. Long after Mescal had retired into her hogan Hare lay awake before her door with his head in his saddle and listened to the low roll, the dull burr, the dreamy hum of the tumbling waters. The place was like the oasis, only infinitely more hidden under the cliffs. A few stars twinkled out of the dark blue, and one hung, beacon-like, on the crest of a noble crag. There were times when he imagined the valley was as silent as the desert night, and other times when he imagined he heard the thundering roll of avalanches and the tramp of armies. Then the voices of Mescal's solitude spoke to him—glorious laughter and low sad wails of woe, sweet songs and whispers and murmurs. His last waking thoughts were of the haunting sound of Thunder River, and that he had come to bear Mescal away from its loneliness.

He bestirred himself at the first glimpse of day, and when the gray mists had lifted to wreathe the crags it was light enough to begin the journey. Mescal shed tears at the grave of the faithful peon. "He loved this cañon," she said, softly. Hare lifted her upon Silvermane. He walked beside the horse and Wolf trotted on before. They travelled awhile under the flowering cottonwoods on a trail bordered with green tufts of grass and great star-shaped lilies. The river was still hidden, but it filled the grove with its soft thunder. Gradually the trees thinned out, hard stony ground encroached upon the sand, bowlders appeared in the way; and presently, when Silvermane stepped out of the shade of the cottonwoods, Hare saw the lower end of the valley with its ragged vent.

"Look back!" said Mescal.

Hare saw the river bursting from the base of the wall in two white streams which soon united below, and leaped down in a continuous cascade. Step by step the stream plunged through the deep gorge, a broken, foaming raceway, and at the lower end of the valley it took its final leap into a blue abyss, and then found its way to the Colorado, hidden underground.

The flower-scented breeze and the rumbling of the river persisted long after the valley lay behind and above, but these failed at length in the close air

of the huge abutting walls. The light grew thick, the
stones cracked like deep bell-strokes; the voices of
man and girl had a hollow sound and echo.
Silvermane clattered down the easy trail at a gait
which urged Hare now and then from walk to run.
Soon the gully opened out upon a plateau through
the centre of which, in a black gulf, wound the red
Colorado, sullen-voiced, booming, never silent nor
restful. Here were distances by which Hare could
begin to comprehend the immensity of the cañon,
and he felt lost among the great terraces leading up
to mesas that dwarfed the Echo Cliffs. All was bare
rock of many hues burning under the sun.

"Jack, this is mescal," said the girl, pointing to
some towering plants.

All over the sunny slopes cacti lifted slender
shafts, unfolding in spiral leaves as they shot upward and bursting at the top into plumes of yellow
flowers. The blossoming stalks waved in the wind,
and black bees circled round them.

"Mescal, I've always wanted to see the Flower of
the Desert from which you're named. It's beautiful."

Hare broke a dead stalk of the cactus and was put
to instant flight by a stream of bees pouring with
angry buzz from the hollow centre. Two big fellows
were so persistent that he had to beat them off with
his hat.

"You shouldn't despoil their homes," said Mescal,
with a peal of laughter.

"I'll break another stalk and get stung, if you'll
laugh again," replied Hare.

They traversed the remaining slope of the plateau, and entering the head of a ravine, descended
a steep cleft of flinty rock, rock so hard that
Silvermane's iron hoofs not so much as scratched
it. Then reaching a level, they passed out to
rounded sand and the river.

"It's a little high," said Hare dubiously. "Mescal, I don't like the looks of those rapids."

Only a few hundred rods of the river could be seen. In front of Hare the current was swift but not broken. Above, where the cañon turned, the river sheered out with a majestic roll and falling in a wide smooth curve suddenly narrowed into a leaping crest of reddish waves. Below Hare was a smaller rapid where the broken water turned toward the nearer side of the river, but with an accompaniment of twisting swirls and vicious waves.

"I guess we'd better risk it," said Hare, grimly recalling the hot rock, the sand, and lava of the desert.

"It's safe, if Silvermane is a good swimmer," replied Mescal. "We can take the river above and cut across so the current will help."

"Silvermane loves the water. He'll make this crossing easily. But he can't carry us both, and it's impossible to make two trips. I'll have to swim."

Without wasting more words and time over a task which would only grow more formidable with every look and thought, Hare led Silvermane up the sandbar to its limit. He removed his coat and strapped it behind the saddle; his belt and revolver and boots he hung over the pommel.

"How about Wolf? I'd forgotten him."

"Never fear for him! He'll stick close to me."

"Now, Mescal, there's the point we want to make, that bar; see it?"

"Surely we can land above that."

"I'll be satisfied if we get even there. You guide him for it. And, Mescal, here's my gun. Try to keep it from getting wet. Balance it on the pommel—so. Come, Silver; come, Wolf."

"Keep up-stream," called Mescal as Hare plunged in. "Don't drift below us."

In two steps Silvermane went in to his saddle, and

he rolled with a splash and a snort, sinking Mescal to her hips. His nose level with the water, mane and tail floating, he swam powerfully with the current.

For Hare the water was just cold enough to be delightful after the long hot descent, but its quality was strange. Keeping up-stream of the horse and even with Mescal, he swam with long regular strokes for perhaps one-quarter of the distance. But when they reached the swirling eddies he found that he was tiring. The water was thick and heavy; it compressed his lungs and dragged at his feet. He whirled round and round in the eddies and saw Silvermane doing the same. Only by main force could he breast his way out of these whirlpools. When a wave slapped his face he tasted sand, and then he knew what the strange feeling meant. There was sand here as on the desert. Even in the depths of the cañon he could not escape it. As the current grew rougher he began to feel that he could scarcely spread his arms in the wide stroke. Changing the stroke he discovered that he could not keep up with Silvermane, and he changed back again. Gradually his feet sank lower and lower, the water pressed tighter round him, his arms seemed to grow useless. Then he remembered a saying of August Naab that the Navajos did not attempt to swim the river when it was in flood and full of sand. He ceased to struggle, and drifting with the current, soon was close to Silvermane, and grasped a saddle strap.

"Not there!" called Mescal. "He might strike you. Hang to his tail!"

Hare dropped behind, and catching Silvermane's tail held on firmly. The stallion towed him easily. The waves dashed over him and lapped at Mescal's waist. The current grew stronger, sweeping Silvermane down out of line with the black wall which had frowned closer and closer. Mescal lifted the rifle, and resting the stock on the saddle, held it upright. The roar of the rapids seemed to lose its volume, and presently it died in the splashing and slapping of broken water closer at hand. Mescal turned to him with bright eyes; curving her hand about her lips she shouted:

"Can't make the bar! We've got to go through this side of the rapids. Hang on!"

In the swelling din Hare felt the resistless pull of the current. As he held on with both hands, hard pressed to keep his grasp, Silvermane dipped over a low fall in the river. Then Hare was riding the rushing water of an incline. It ended below in a red-crested wave, and beyond was a chaos of curling breakers. Hare had one glimpse of Mescal crouching low, shoulders narrowed and head bent; then, with one white flash of the stallion's mane against her flying black hair, she went out of sight in leaping waves and spray. Hare was thrown forward into the back-lash of the wave. The shock blinded him, stunned him, almost tore his arms from his body, but his hands were so twisted in Silvermane's tail that even this could not loosen them. The current threw him from wave to wave. He was dragged through a caldron, blind from stinging blows, deaf from the tremendous roar. Then the fierce contention of waves lessened, the threshing of cross-currents straightened, and he could breathe once more. Silvermane dragged him steadily; and, finally, his feet touched the ground. He could scarcely see, so full were his eyes of the sandy water, but he made out Mescal rising from the river on Silvermane, as with loud snorts he climbed to a bar. Hare staggered up and fell on the sand.

"Jack, are you all right?" inquired Mescal.

"All right, only pounded out of breath, and my eyes are full of sand. How about you?"

"I don't think I ever was any wetter," replied Mescal, laughing. "It was hard to stick on holding the rifle. That first wave almost unseated me. I was afraid we might strike the rocks, but the water was deep. Silvermane is grand, Jack. Wolf swam out above the rapids and was waiting for us when we landed."

Hare wiped the sand out of his eyes and rose to his feet, finding himself little the worse for the adventure. Mescal was wringing the water from the long straight braids of her hair. She was smiling, and a tint of color showed in her cheeks. The wet buckskin blouse and short skirt clung tightly to her slender form. She made so pretty a picture and appeared so little affected by the peril they had just passed through that Hare, yielding to a tender rush of pride and possession, kissed the pink cheeks till they flamed.

"All wet," said he, "you and I, clothes, food, guns—everything."

"It's hot and we'll soon dry," returned Mescal. "Here's the cañon and creek we must follow up to Coconina. My peon mapped them in the sand for me one day. It'll probably be a long climb."

Hare poured the water out of his boots, pulled them on, and helping Mescal to mount Silvermane, he took the bridle over his arm and led the way into a black-mouthed cañon, through which flowed a stream of clear water. Wolf splashed and pattered along beside him. Beyond the marble rock this cañon opened out to great breadth and wonderful walls. Hare had eyes only for the gravelly bars and shallow levels of the creek; intent on finding the easy going for his horse he strode on and on thoughtless of time. Nor did he talk to Mescal, for the work was hard, and he needed his breath. Splashing the water, hammering the stones, Silvermane ever kept his nose at Hare's elbow. They climbed little ridges, making short cuts from point to point, they threaded miles of narrow winding creek floor, and passed under ferny cliffs and over grassy banks and through thickets of yellow willow. As they wound along the course of the creek, always up and up, the great walls imperceptibly lowered their rims. The warm sun soared to the zenith. Jumble of bowlders, stretches of white gravel, ridges of sage, blocks of granite, thickets of manzanita, long yellow slopes, crumbling crags, clumps of cedar and lines of piñon—all were passed in the persistent plodding climb. The cañon grew narrower toward its source; the creek lost its volume; patches of snow gleamed in sheltered places. At last the yellow-streaked walls edged out upon a grassy hollow and the great dark pines of Coconina shadowed the snow.

"We're up," panted Hare. "What a climb! Five hours! One more day—then home!"

Silvermane's ears shot up and Wolf barked. Two gray deer loped out of a thicket and turned inquisitively. Reaching for his rifle Hare threw back the lever, but the action clogged, it rasped with the sound of crunching sand, and the cartridge could not be pressed into the chamber or ejected. He fumbled about the breach of the gun and his brow clouded.

"Sand! Out of commission!" he exclaimed. "Mescal, I don't like that."

"Use your Colt," suggested Mescal.

The distance was too great. Hare missed, and the deer bounded away into the forest.

Hare built a fire under a sheltering pine where no snow covered the soft mat of needles, and while Mescal dried the blankets and roasted the last portion of meat he made a wind-break of spruce boughs. When they had eaten, not forgetting to give Wolf a portion, Hare fed Silvermane the last few handfuls of grain, and tied him with a long halter on the grassy bank. The daylight failed and darkness came on apace. The old familiar roar of the wind in the pines was disturbing; it might mean only the lull and crash of the breaking night-gusts, and it might mean the north wind, storm, and snow. It whooped down the hollow, scattering the few scrub-oak leaves; it whirled the red embers of the fire away into the dark to sputter in the snow, and blew the burning logs into a white glow. Mescal slept in the shelter of the spruce boughs with Wolf snug and warm beside her. Hare stretched his tired limbs in the heat of the blaze.

When he awakened the fire was low and he was numb with cold. He took care to put on logs enough to last until morning; then he lay down once more, but did not sleep. The dawn came with a gray shade in the forest; it was a cloud, and it rolled over him soft, tangible, moist, and cool, and passed away under the pines. With its vanishing the dawn lightened. "Mescal, if we're on the spur of Coconina, it's only ten miles or so to Silver Cup," said Hare, as he saddled Silvermane. "Mount now and we'll go up out of the hollow and get our bearings."

While ascending the last step to the rim Hare revolved in his mind the probabilities of marking a straight course to Silver Cup.

"Oh! Jack!" exclaimed Mescal, suddenly. "Vermillion Cliffs and home!"

"I've travelled in a circle!" replied Hare.

Mescal was enraptured at the scene. Vermillion Cliffs shone red as a rose. The split in the wall marking the oasis defined its outlines sharply against the sky. Miles of the Colorado River lay in sight. Hare knew he stood on the highest point of Coconina overhanging the Grand Cañon and the Painted Desert, thousands of feet below. He noted the wondrous abyss sleeping in blue mist at his feet, while he gazed across to the desert awakening in the first red rays of the rising sun.

"Mescal, your Thunder River Cañon is only one

little crack in the rocks. It is lost in this chasm," said Hare.

"It's lost, surely. I can't even see the tip of the peak that stood so high over the valley."

Once more turning to the left Hare ran his eye over the Vermillion Cliffs, and the strip of red sand shining under them, and so calculating his bearings he headed due north for Silver Cup. What with the snow and the soggy ground the first mile was hard going for Hare, and Silvermane often sank deep. Once off the level spur of the mountain they made better time, for the snow thinned out on the slope and gradually gave way to the brown dry aisles of the forest. Hare mounted in front of Mescal, and put the stallion to an easy trot; after two hours of riding they struck a bridle-trail which Hare recognized as one leading down to the spring. In another hour they reached the steep slope of Coconina, and saw the familiar red wall across the valley, and caught glimpses of gray sage patches down through the pines.

"I smell smoke," said Hare.

"The boys must be at the spring," rejoined Mescal.

"Maybe. I want to be sure who's there. We'll leave the trail and slip down through the woods to the left. I wish we could get down on the home side of the spring. But we can't; we've got to pass it."

With many a pause to peer through openings in the pines Hare traversed a diagonal course down the slope, crossed the line of cedars, and reached the edge of the valley a mile or more above Silver Cup. Then he turned toward it, still cautiously leading Silvermane under cover of the fringe of cedars.

"Mescal, there are too many cattle in the valley," he said, looking at her significantly.

"They can't all be ours, that's sure," she replied. "What do you think?"

"Holderness!" With the word Hare's face grew set

and stern. He kept on, cautiously leading the horse under the cedars, careful to avoid breaking brush or rattling stones, occasionally whispering to Wolf; and so worked his way along the curve of the woody slope till further progress was checked by the bulging wall of rock.

"Only cattle in the valley, no horses," he said. "I've a good chance to cut across this curve and reach the trail. If I take time to climb up and see who's at the spring maybe the chance will be gone. I don't believe Dave and the boys are there."

He pondered a moment, then climbed up in front of Mescal, and directed the gray out upon the valley. Soon he was among the grazing cattle. He felt no surprise to see the H brand on their flanks.

"Jack, look at that brand," said Mescal, pointing to a white-flanked steer. "There's an old brand like a cross, Father Naab's cross, and a new brand, a single bar. Together they make an H!"

"Mescal! You've hit it. I remember that steer. He was a very devil to brand. He's the property of August Naab, and Holderness has added the bar, making a clumsy H. What a rustler's trick! It wouldn't deceive a child."

They had reached the cedars and the trail when Wolf began to sniff suspiciously at the wind.

"Look!" whispered Mescal, calling Hare's attention from the dog. "Look! A new corral!"

Bending back to get in line with her pointing finger Hare looked through a network of cedar boughs to see a fence of stripped pines. Farther up were piles of unstripped logs, and close by the spring there was a new cabin with smoke curling from a stone chimney. Hare guided Silvermane off of the trail to softer ground and went on. He climbed the slope, passed the old pool, now a mud-puddle, and crossed the dry wash to be brought suddenly to a halt. Wolf had made an uneasy stand with his nose pointing to the left, and Silvermane pricked up his ears. Presently Hare heard the stamping of hoofs off in the cedars, and before he had fully determined the direction from which the sound came three horses and a man stepped from the shade into a sunlit space.

As luck would have it Hare happened to be well screened by a thick cedar; and since there was a possibility that he might remain unseen he chose to take it. Silvermane and Wolf stood still in their tracks. Hare felt Mescal's hands tighten on his coat and he pressed them to reassure her. Peeping out from his covert he saw a man in his shirt-sleeves leading the horses—a slender, clean-faced, dark-haired man—Dene! The blood beat hotly in Hare's temples and he gripped the handle of his Colt. It seemed a fatal chance that sent the outlaw to that trail. He was whistling; he had two halters in one hand and with the other he led his bay horse by the mane. Then Hare saw that he wore no belt; he was unarmed; on the horses were only the halters and clinking hobbles. Hare dropped his Colt back into its holster.

Dene sauntered on, whistling "Dixie." When he reached the trail, instead of crossing it, as Hare had hoped, he turned into it and came down.

Hare swung the switch he had broken from an aspen and struck Silvermane a stinging blow on the flanks. The gray leaped forward. The crash of brush and rattle of hoofs stampeded Dene's horses in a twinkling. But the outlaw paled to a ghastly white and seemed rooted to the trail. It was not fear of a man or a horse that held Dene fixed; in his starting eyes was the terror of the supernatural.

The shoulder of the charging stallion struck Dene and sent him spinning out of the trail. In a backward glance Hare saw the outlaw fall, then rise unhurt to shake his fists wildly and to run yelling toward the cabin.

CHAPTER XVII

The Swoop of the Hawk

"JACK! THE saddle's slipping!" cried Mescal, clinging closer to him.

"What luck!" Hare muttered through clinched teeth, and pulled hard on the bridle. But the mouth of the stallion was iron; regardless of the sawing bit, he galloped on. Hare called steadily: "Whoa there, Silver! Whoa—slow now—whoa—easy!" and finally halted him. Hare swung down, and as he lifted Mescal off, the saddle slipped to the ground.

"Lucky not to get a spill! The girth snapped. It was wet, and dried out." Hare hurriedly began to repair the break with buckskin thongs that he found in a saddle-bag.

"Listen! Hear the yells! Oh! hurry!" cried Mescal.

"I've never ridden bareback. Suppose you go ahead with Silver, and I'll hide in the cedars till dark, then walk home!"

"No— No. There's time, but hurry."

"It's got to be strong," muttered Hare, holding the

strap over his knee and pulling the laced knot with all his strength, "for we'll have to ride some. If it comes loose—Good-bye!"

Silvermane's broad chest muscles rippled and he stamped restlessly. The dog whined and looked back. Mescal had the blanket smooth on the gray when Hare threw the saddle over him. The yells had ceased, but clattering hoofs on the stony trail were a greater menace. While Hare's brown hands worked swiftly over buckle and strap Mescal climbed to a seat behind the saddle.

"Get into the saddle," said Hare, leaping astride and pressing forward over the pommel. "Slip down—there! and hold to me. Go! Silver!"

The rapid pounding of the stallion's hoofs drowned the clatter coming up the trail. A backward glance relieved Hare, for dust-clouds some few hundred yards in the rear showed the position of the pursuing horesmen. He held in Silvermane to a steady gallop. The trail was up-hill, and steep enough to wind even a desert racer, if put to his limit.

"Look back!" cried Mescal. "Can you see them? Is Snap with them?"

"I can't see for trees," replied Hare, over his shoulder. "There's dust—we're far in the lead—never fear, Mescal. The lead's all we want."

Cedars grew thickly all the way up the steeper part of the divide, and ended abruptly at a pathway of stone, where the ascent became gradual. When Silvermane struck out of the grove upon this slope Hare kept turning keen glances rearward. The dust-cloud rolled to the edge of the cedars, and out of it trooped half-a-dozen horsemen who began to shoot as soon as they had reached the open. Bullets zipped along the red stone, cutting little puffs of red dust, and sung through the air.

"Good God!" cried Hare. "They're firing on us! They'd shoot a woman!"

"Has it taken you so long to learn that?"

Hare slashed his steed with the switch. But Silvermane needed no goad or spur; he had been shot at before, and the whistle of one bullet was sufficient to stretch his gallop into a run. Then distance between him and his pursuers grew wider and wider and soon he was out of range. The yells of the rustlers seemed at first to come from baffled rage, but Mescal's startled cry showed their meaning. Other horsemen appeared ahead and to the right of him, tearing down the ridge to the divide. Evidently they had been returning from the western curve of Coconina.

The direction in which Silvermane was stretching was the only possible one for Hare. If he swerved off the trail to the left it would be upon rough rising ground. Not only must he outride this second band to the point where the trail went down on the other side of the divide, but also he must get beyond it before they came within rifle range.

"Now! Silver! Go! Go!" Fast as the noble stallion was speeding he answered to the call. He was in the open now, free of stones and brush, with the spang of rifles in the air. The wind rushed into Hare's ears, filling them with a hollow roar; the ground blurred by in reddish sheets. The horsemen cut down the half mile to a quarter, lessened that, swept closer and closer, till Hare recognized Chance and Culver, and Snap Naab on his cream-colored pinto. Seeing that they could not head the invincible stallion they sheered more to the right. But Silvermane thundered on, crossing the line ahead of them at full three hundred yards, and went over the divide, drawing them in behind him.

Then, at the sharp crack of the rifles, leaden messengers whizzed high in the air over horse and riders, and skipped along the red shale in front of the running dog.

"Oh—Silvermane!" cried Hare. It was just a call, as if the horse were human, and knew what that pace meant to his master. The stern business of the race had ceased to rest on Hare. Silvermane was out to the front! He was like a level-rushing thunderbolt. Hare felt the instantaneous pause between his long low leaps, the gather of mighty muscles, the strain, the tension, then the quivering expulsion of force. It was a perilous ride down that red slope, not so much from the hissing bullets as from the washes and gullies which Silvermane sailed over in magnificent leaps. Hare thrilled with savage delight in the wonderful prowess of his desert king, in the primal instinct of joy at escaping with the woman he loved.

"Outrun!" he cried, with blazing eyes. Mescal's white face was pressed close to his shoulder. "Silver has beaten them. They'll hang on till we reach the sand-strip, hoping the slow-down will let them come up in time. But they'll be far too late."

The rustlers continued on the trail, firing desultorily, till Silvermane so far distanced them that even the necessary lapse into a walk in the red sand placed him beyond range when they arrived at the strip.

"They've turned back, Mescal. We're safe. Why, you look as you did the day the bear ran for you."

"I'd rather a bear got me than Snap. Jack, did you see him?"

"See him? Rather! I'll bet he nearly killed his pinto. Mescal, what do you think of Silvermane now? Can he run? Can he outrun Bolly?"

"Yes—yes. Oh! Jack! how I'll love him! Look back again. Are we safe? Will we ever be safe?"

It was still daylight when they rounded the portal of the oasis and entered the lane with the familiar wall on one side, the peeled fence-pickets on the other. Wolf dashed on ahead, and presently a chorus of barks announced that he had been met by the other dogs. Silvermane neighed shrilly, and the horses and mustangs in the corrals trooped noisily to the lower sides and hung inquisitive heads over the top bars.

A Navajo whom Hare remembered stared with axe idle by the woodpile, then Judith Naab dropped a bundle of sticks and with a cry of gladness ran from the house. Before Silvermane had come to a full stop Mescal was off. She put her arms around his neck and kissed him, then she left Judith to dart to the corral where a little black mustang had begun to whistle and stamp and try to climb over the bars.

August Naab, bareheaded, with shaggy locks shaking at every step, strode off the porch and his great hands lifted Hare from the saddle.

"Every day I've watched the river for you," he said. His eyes were warm and his grasp like a vise. "Mescal—child!" he continued, as she came running to him. "Safe and well. He's brought you back. Thank the Lord!" He took her to his breast and bent his gray head over her.

Then the crowd of big and little Naabs burst from the house and came under the cottonwoods to offer noisy welcome to Mescal and Hare.

"Jack, you look done up," said Dave Naab solicitously, when the first greetings had been spoken and Mother Ruth had led Mescal indoors. "Silvermane, too—he's wet and winded. He's been running?"

"Yes, a little," replied Hare, as he removed the saddle from the weary horse.

"Ah! What's this?" questioned August Naab, with his hand on Silvermane's flank. He touched a raw groove, and the stallion flinched. "Hare, a bullet made that!"

"Yes."

"Then you didn't ride in by the Navajo crossing?"

"No. I came by Silver Cup."

"Silver Cup? How on earth did you get down there?"

"We climbed out of the cañon up over Coconina, and so made the spring."

Naab whistled in surprise and he flashed another keen glance over Hare and his horse. "Your story can wait. I know about what it is—after you reached Silver Cup. Come in, come in, Dave will look out for the stallion."

But Hare would allow no one else to attend to Silvermane. He rubbed the tired gray, gave him a drink at the trough, led him to the corral, and took leave of him with a caress like Mescal's. Then he went to his room and bathed himself and changed his clothes, afterward presenting himself at the supper-table to eat like one famished. Mescal and he ate alone, as they had been too late for the regular hour. The women-folk waited upon them as if they could not do enough. There were pleasant words and smiles; but in spite of them something sombre attended the meal. There was a shadow in each face, each step was slow, each voice subdued. Naab and his sons were waiting for Hare when he entered the sitting-room, and after his entrance the door was closed. They were all quiet and stern, especially the father. "Tell us all," said Naab, simply.

While Hare was telling his adventures not a word or a move interrupted him till he spoke of Silvermane's running Dene down.

"That's the second time!" rolled out Naab. "The stallion will kill him yet!"

Hare finished his story.

"What don't you owe to that whirlwind of a horse!" exclaimed Dave Naab. No other comment on Hare or Silvermane was offered by the Naabs.

"You knew Holderness had taken in Silver Cup?" inquired Hare.

August Naab nodded gloomily.

"I guess we knew it," replied Dave for him. "While I was in White Sage and the boys were here at home, Holderness rode to the spring and took possession. I called to see him on my way back, but he wasn't around. Snap was there, the boss of a bunch of riders. Dene, too, was there."

"Did you go right into camp?" asked Hare.

"Sure. I was looking for Holderness. There were eighteen or twenty riders in the bunch. I talked to several of them, Mormons, good fellows, they used to be. Also I had some words with Dene. He said: 'I shore was sorry Snap got to my spy first. I wanted him bad, an' I'm shore goin' to have his white horse.' Snap and Dene, all of them, thought you were number thirty-one in Dad's cemetery."

"Not yet," said Hare. "Dene certainly looked as if he saw a ghost when Silvermane jumped for him. Well, he's at Silver Cup now. They're all there. What's to be done about it? They're openly thieves. The new brand on all your stock proves that."

"Such a trick we never heard of," replied August Naab. "If we had we might have spared ourselves the labor of branding the stock."

"But that new brand of Holderness's upon yours proves his guilt."

"It's not now a question of proof. It's one of possession. Holderness has stolen my water and my stock."

"They are worse than rustlers; firing on Mescal and me proves that."

"Why didn't you unlimber the long rifle?" interposed Dave, curiously.

"I got it full of water and sand. That reminds me I must see about cleaning it. I never thought of shooting back. Silvermane was running too fast."

"Jack, you can see I am in the worst fix of my life," said August Naab. "My sons have persuaded me that I was pushed off my ranges too easily. I've come to believe Martin Cole; certainly his prophecy has come true. Dave brought news from White Sage, and it's almost unbelievable. Holderness has proclaimed himself or has actually got himself elected sheriff. He holds office over the Mormons from whom he steals. Scarcely a day goes by in the village without a killing. The Mormons north of Lund finally banded together, hanged some rustlers, and drove the others out. Many of them have come down into our country, and Holderness now has a strong force. But the Mormons will rise against him. I know it; I see it. I am waiting for it. We are God-fearing, life-loving men, slow to wrath. But—"

The deep rolling burr in his voice showed emotion too deep for words.

"They need a leader," replied Hare, sharply.

August Naab rose with haggard face and his eyes had the look of a man accused.

"Dad figures this way," put in Dave. "On the one hand we lose our water and stock without bloodshed. We have a living in the oasis. There's little here to attract rustlers, so we may live in peace if we give up our rights. On the other hand, suppose Dad gets the Navajos down here and we join them and go after Holderness and his gang. There's going to be an all-fired bloody fight. Of course we'd wipe out the rustlers, but some of us would get killed— and there are the wives and kids. See!"

The force of August Naab's argument for peace, entirely aside from his Christian repugnance to the shedding of blood, was plainly unassailable.

"Remember what Snap said?" asked Hare, suddenly. "One man to kill Dene! Therefore one man to kill Holderness! That would break the power of this band."

"Ah! you've said it," replied Dave, raising a tense arm. "It's a one-man job. Damn Snap! He could have done it, if he hadn't gone to the bad. But it won't be easy. I tried to get Holderness. He was wise, and his men politely said they had enjoyed my call, but I wasn't to come again."

"One man to kill Holderness!" repeated Hare.

August Naab cast at the speaker one of his far-seeing glances; then he shook himself, as if to throw off the grip of something hard and inevitable. "I'm still master here," he said, and his voice showed the conquest of his passions. "I give up Silver Cup and my stock. Maybe that will content Holderness."

Some days went by pleasantly for Hare, as he rested from his long exertions. Naab's former cheer and that of his family reasserted itself once the decision was made, and the daily life went on as usual. The sons worked in the fields by day, and in the evening played at pitching horseshoes on the bare circle where the children romped. The women went on baking, sewing, and singing. August Naab's prayers were more fervent than ever, and he even prayed for the soul of the man who had robbed him. Mescal's cheeks soon rounded out to their old contour and her eyes shone with a happier light than Hare had ever seen there. The races between Silvermane and Black Bolly were renewed on the long stretch under the wall, and Mescal forgot that she had once acknowledged the superiority of the gray. The cottonwoods showered silken floss till the cabins and grass were white; the birds returned to the oasis; the sun kissed warm color into the cherries, and the distant noise of the river seemed like the humming of a swarm of bees.

"Here, Jack," said August Naab, one morning, "get a spade and come with me. There's a break somewhere in the ditch."

Hare went with him out along the fence by the alfalfa-fields, and round the corner of red wall toward the irrigating-dam.

"Well, Jack, I suppose you'll be asking me for Mescal one of these days," said Naab.

"Yes," replied Hare.

"There's a little story to tell you about Mescal, when the day comes."

"Tell it now."

"No. Not yet. I'm glad you found her. I never knew her to be so happy, not even when she was a child. But somehow there's a better feeling between her and my women-folk. The old antagonism is gone. Well, well, life is so. I pray that things may turn out well for you and her. But I fear—I seem to see— Hare, I'm a poor man once more. I can't do for you what I'd like. Still we'll see, we'll hope."

Hare was perfectly happy. The old Mormon's hint did not disturb him; even the thought of Snap Naab did not return to trouble his contentment. The full present was sufficient for Hare, and his joy bubbled over, bringing smiles to August's grave face. Never had a summer afternoon in the oasis been so fair. The green fields, the red walls, the blue sky, all seemed drenched in deeper, richer hues. The windsong in the crags, the river-murmur from the cañon, filled Hare's ears with music. To be alive, to feel the sun, to see the colors, to hear the sounds, was beautiful; and to know that Mescal awaited him was enough.

Work on the washed-out bank of the ditch had not gone far when Naab raised his head as if listening.

"Did you hear anything?" he asked.

"No," replied Hare.

"The roar of the river is heavy here. Maybe I was mistaken. I thought I heard shots." Then he went on spading clay into the break, but he stopped every moment or so, uneasily, as if he could not get rid of some disturbing thought. Suddenly he dropped the spade and his eyes flashed.

"Judith! Judith! Here!" he called. Wheeling with a sudden premonition of evil Hare saw the girl running along the wall toward them. Her face was white as death; she wrung her hands and her cries rose above the sound of the river. Naab sprang toward her and Hare ran at his heels.

"Father!— Father!" she panted. "Come—quick— the rustlers!—the rustlers! Snap!—Dene— Oh— hurry! They've killed Dave—they've got Mescal!"

Death itself shuddered through Hare's veins and then a raging flood of fire. He bounded forward to be flung back by Naab's arm.

"Fool! Would you throw away your life? Go slowly. We'll slip through the fields, under the trees."

Sick and cold, Hare hurried by Naab's side round the wall and into the alfalfa. There were moments when he was weak and trembling; others when he could have leaped like a tiger to rend and kill.

They left the fields and went on more cautiously into the grove. The screaming and wailing of women added certainty to their doubt and dread.

"I see only the women—the children—no—there's a man—Zeke," said Hare, bending low to gaze under the branches.

"Go slow," muttered Naab.

"The rustlers rode off—after Mescal—she's gone!" panted Judith.

Hare, spurred by the possibilities in the half-crazed girl's speech, cast caution to the winds and dashed forward into the glade. Naab's heavy steps thudded behind him.

In the corner of the porch scared and stupefied children huddled in a heap. George and Billy bent over Dave, who sat white-faced against the steps. Blood oozed through the fingers pressed to his breast. Zeke was trying to calm the women.

"My God! Dave!" cried Hare. "You're not hard hit? Don't say it!"

"Hard hit—Jack—old fellow," replied Dave, with a pale smile. His face was white and clammy.

August Naab looked once at him and groaned, "My son! My son!"

"Dad—I got Chance and Culver—there they lie in the road—not bungled, either!"

Hare saw the inert forms of two men lying near the gate; one rested on his face, arm outstretched with a Colt gripped in the stiff hand; the other lay on his back, his spurs deep in the ground, as if driven there in his last convulsion.

August Naab and Zeke carried the injured man into the house. The women and children followed, and Hare, with Billy and George, entered last.

"Dad—I'm shot clean through—low down," said Dave, as they laid him on a couch. "It's just as well I—as any one—somebody had to—start this fight."

Naab got the children and the girls out of the room. The women were silent now, except Dave's wife, who clung to him with low moans. He smiled upon all with a quick intent smile, then he held out a hand to Hare.

"Jack, we got—to be—good friends. Don't forget—that—when you meet—Holderness. He shot me—from behind Chance and Culver—and after I fell—I killed them both—trying to get him. You—won't hang up—your gun—again—will you?"

Hare wrung the cold hand clasping his so feebly. "No! Dave, no!" Then he fled from the room. For an hour he stood on the porch waiting in dumb misery. George and Zeke came noiselessly out, followed by their father.

"It's all over, Hare." Another tragedy had passed by this man of the desert, and left his strength unshaken, but his deadly quiet and the gloom of his iron face were more terrible to see than any grief.

"Father, and you, Hare, come out into the road," said George.

Another motionless form lay beyond Chance and Culver. It was that of a slight man, flat on his back, his arms wide, his long black hair in the dust. Under the white level brow the face had been crushed into a bloody curve.

"Dene!" burst from Hare, in a whisper.

"Killed by a horse!" exclaimed August Naab. "Ah! What horse?"

"Silvermane!" replied George.

"Who rode my horse—tell me—quick!" cried Hare, in a frenzy.

"It was Mescal. Listen. Let me tell you how it all happened. I was out at the forge when I heard a bunch of horses coming up the lane. I wasn't packing my gun, but I ran anyway. When I got to the house there was Dave facing Snap, Dene, and a bunch of rustlers. I saw Chance at first, but not Holderness. There must have been twenty men.

" 'I came after Mescal, that's what,' Snap was saying.

" 'You can't have her,' Dave answered.

" 'We'll shore take her, an' we want Silvermane, too,' said Dene.

" 'So you're a horse-thief as well as a rustler?' asked Dave.

" 'Naab, I ain't in any mind to fool. Snap wants the girl, an' I want Silvermane, an' that damned spy that come back to life.'

"Then Holderness spoke from the back of the crowd: 'Naab, you'd better hurry, if you don't want the house burned!'

"Dave drew and Holderness fired from behind the men. Dave fell, raised up and shot Chance and Culver, then dropped his gun.

"With that the women in the house began to scream, and Mescal ran out saying she'd go with Snap if they'd do no more harm.

" 'All right,' said Snap, 'get a horse, hurry—hurry!'

"Then Dene dismounted and went toward the corral saying, 'I shore want Silvermane.'

"Mescal reached the gate ahead of Dene. 'Let me get Silvermane. He's wild; he doesn't know you; he'll kick you if you go near him.' She dropped the bars and went up to the horse. He was rearing and snorting. She coaxed him down and then stepped up on the fence to untie him. When she had him loose she leaped off the fence to his back, screaming as she hit him with the halter. Silvermane snorted and jumped, and in three jumps he was going like a bullet. Dene tried to stop him, and was knocked twenty feet. He was raising up when the stallion ran over him. He never moved again. Once in the lane Silvermane got going—Lord! how he did run! Mescal hung low over his neck like an Indian. He was gone in a cloud of dust before Snap and the rustlers knew what had happened. Snap came to first and, yelling and waving his gun, spurred down the lane. The rest of the rustlers galloped after him."

August Naab placed a sympathetic hand on Hare's shaking shoulder.

"You see, lad, things are never so bad as they seem at first. Snap might as well try to catch a bird as Silvermane."

CHAPTER XVIII

The Heritage of the Desert

"MESCAL'S FAR out in front by this time. Depend on it, Hare," went on Naab. "That trick was the cunning Indian of her. She'll ride Silvermane into White Sage to-morrow night. Then she'll hide from Snap. The Bishop will take care of her. She'll be safe for the present in White Sage. Now we must bury these men. To-morrow—my son. Then—"

"What then?" Hare straightened up.

Unutterable pain darkened the flame in the Mormon's gaze. For an instant his face worked spasmodically, only to stiffen into a stony mask. It was the old conflict once more, the never-ending war between flesh and spirit. And now the flesh had prevailed.

"The time has come!" said George Naab.

"Yes," replied his father, harshly.

A great calm settled over Hare; his blood ceased to race, his mind to riot; in August Naab's momentous word he knew the old man had found himself.

At last he had learned the lesson of the desert—to strike first and hard.

"Zeke, hitch up a team," said August Naab. "No—wait a moment. Here comes Piute. Let's hear what he has to say."

Piute appeared on the zigzag cliff-trail, driving a burro at dangerous speed.

"He's sighted Silvermane and the rustlers," suggested George, as the shepherd approached.

Naab translated the excited Indian's mingling of Navajo and Piute languages to mean just what George had said. "Snap ahead of riders—Silvermane far, far ahead of Snap—running fast—damn!"

"Mescal pushing him hard to make the sand-strip," said George.

"Piute—three fires to-night—Lookout Point!" This order meant the execution of August Naab's hurry-signal for the Navajos, and after he had given it, he waved the Indian toward the cliff, and lapsed into a silence which no one dared to break.

Naab consigned the bodies of the rustlers to the famous cemetery under the red wall. He laid Dene in grave thirty-one. It was the grave that the outlaw had promised as the last resting-place of Dene's spy. Chance and Culver he buried together. It was note-worthy that no Mormon rites were conferred on Culver, once a Mormon in good standing, nor were any prayers spoken over the open graves.

What did August Naab intend to do? That was the question in Hare's mind as he left the house. It was a silent day, warm as summer, though the sun was overcast with gray clouds; the birds were quiet in the trees; there was no bray of burro or clarion-call of peacock, even the hum of the river had fallen into silence. Hare wandered over the farm and down the red lane, brooding over the issue. Naab's few words had been full of meaning; the cold gloom, so foreign to his nature, had been even more impressive. His had been the revolt of the meek. The gentle, the loving, the administering, the spiritual uses of his life had failed.

Hare recalled what the desert had done to his own nature, how it had bred in him its impulse to fight, to resist, to survive. If he, a stranger of a few years, could be moulded in the flaming furnace of its fiery life, what then must be the cast of August Naab, born on the desert, and sleeping five nights out of seven on the sands for sixty years?

The desert! Hare trembled as he grasped all its meaning. Then he slowly resolved that meaning. There were the measureless distances to narrow the eye and teach restraint; the untrodden trails, the shifting sands, the thorny brakes, the broken lava to pierce the flesh; the heights and depths, unscalable and unplumbed. And over all the sun, red and burning.

The parched plants of the desert fought for life, growing far apart, sending enormous roots deep to pierce the sand and split the rock for moisture, arming every leaf with a barbed thorn or poisoned sap, never thriving and ever thirsting.

The creatures of the desert endured the sun and lived without water, and were at endless war. The hawk had a keener eye than his fellow of more fruitful lands, sharper beak, greater spread of wings, and claws of deeper curve. For him there was little to eat, a rabbit now, a rock-rat then; nature made his swoop like lightning and it never missed its aim. The gaunt wolf never failed in his sure scent, in his silent hunt. The lizard flicked an invisible tongue into the heart of a flower; and the bee he caught stung with a poisoned sting. The battle of life went to the strong.

So the desert trained each of its wild things to survive. No eye of the desert but burned with the flame of the sun to kill or to escape death—that was the dominant motive. To fight barrenness and heat—that was stern enough, but each creature must fight his fellow.

What then of the men who drifted into the desert and survived? They must of necessity endure the wind and heat, the drouth and famine; they must grow lean and hard, keen-eyed and silent. The weak, the humble, the sacrificing must be winnowed from among them. As each man developed he took on some aspect of the desert—Holderness had the amber clearness of its distances in his eyes, its deceit in his soul; August Naab, the magnificence of the desert-pine in his giant form, its strength in his heart; Snap Naab, the cast of the hawk-beak in his face, its cruelty in his nature. But all shared alike in the common element of survival—ferocity. August Naab had subdued his to the promptings of a Christ-like spirit; yet did not his very energy, his wonderful tirelessness, his will to achieve, his power to resist, partake of that fierceness? Moreover, after many struggles, he too had been overcome by the desert's call for blood. His mystery was no longer a mystery. Always in those moments of revelation which he disclaimed, he had seen himself as faithful to the desert in the end.

Hare's slumbers that night were broken. He dreamed of a great gray horse leaping in the sky from cloud to cloud with the lightning and the thunder under his hoofs, the storm-winds sweeping from his silver mane. He dreamed of Mescal's brooding eyes. They were dark gateways of the desert open only to him, and he entered to chase the alluring stars deep into the purple distance. He dreamed of himself waiting in serene confidence for some unknown thing to pass. He awakened late in the morning and found the house hushed. The day wore on in a repose unstirred by breeze and sound, in accord with the mourning of August Naab. At noon a solemn procession wended its slow course to the shadow of the red cliff, and as solemnly returned.

Then a long-drawn piercing Indian whoop broke the midday hush. It heralded the approach of the Navajos. In single-file they rode up the lane, and when the falcon-eyed Eschtah dismounted before his white friend, the line of his warriors still turned the corner of the red wall. Next to the chieftain rode Scarbreast, a grim war-lord of the Navajos. His followers trailed into the grove. Their sinewy bronze bodies, almost naked, glistened wet from the river. Full a hundred strong were they, a silent, lean-limbed desert troop.

"The White Prophet's fires burned bright," said the chieftain. "Eschtah is here."

"The Navajo is a friend," replied Naab. "The white man needs counsel and help. He has fallen upon evil days."

"Eschtah sees war in the eyes of his friend."

"War, chief, war! Let the Navajo and his warriors rest and eat. Then we shall speak."

A single command from the Navajo broke the waiting files of warriors. Mustangs were turned into the fields, packs were unstrapped from the burros, blankets spread under the cottonwoods. When the afternoon waned and the shade from the western wall crept into the oasis, August Naab came from his cabin clad in buckskins, with a large blue Colt swinging handle outward from his left hip. He ordered his sons to replenish the fire which had been built in the circle, and when the fierce-eyed Indians gathered round the blaze he called to his women to bring meat and drink.

Hare's unnatural calmness had prevailed until he saw Naab stride out to front the waiting Indians. Then a ripple of cold passed over him. He leaned against a tree in the shadow and watched the gray-faced giant stalking to and fro before his Indian friends. A long while he strode in the circle of light to pause at length before the chieftains and to break the impressive silence with his deep voice.

"Eschtah sees before him a friend stung to his heart. Men of his own color have long injured him, yet have lived. The Mormon loved his fellows and forgave. Five sons he laid in their graves, yet his heart was not hardened. His first-born went the trail of the fire-water and is an outcast from his people. Many enemies has he and one is a chief. He has killed the white man's friends, stolen his cattle, and his water. To-day the white man laid another son in his grave. What thinks the chief? Would he not crush the scorpion that stung him?"

The old Navajo answered in speech which, when translated, was as stately as the Mormon's.

"Eschtah respects his friend, but he has not thought him wise. The White Prophet sees visions of things to come, but his blood is cold. He asks too much of the white man's God. He is a chief; he has an eye like the lightning, an arm strong as the pine, yet he has not struck. Eschtah grieves. He does not wish to shed blood for pleasure. But Eschtah's friend has let too many selfish men cross his range and drink at his springs. Only a few can live on the desert. Let him who has found the springs and the trails keep them for his own. Let him who came too late go away to find for himself, to prove himself a warrior, or let his bones whiten in the sand. The Navajo counsels his white friend to kill."

"The great Eschtah speaks wise words," said Naab. "The White Prophet is richer for them. He will lay aside the prayers to his unseeing God, and will seek his foe."

"It is well."

"The white man's foe is strong," went on the Mormon; "he has many men, they will fight. If Eschtah sends his braves with his friend there will be war.

Many braves will fall. The White Prophet wishes to save them if he can. He will go forth alone to kill his foe. If the sun sets four times and the white man is not here, then Eschtah will send his great war-chief and his warriors. They will kill whom they find at the white man's springs. And thereafter half of all the white man's cattle that were stolen shall be Eschtah's, so that he watch over the water and range."

"Eschtah greets a chief," answered the Indian. "The White Prophet knows he will kill his enemy, but he is not sure he will return. He is not sure that the little braves of his foe will fly like the winds, yet he hopes. So he holds the Navajo back to the last. Eschtah will watch the sun set four times. If his white friend returns he will rejoice. If he does not return the Navajo will send his warriors on the trail."

August Naab walked swiftly from the circle of light into the darkness; his heavy steps sounded on the porch, and in the hallway. His three sons went toward their cabins with bowed heads and silent tongues. Eschtah folded his blanket about him and stalked off into the gloom of the grove, followed by his warriors.

Hare remained in the shadow of the cottonwood where he had stood unnoticed. He had not moved a muscle since he had heard August Naab's declaration. That one word of Naab's intention, "Alone!" had arrested him. For it had struck into his heart and mind. It had paralyzed him with the revelation it brought; for Hare now knew as he had never known anything before, that he would forestall August Naab, avenge the death of Dave, and kill the rustler Holderness. Through blinding shock he passed slowly into cold acceptance of his heritage from the desert.

The two long years of his desert training were as

an open page to Hare's unveiled eyes. The life he owed to August Naab, the strength built up by the old man's knowledge of the healing power of plateau and range—these lay in a long curve between the day Naab had lifted him out of the White Sage trail and this day of the Mormon's extremity. A long curve with Holderness's insulting blow at the beginning, his murder of a beloved friend at the end! For Hare remembered the blow, and never would he forget Dave's last words. Yet unforgettable as these were, it was duty rather than revenge that called him. This was August Naab's hour of need. Hare knew himself to be the tool of inscrutable fate; he was the one to fight the old desert-scarred Mormon's battle. Hare recalled how humbly he had expressed his gratitude to Naab, and the apparent impossibility of ever repaying him, and then Naab's reply: "Lad, you can never tell how one man may repay another." Hare could pay his own debt and that of the many wanderers who had drifted across the sands to find a home with the Mormon. These men stirred in their graves, and from out the shadow of the cliff whispered the voice of Mescal's nameless father: "Is there no one to rise up for this old hero of the desert?"

Softly Hare slipped into his room. Putting on coat and belt and catching up his rifle he stole out again stealthily, like an Indian. In the darkness of the wagon-shed he felt for his saddle, and finding it, he groped with eager hands for the grain-box; raising the lid he filled a measure with grain, and emptied it into his saddle-bag. Then lifting the saddle he carried it out of the yard, through the gate and across the lane to the corrals. The wilder mustangs in the far corral began to kick and snort, and those in the corral where Black Bolly was kept trooped noisily to the bars. Bolly whinnied and thrust her black muzzle over the fence. Hare placed a caressing hand on her while he waited listening and watching. It was not unusual for the mustangs to get restless at any time, and Hare was confident that this would pass without investigation.

Gradually the restless stampings and suspicious snortings ceased, and Hare, letting down the bars, led Bolly out into the lane. It was the work of a moment to saddle her; his bridle hung where he always kept it, on the pommel, and with nimble fingers he shortened the several straps to fit Bolly's head, and slipped the bit between her teeth. Then he put up the bars of the gate.

Before mounting he stood a moment thinking coolly, deliberately numbering the several necessities he must not forget—grain for Bolly, food for himself, his Colt and Winchester, cartridges, canteen, matches, knife. He inserted a hand into one of his saddle-bags expecting to find some strips of meat. The bag was empty. He felt in the other one, and under the grain he found what he sought. The canteen lay in the coil of his lasso tied to the saddle, and its heavy canvas covering was damp to his touch. With that he thrust the long Winchester into its saddle-sheath, and swung his leg over the mustang.

The house of the Naabs was dark and still. The dying council-fire cast flickering shadows under the black cottonwoods where the Navajos slept. The faint breeze that rustled the leaves brought the low sullen roar of the river.

Hare guided Bolly into the thick dust of the lane, laid the bridle loosely on her neck for her to choose the trail, and silently rode out into the lonely desert night.

CHAPTER XIX

Unleashed

HARE, LISTENING breathlessly, rode on toward the gateway of the cliffs, and when he had passed the corner of the wall he sighed in relief. Spurring Bolly into a trot he rode forward with a strange elation. He had slipped out of the oasis unheard, and it would be morning before August Naab discovered his absence, perhaps longer before he divined his purpose. Then Hare would have a long start. He thrilled with something akin to fear when he pictured the old man's rage, and wondered what change it would make in his plans. Hare saw in mind Naab and his sons, and the Navajos sweeping in pursuit to save him from the rustlers.

But the future must take care of itself, and he addressed all the faculties at his command to cool consideration of the present. The strip of sand under the Blue Star had to be crossed at night—a feat which even the Navajos did not have to their credit. Yet Hare had no shrinking; he had no doubt;

he must go on. As he had been drawn to the Painted Desert by a voiceless call, so now he was urged forward by something nameless.

In the blackness of the night it seemed as if he were riding through a vaulted hall swept by a current of air. The night had turned cold, the stars had brightened icily, the rumble of the river had died away when Bolly's ringing trot suddenly changed to a noiseless floundering walk. She had come upon the sand. Hare saw the Blue Star in the cliff, and once more loosed the rein on Bolly's neck. She stopped and champed her bit, and turned her black head to him as if to intimate that she wanted the guidance of a sure arm. But as it was not forthcoming she stepped onward into the yielding sand.

With hands resting idly on the pommel Hare sat at ease in the saddle. The billowy dunes reflected the pale starlight and fell away from him to darken in obscurity. So long as the Blue Star remained in sight he kept his sense of direction; when it had disappeared he felt himself lost. Bolly's course seemed as crooked as the jagged outline of the cliffs. She climbed straight up little knolls, descended them at an angle, turned sharply at wind-washed gullies, made winding detours, zigzagged levels that shone like a polished floor; and at last (so it seemed to Hare) she doubled back on her trail. The black cliff receded over the waves of sand; the stars changed positions, travelled round in the blue dome, and the few that he knew finally sank below the horizon. Bolly never lagged; she was like the homeward-bound horse, indifferent to direction because sure of it, eager to finish the journey because now it was short. Hare was glad though not surprised when she snorted and cracked her iron-shod hoof on a stone at the edge of the sand. He smiled with tightening lips as he rode into the shadow of a rock which he recognized. Bolly had crossed the treach-

erous belt of dunes and washes and had struck the
trail on the other side.

The long level of wind-carved rocks under the
cliffs, the ridges of the desert, the miles of slow ascent up to the rough divide, the gradual descent to
the cedars—these stretches of his journey took the
night hours and ended with the brightening gray in
the east. Within a mile of Silver Cup Spring Hare dismounted, to tie folded pads of buckskin on Bolly's
hoofs. When her feet were muffled, he cautiously
advanced on the trail for the matter of a hundred
rods or more; then sheered off to the right into the
cedars. He led Bolly slowly, without rattling a stone
or snapping a twig, and stopped every few paces to
listen. There was no sound other than the wind in
the cedars. Presently, with a gasp, he caught the
dull gleam of a burned-out camp-fire. Then his
movements became as guarded, as noiseless as
those of a scouting Indian. The dawn broke over the
red wall as he gained the trail beyond the spring.

He skirted the curve of the valley and led Bolly a
little way up the wooded slope to a dense thicket of
aspens in a hollow. This thicket encircled a patch of
grass. Hare pressed the lithe aspens aside to admit
Bolly and left her there free. He drew his rifle from
its sheath and, after assuring himself that the mustang could not be seen or heard from below, he
bent his steps diagonally up the slope.

Every foot of this ground he knew, and he
climbed swiftly until he struck the mountain trail.
Then, descending, he entered the cedars. At last he
reached a point directly above the cliff-camp where
he had spent so many days, and this he knew overhung the cabin built by Holderness. He stole down
from tree to tree and slipped from thicket to
thicket. The sun, red as blood, raised a bright cres-
cent over the red wall; the soft mists of the valley
began to glow and move; cattle were working in to-

ward the spring. Never brushing a branch, never dislodging a stone, Hare descended the slope, his eyes keener, his ears sharper with every step. Soon the edge of the gray stone cliff below shut out the lower level of cedars. While resting he listened. Then he marked his course down the last bit of slanting ground to the cliff bench which faced the valley. This space was open, rough with crumbling rock and dead cedar brush—a difficult place to cross without sound. Deliberate in his choice of steps, very slow in moving, Hare went on with a stealth which satisfied even his intent ear. When the wide gray strip of stone drew slowly into the circle of his downcast gaze he sank to the ground with a slight trembling in all his limbs. There was a thick bush on the edge of the cliff; in three steps he could reach it and, unseen himself, look down upon the camp.

A little cloud of smoke rose lazily and capped a slender column of blue. Sounds were wafted softly upward, the low voices of men in conversation, a merry whistle, and then the humming of a tune. Hare's mouth was dry and his temples throbbed as he asked himself what it was best to do. The answer came instantaneously as though it had lain just below the level of his conscious thought. "I'll watch till Holderness walks out into sight, jump up with a yell when he comes, give him time to see me, to draw his gun—then kill him!"

Hare slipped to the bush, drew in a deep long breath that stilled his agitation, and peered over the cliff. The crude shingles of the cabin first rose into sight; then beyond he saw the corral with a number of shaggy mustangs and a great gray horse. Hare stared blankly. As in a dream he saw the proud arch of a splendid neck, the graceful wave of a white-crested mane.

"Silvermane! ... My God!" he gasped, suddenly.
"They caught him—after all!"

He fell backward upon the cliff and lay there with
hands clinching his rifle, shudderingly conscious of
a blow, trying to comprehend its meaning.

"Silvermane! ... they caught him—after all!" he
kept repeating; then in a flash of agonized understanding he whispered: "Mescal ... Mescal!"

He rolled upon his face, shutting out the blue sky;
his body stretched stiff as a bent spring released
from its compress, and his nails dented the stock of
his rifle. Then this rigidity softened to sobs that
shook him from head to foot. He sat up, haggard
and wild-eyed.

Silvermane had been captured, probably by rustlers waiting at the western edge of the sand-strip.
Mescal had fallen into the hands of Snap Naab. But
Mescal was surely alive and Snap was there to be
killed; his long career of unrestrained cruelty was in
its last day—something told Hare that this thing
must and should be. The stern deliberation of his
intent to kill Holderness, the passion of his purpose
to pay his debt to August Naab, were as nothing
compared to the gathering might of this new resolve; suddenly he felt free and strong as an untamed lion broken free from his captors.

From the cover of the bush he peered again over
the cliff. The cabin with its closed door facing him
was scarcely two hundred feet down from his hiding-
place. One of the rustlers sang as he bent over the
camp-fire and raked the coals around the pots; others
lounged on a bench waiting for breakfast; some rolled
out of their blankets; they stretched and yawned, and
pulling on their boots made for the spring. The last
man to rise was Snap Naab, and he had slept with his
head on the threshold of the door. Evidently Snap
had made Mescal a prisoner in the cabin, and no one
could go in or out without stepping upon him. The

rustler-foreman of Holderness's company had slept with his belt containing two Colts, nor had he removed his boots. Hare noted these details with grim humor. Now the tall Holderness, face shining, gold-red beard agleam, rounded the cabin whistling. Hare watched the rustlers sit down to breakfast, and here and there caught a loud-spoken word, and marked their leisurely care-free manner. Snap Naab took up a pan of food and a cup of coffee, carried them into the cabin, and came out, shutting the door.

After breakfast most of the rustlers set themselves to their various tasks. Hare watched them with the eyes of a lynx watching deer. Several men were arranging articles for packing, and their actions were slow to the point of laziness; others trooped down toward the corral. Holderness rolled a cigarette and stooped over the camp-fire to reach a burning stick. Snap Naab stalked to and fro before the door of the cabin. He alone of the rustler's band showed restlessness, and more than once he glanced up the trail that led over the divide toward his father's oasis. Holderness sent expectant glances in the other direction toward Seeping Springs. Once his clear voice rang out:

"I tell you, Naab, there's no hurry. We'll ride in tomorrow."

A thousand thoughts flitted through Hare's mind—a steady stream of questions and answers. Why did Snap look anxiously along the oasis trail? It was not that he feared his father or his brothers alone, but there was always the menace of the Navajos. Why was Holderness in no hurry to leave Silver Cup? Why did he lag at the spring when, if he expected riders from his ranch, he could have gone on to meet them, obviously saving time and putting greater distance between him and the men he had wronged? Was it utter fearlessness or only a deep-played game? Holderness and his rustlers, all except the gloomy Naab, were blind to the peril that lay beyond the divide. How soon would August Naab strike out on the White Sage trail? Would he come alone? Whether he came alone or at the head of his hard-riding Navajos he would arrive too late. Holderness's life was not worth a pinch of the ashes he flecked so carelessly from his cigarette. Snap Naab's gloom, his long stride, his nervous hand always on or near the butt of his Colt, spoke the keenness of his desert instinct. For him the sun had arisen red over the red wall. Had he harmed Mescal? Why did he keep the cabin door shut and guard it so closely?

While Hare watched and thought the hours sped by. Holderness lounged about and Snap kept silent guard. The rustlers smoked, slept, and moved about; the day waned, and the shadow of the cliff crept over the cabin. To Hare the time had been as a moment; he was amazed to find the sun had gone down behind Coconina. If August Naab had left the oasis at dawn he must now be near the divide, unless he had been delayed by a wind-storm at the strip of sand. Hare longed to see the roan charger come up over the crest; he longed to see a file of Navajos, plumes waving, dark mustangs gleaming in the red light, sweep down the stony ridge toward the cedars. "If they come," he whispered, "I'll kill Holderness and Snap and any man who tries to open that cabin door."

So he waited in tense watchfulness, his gaze alternating between the wavy line of the divide and the camp glade. Out in the valley it was still daylight, but under the cliff twilight had fallen. All day Hare had strained his ears to hear the talk of the rustlers, and it now occurred to him that if he climbed down through the split in the cliff to the bench where Dave and George had always hidden to watch the spring he would be just above the camp. This descent involved risk, but since it would enable him to see the cabin door when darkness set in, he decided to venture. The moment was propitious, for the rustlers were bustling around, cooking dinner, unrolling blankets, and moving to and fro from spring and corral. Hare crawled back a few yards and along the cliff until he reached the split. It was a narrow steep crack which he well remembered. Going down was attended with two dangers—losing his hold, and the possible rattling of stones. Face foremost he slipped downward with the gliding, sinuous movement of a snake, and reaching the grassy bench he lay quiet. Jesting voices and loud laughter from below reassured him. He had not been heard. His new position afforded every chance to see and hear, and also gave means of rapid, noiseless retreat along the bench to the cedars. Lying flat he crawled stealthily to the bushy fringe of the bench.

A bright fire blazed under the cliff. Men were moving and laughing. The cabin door was open. Mescal stood leaning back from Snap Naab, struggling to release her hands.

"Let me untie them, I say," growled Snap.

Mescal tore loose from him and stepped back. Her hands were bound before her, and twisting them outward, she warded him off. Her dishevelled hair almost hid her dark eyes. They burned in a level glance of hate and defiance. She was a little lioness, quivering with fiery life, fight in every line of her form.

"All right, don't eat then—starve!" said Snap.

"I'll starve before I eat what you give me."

The rustlers laughed. Holderness blew out a puff of smoke and smiled. Snap glowered upon Mescal and then upon his amiable companions. One of them, a ruddy-faced fellow, walked toward Mescal.

"Cool down, Snap, cool down," he said. "We're

not goin' to stand for a girl starvin'. She ain't eat a bite yet. Here, Miss, let me untie your hands— there. . . . Say! Naab, damn you, her wrists are black an' blue!"

"Look out! Your gun!" yelled Snap.

With a swift movement Mescal snatched the man's Colt from its holster and was raising it when he grasped her arm. She winced and dropped the weapon.

"You little Indian devil!" exclaimed the rustler, in a rapt admiration. "Sorry to hurt you, an' more'n sorry to spoil your aim. Thet wasn't kind to throw my own gun on me, jest after I'd played the gentleman, now, was it?"

"I didn't—intend—to shoot—you," panted Mescal.

"Naab, if this's your Mormon kind of wife— excuse me! Though I ain't denyin' she's the sassiest an' sweetest little cat I ever seen!"

"We Mormons don't talk about our women or hear any talk," returned Snap, a dancing fury in his pale eyes. "You're from Nebraska?"

"Yep, jest a plain Nebraska rustler, cattle-thief, an' all round no-good customer, though I ain't taken to houndin' women yet."

For answer Snap Naab's right hand slowly curved upward before him and stopped taut and inflexible, while his strange eyes seemed to shoot sparks.

"See here, Naab, why do you want to throw a gun on me?" asked the rustler, coolly. "Hevn't you shot enough of your friends yet? I reckon I've no right to interfere in your affairs. I was only protestin' friendly like, for the little lady. She's game, an' she's called your hand. An' it's not a straight hand. Thet's all, an' damn if I care whether you are a Mormon or not. I'll bet a hoss Holderness will back me up."

"Snap, he's right," put in Holderness, smoothly. "You needn't be so touchy about Mescal. She's showed what little use she's got for you. If you must rope her around like you do a mustang, be easy about it. Let's have supper. Now, Mescal, you sit here on the bench and behave yourself. I don't want you shooting up my camp."

Snap turned sullenly aside while Holderness seated Mescal near the door and fetched her food and drink. The rustlers squatted round the camp-fire, and conversation ceased in the business of the meal.

To Hare the scene had brought a storm of emotions. Joy at the sight of Mescal, blessed relief to see her unscathed, pride in her fighting spirit—these came side by side with gratitude to the kind Nebraska rustler, strange deepening insight into Holderness's game, unextinguishable white-hot hatred of Snap Naab. And binding all was the ever-mounting will to rescue Mescal, which was held in check by an inexorable judgment; he must continue to wait. And he did wait with blind faith in the something to be, keeping ever in mind the last resort—the rifle he clutched with eager hands. Meanwhile the darkness descended, the fire sent forth a brighter blaze, and the rustlers finished their supper. Mescal arose and stepped across the threshold of the cabin door.

"Hold on!" ordered Snap, as he approached with swift strides. "Stick out your hands!"

Some of the rustlers grumbled; and one blurted out: "Aw no, Snap, don't tie her up—no!"

"Who says so?" hissed the Mormon, with snapping teeth. As he wheeled upon them his Colt seemed to leap forward, and suddenly quivered at arm's-length, gleaming in the ruddy fire-rays.

Holderness laughed in the muzzle of the weapon. "Go ahead, Snap, tie up your lady love. What a tame little wife she's going to make you! Tie her up, but do it without hurting her."

The rustlers growled or laughed at their leader's order. Snap turned to his task. Mescal stood in the doorway and shrinkingly extended her clasped hands. Holderness whirled to the fire with a look which betrayed his game. Snap bound Mescal's hands securely, thrust her inside the cabin, and after hesitating for a long moment, finally shut the door.

"It's funny about a woman, now, ain't it?" said Nebraska, confidentially, to a companion. "One minnit she'll snatch you bald-headed; the next, she'll melt in your mouth like sugar. An' I'll be darned if the changeablest one ain't the kind to hold a feller longest. But it's hell. I was married onct. Not any more for mine! A pal I had used to say thet whiskey riled him, thet rattlesnake pisen het up his blood some, but it took a woman to make him plumb bad. Damn if it ain't so. When there's a woman around there's somethin' allus comin' off."

But the strain, instead of relaxing, became portentous. Holderness suddenly showed he was ill at ease; he appeared to be expecting arrivals from the direction of Seeping Springs. Snap Naab leaned against the side of the door, his narrow gaze cunningly studying the rustlers before him. More than any other he had caught a foreshadowing. Like the desert-hawk he could see afar. Suddenly he pressed back against the door, half opening it while he faced the men.

"Stop!" commanded Holderness. The change in his voice was as if it had come from another man. "You don't go in there!"

"I'm going to take the girl and ride to White Sage," replied Naab, in slow deliberation.

"Bah! You say that only for the excuse to get into the cabin with her. You tried it last night and I blocked you. Shut the door, Naab, or something'll happen."

"There's more going to happen than ever you think of, Holderness. Don't interfere now, I'm going."

"Well, go ahead—but you won't take the girl!"

Snap Naab swung off the step, slamming the door behind him.

"So-ho!" he exclaimed, sneeringly. "That's why you've made me foreman, eh?" His claw-like hand moved almost imperceptibly upward while his pale eyes strove to pierce the strength behind Holderness's effrontery. The rustler chief had a trump card to play; one that showed in his sardonic smile.

"Naab, you don't get the girl."

"Maybe you'll get her?" hissed Snap.

"I always intended to."

Surely never before had passion driven Snap's hand to such speed. His Colt gleamed in the campfire light. Click! Click! Click! The hammer fell upon empty chambers.

"Hell!" he shrieked.

Holderness laughed sarcastically.

"That's where you're going!" he cried. "Here's to Naab's trick with a gun— Bah!" And he shot his foreman through the heart.

Snap plunged upon his face. His hands beat the ground like the shuffling wings of a wounded partridge. His fingers gripped the dust, spread convulsively, straightened, and sank limp.

Holderness called through the door of the cabin. "Mescal, I've rid you of your would-be husband. Cheer-up!" Then, pointing to the fallen man, he said to the nearest bystanders: "Some of you drag that out for the coyotes."

The first fellow who bent over Snap happened to be the Nebraska rustler, and he curiously opened the breech of the six-shooter he picked up. "No shells!" he said. He pulled Snap's second Colt from his belt, and unbreeched that. "No shells! Well, damn me!" He surveyed the group of grim men, not one of whom had any reply. Holderness again laughed harshly, and turning to the cabin he fastened the door with a lasso.

It was a long time before Hare recovered from the startling revelation of the plot which had put Mescal into Holderness's power. Bad as Snap Naab had been he would have married her, and such a fate was infinitely preferable to the one that now menaced her. Hare changed his position and settled himself to watch and wait out the night. Every hour Holderness and his men tarried at Silver Cup hastened their approaching doom. Hare's strange prescience of the fatality that overshadowed these men had received its first verification in the sudden taking off of Snap Naab. The deep-scheming Holderness, confident that his strong band meant sure protection, sat and smoked and smiled beside the camp-fire. He had not caught even a hint of Snap Naab's suggested warning. Yet somewhere out on the oasis trail rode a man who, once turned from the saving of life to the lust to kill, would be as immutable as death itself. Behind him waited a troop of Navajos, swift as eagles, merciless as wolves, desert warriors with the sun-heated blood of generations in their veins. As Hare waited and watched with all his inner being cold, he could almost feel pity for Holderness. His doom was close. Twice, when the rustler chief had sauntered nearer to the cabin door, as if to enter, Hare had covered him with the rifle, waiting, waiting for the step upon the threshold. But Holderness always checked himself in time, and Hare's finger eased its pressure upon the trigger.

The night closed in black; the clouded sky gave forth no starlight; the wind rose and moaned through the cedars. One by one the rustlers rolled in their blankets and all dropped into slumber while the camp-fire slowly burned down. The night hours wore on to the soft wail of the breeze and the wild notes of far-off trailing coyotes.

Hare, watching sleeplessly, saw one of the prone figures stir. The man raised himself very cautiously; he glanced at his companions, and looked long at Holderness, who lay squarely in the dimming light. Then he softly lowered himself. Hare wondered what the rustler meant to do. Presently he again lifted his head and turned it as if listening intently. His companions were motionless in deep-breathing sleep. Gently he slipped aside his blankets and began to rise. He was slow and guarded of movement; it took him long to stand erect. He stepped between the rustlers with stockinged feet which were as noiseless as an Indian's, and he went toward the cabin door.

He softly edged round the sleeping Holderness, showing a glinting six-shooter in his hand. Hare's resolve to kill him before he reached the door was checked. What did it mean, this rustler's stealthy movements, his passing by Holderness with his drawn weapon! Again doom hovered over the rustler chief. If he stirred!—Hare knew instantly that this softly stepping man was a Mormon; he was true to Snap Naab, to the woman pledged in his creed. He meant to free Mescal.

If ever Hare breathed a prayer it was then. What if one of the band awakened! As the rustler turned at the door his dark face gleamed in the flickering light. He unwound the lasso and opened the door without a sound.

Hare whispered: "Heavens! if he goes in she'll scream! that will wake Holderness—then I must shoot—I must!"

But the Mormon rustler added wisdom to this cunning and stealth.

"Hist!" he whispered into the cabin. "Hist!"

Mescal must have been awake; she must have guessed instantly the meaning of that low whisper, for silently she appeared in the doorway, silently she held forth her bound hands. The man untied the bonds and pointed into the cedars toward the corral. Swift and soundless as a flitting shadow Mescal vanished in the gloom. The Mormon stole with wary, unhurried steps back to his bed and rolled in his blankets.

Hare rose unsteadily, wavering in the hot grip of a moment that seemed to have but one issue—the killing of Holderness. Mescal would soon be upon Silvermane, far out on the White Sage trail, and this time there would be no sand-strip to trap her. But Hare could not kill the rustler while he was sleeping; and he could not awaken him without revealing to his men the escape of the girl. Hare stood there on the bench, gazing down on the blanketed Holderness. Why not kill him now, ending forever his power, and trust to chance for the rest? No, no! Hare flung the temptation from him. To ward off pursuit as long as possible, to aid Mescal in every way to some safe hiding-place, and *then* to seek Holderness—that was the forethought of a man who had learned to wait.

Under the dark projection of the upper cliff Hare felt his way to the cedar slope, and the trail, and then he went swiftly down into the little hollow where he had left Bolly. The darkness of the forest hindered him, but he came at length to the edge of the aspen thicket; he penetrated it, and guided toward Bolly by a suspicious stamp and neigh, he found her and quieted her with a word. He rode down the hollow, out upon the level valley.

The clouds had broken somewhat, letting pale light down through rifts. All about him cattle were lying in a thick gloom. It was penetrable for only a few rods. The ground was like a cushion under

Bolly's hoofs, giving forth no sound. The mustang threw up her head, causing Hare to peer into the night-fog. Rapid hoof-beats broke the silence, a vague gray shadow moved into sight. He saw Silvermane and called as loudly as he dared. The stallion melted into the misty curtain, the beating of hoofs softened and ceased. Hare spurred Bolly to her fleetest. He had a long, silent chase, but it was futile, and unnecessarily hard on the mustang; so he pulled her in to a trot.

Hare kept Bolly to this gait the remainder of the night, and when the eastern sky lightened he found the trail and reached Seeping Springs at dawn. Silvermane's tracks were deep in the clay at the drinking-trough. He rested a few moments, gave Bolly sparingly of grain and water, and once more took to the trail.

From the ridge below the spring he saw Silvermane beyond the valley, miles ahead of him. This day seemed shorter than the foregoing one; it passed while he watched Silvermane grow smaller and smaller and disappear on the looming slope of Coconina. Hare's fear that Mescal would run into the riders Holderness expected from his ranch grew less and less after she had reached the cover of the cedars. That she would rest the stallion at the Navajo pool on the mountain he made certain. Late in the night he came to the camping spot and found no trace to prove that she had halted there even to let Silvermane drink. So he tied the tired mustang and slept until daylight.

He crossed the plateau and began the descent. Before he was half-way down the warm bright sun had cleared the valley of vapor and shadow. Far along the winding white trail shone a speck. It was Silvermane almost out of sight.

"Ten miles—fifteen, more maybe," said Hare. "Mescal will soon be in the village."

Again hours of travel flew by like winged moments. Thoughts of time, distance, monotony, fatigue, purpose, were shut out from his mind. A rushing kaleidoscopic dance of images filled his consciousness, but they were all of Mescal. Safety for her had unsealed the fountain of happiness.

It was near sundown when he rode Black Bolly into White Sage, and took the back road, and the pasture lane to Bishop Caldwell's cottage. John, one of the Bishop's sons, was in the barn-yard and ran to open the gate.

"Mescal!" cried Hare.

"Safe," replied the Mormon.

"Have you hidden her?"

"She's in a secret cave, a Mormon hiding-place for women. Only a few men know of its existence. Rest easy, for she's absolutely safe."

"Thank God! . . . then that's settled." Hare drew a long, deep breath.

"Mescal told us what happened, how she got caught at the sand-strip and escaped from Holderness at Silver Cup. Was Dene hurt?"

"Silvermane killed him."

"Good God! How things come about! I saw you run Dene down that time here in White Sage. It must have been written. Did Holderness shoot Snap Naab?"

"Yes."

"What of old Naab? Won't he come down here now to lead us Mormons against the rustlers?"

"He called the Navajos across the river. He meant to take the trail alone and kill Holderness, keeping the Indians back a few days. If he failed to return then they were to ride out on the rustlers. But his plan must be changed, for I came ahead of him."

"For what? Mescal?"

"No. For Holderness."

"You'll kill him!"

"Yes."

"He'll be coming soon!— When?"

"To-morrow, possibly by daylight.. He wants Mescal. There's a chance Naab may have reached Silver Cup before Holderness left, but I doubt it."

"May I know your plan?" The Mormon hesitated while his strong brown face flashed with daring inspiration. "I—I've a good reason."

"Plan?— Yes. Hide Bolly and Silvermane in the little arbor down in the orchard. I'll stay outside tonight, sleep a little—for I'm dead tired—and watch in the morning. Holderness will come here with his men, perhaps not openly at first, to drag Mescal away. He'll mean to use strategy. I'll meet him when he comes—that's all."

"It's well. I ask you not to mention this to my father. Come in, now. You need food and rest. Later I'll hide Bolly and Silvermane in the arbor."

Hare met the Bishop and his family with composure, but his arrival following so closely upon Mescal's, increased their alarm. They seemed repelled yet fascinated by his face. Hare ate in silence. John Caldwell did not come in to supper; his brothers mysteriously left the table before finishing the meal. A subdued murmur of voices floated in at the open window.

Darkness found Hare wrapped in a blanket under the trees. He needed sleep that would loose the strange deadlock of his thoughts, clear the blur from his eyes, ease the pain in his head and weariness of limbs—all these weaknesses of which he had suddenly become conscious. Time and again he had almost wooed slumber to him when soft footsteps on the gravel paths, low voices, the gentle closing of the gate, brought him back to the unreal listening wakefulness. The sounds continued late into the night, and when he did fall asleep he dreamed of them. He awoke to a dawn clearer than the light from the noonday sun. In his ears was the ringing of a bell. He could not stand still, and his movements were subtle and swift. His hands took a peculiar, tenacious, hold of everything he chanced to touch. He paced his hidden walk behind the arbor, at every turn glancing sharply up and down the road. Thoughts came to him clearly, yet one was dominant. The morning was curiously quiet, the sons of the Bishop had strangely disappeared—a sense of imminent catastrophe was in the air.

A band of horsemen closely grouped turned into the road and trotted forward. Some of the men wore black masks. Holderness rode at the front, his red-gold beard shining in the sunlight. The steady clip-clop of hoofs and clinking of iron stirrups broke the morning quiet. Holderness, with two of his men, dismounted before the Bishop's gate; the others of the band trotted on down the road. The ring of Holderness's laugh preceded the snap of the gate-latch.

Hare stood calm and cold behind his green covert watching the three men stroll up the garden path. Holderness took a cigarette from his lips as he neared the porch and blew out circles of white smoke. Bishop Caldwell tottered from the cottage rapping the porch-floor with his cane.

"Good-morning, Bishop," greeted Holderness, blandly, baring his head.

"To you, sir," quavered the old man, with his wavering blue eyes fixed on the spurred and belted rustler. Holderness stepped out in front of his companions, a superb man, courteous, smiling, entirely at his ease.

"I rode in to—"

Hare leaped from his hiding-place.

"Holderness!"

The rustler pivoted on whirling heels.

"Dene's spy!" he exclaimed, aghast. Swift changes swept his mobile features. Fear flickered in his eyes as he faced his foe; then came wonder, a glint of amusement, dark anger, and the terrible instinct of death impending.

"Naab's trick!" hissed Hare, with his hand held high. The suggestion in his words, the meaning in his look, held the three rustlers transfixed. The surprise was his strength.

In Holderness's amber eyes shone his desperate calculation of chances. Hare's fateful glance, impossible to elude, his strung form slightly crouched, his cold deliberate mention of Naab's trick, and more than all the poise of that quivering hand, filled the rustler with a terror that he could not hide. He had been bidden to draw and he could not summon the force.

"Naab's trick!" repeated Hare, mockingly.

Suddenly Holderness reached for his gun.

Hare's hand leapt like a lightning stroke. Gleam of blue—spurt of red—crash!

Holderness swayed with blond head swinging backward, the amber of his eyes suddenly darkened; the life in them glazed; like a log he fell clutching the weapon he had half drawn.

CHAPTER XX

The Rage of the Old Lion

"TAKE HOLDERNESS away—quick!" ordered Hare. A thin curl of blue smoke floated from the muzzle of his raised weapon.

The rustlers started out of their statue-like immobility, and lifting their dead leader dragged him down the garden path with his spurs clinking on the gravel and ploughing little furrows.

"Bishop, go in now. They may return," said Hare. He hurried up the steps to place his arm round the tottering old man.

"Was that Holderness?"

"Yes," replied Hare.

"The deeds of the wicked return unto them! God's will!"

Hare led the Bishop indoors. The sitting-room was full of wailing women and crying children. None of the young men were present. Again Hare made note of their inexplicable absence. He spoke soothingly to the frightened family. The little boys and girls yielded readily to his persuasion, but the women took no heed of him.

"Where are your sons?" asked Hare.

"I don't know," replied the Bishop. "They should be here to stand by you. It's strange. I don't understand. Last night my sons were visited by many men, coming and going in twos and threes till late. They didn't sleep in their beds. I know not what to think."

Hare remembered John Caldwell's enigmatic face.

"Have the rustlers really come?" asked a young woman, whose eyes were red and cheeks tear-stained.

"They have. Nineteen in all. I counted them," answered Hare.

The young woman burst out weeping afresh, and the wailing of the others answered her. Hare left the cottage. He picked up his rifle and went down through the orchard to the hiding-place of the horses. Silvermane pranced and snorted his gladness at sight of his master. The desert king was fit for a grueling race. Black Bolly quietly cropped the long grass. Hare saddled the stallion to have him in instant readiness, and then returned to the front of the yard.

He heard the sound of a gun down the road, then another, and several shots following in quick succession. A distant angry murmuring and trampling of many feet drew Hare to the gate. Riderless mustangs were galloping down the road; several frightened boys were fleeing across the square; not a man was in sight. Three more shots cracked, and the low murmur and trampling swelled into a hoarse uproar. Hare had heard that sound before; it was the tumult of mob-violence. A black dense throng of men appeared crowding into the main street, and crossing toward the square. The procession had some order; it was led and flanked by mounted men. But the upflinging of many arms, the craning of necks, and the leaping of men on the out-skirts of the mass, the pressure inward and the hideous roar, proclaimed its real character.

"By Heaven!" cried Hare. "The Mormons have risen against the rustlers. I understand now. John Caldwell spent last night in secretly rousing his neighbors. They have surprised the rustlers. Now what?"

Hare vaulted the fence and ran down the road. A compact mob of men, a hundred or more, had halted in the village under the wide-spreading cot-tonwoods. Hare suddenly grasped the terrible significance of those outstretched branches, and out of the thought grew another which made him run at bursting break-neck speed.

"Open up! Let me in!" he yelled to the thickly thronged circle. Right and left he flung men. "Make way!" His piercing voice stilled the angry murmur. Fierce men with weapons held aloft fell back from his face.

"Dene's spy!" they cried.

The circle opened and closed upon him. He saw bound rustlers under armed guard. Four still forms were on the ground. Holderness lay outstretched, a dark-red blot staining his gray shirt. Flinty-faced Mormons, ruthless now as they had once been mild, surrounded the rustlers. John Caldwell stood foremost, with ashen lips breaking bitterly into speech:

"Mormons, this is Dene's spy, the man who killed Holderness!"

The listeners burst into the short stern shout of men proclaiming a leader in war.

"What's the game?" demanded Hare.

"A fair trial for the rustlers, then a rope," replied John Caldwell. The low ominous murmur swelled through the crowd again.

"There are two men here who have befriended me. I won't see them hanged."

"Pick them out!" A strange ripple of emotion made a fleeting break in John Caldwell's hard face.

Hare eyed the prisoners.

"Nebraska, step out here," said he.

"I reckon you're mistaken," replied the rustler, his blue eyes intently on Hare. "I never seen you before. An' I ain't the kind of a feller to cheat the man you mean."

"I saw you untie the girl's hands."

"You did? Well, damn me!"

"Nebraska, if I save your life will you quit rustling cattle? You weren't cut out for a thief."

"Will I? Damn me! I'll be straight an' decent. I'll take a job ridin' for you, stranger, an' prove it."

"Cut him loose from the others," said Hare. He scrutinized the line of rustlers. Several were masked in black. "Take off those masks!"

"No! Those men go to their graves masked." Again the strange twinge of pain crossed John Caldwell's face.

"Ah! I see," exclaimed Hare. Then quickly: "I couldn't recognize the other man anyhow; I don't know him. But Mescal can tell. He saved her and I'll save him. But how?"

Every rustler, except the masked ones standing stern and silent, clamored that he was the one to be saved.

"Hurry back home," said Caldwell in Hare's ear. "Tell them to fetch Mescal. Find out and hurry back. Time presses. The Mormons are wavering. You've got only a few minutes."

Hare slipped out of the crowd, sped up the road, jumped the fence on the run, and burst in upon the Bishop and his family.

"No danger—don't be alarmed—all's well," he

panted. "The rustlers are captured. I want Mescal. Quick! Where is she? Fetch her, somebody."

One of the women glided from the room. Hare caught the clicking of a latch, the closing of a door, hollow footfalls descending on stone, and dying away under the cottage. They rose again, ending in swiftly pattering footsteps. Like a whirlwind Mescal came through the hall, black hair flying, dark eyes beaming.

"My darling!" Oblivious of the Mormons he swung her up and held her in his arms. "Mescal! Mescal!" When he raised his face from the tumbling mass of her black hair, the Bishop and his family had left the room.

"Listen, Mescal. Be calm. I'm safe. The rustlers are prisoners. One of them released you from Holderness. Tell me which one?"

"I don't know," replied Mescal. "I've tried to think. I didn't see his face; I can't remember his voice."

"Think! Think! He'll be hanged if you don't recall something to identify him. He deserves a chance. Holderness's crowd are thieves, murderers. But two men were not all bad. That showed the night you were at Silver Cup. I saved Nebraska—"

"Were you at Silver Cup? Jack!"

"Hush! don't interrupt me. We must save this man who saved you. Think! Mescal! Think!"

"Oh! I can't. What—how shall I remember?"

"Something about him. Think of his coat, his sleeve. You must remember something. Did you see his hands?"

"Yes, I did—when he was loosing the cords," said Mescal, eagerly. "Long, strong fingers. I felt them too. He has a sharp rough wart on one hand, I don't know which. He wears a leather wristband."

"That's enough!" Hare bounded out upon the garden walk and raced back to the crowded square.

The uneasy circle stirred and opened for him to enter. He stumbled over a pile of lassoes which had not been there when he left. The stony Mormons waited; the rustlers coughed and shifted their feet. John Caldwell turned a gray face. Hare bent over the three dead rustlers lying with Holderness, and after a moment of anxious scrutiny he rose to confront the line of prisoners.

"Hold out your hands."

One by one they complied. The sixth rustler in the line, a tall fellow, completely masked, refused to do as he was bidden. Twice Hare spoke. The rustler twisted his bound hands under his coat.

"Let's see them," said Hare, quickly. He grasped the fellow's arm and received a violent push that almost knocked him over. Grappling with the rustler, he pulled up the bound hands, in spite of fierce resistance, and there were the long fingers, the sharp wart, the laced wristband. "Here's my man!" he said.

"No," hoarsely mumbled the rustler. The perspiration ran down his corded neck; his breast heaved convulsively.

"You fool!" cried Hare, dumbfounded and resentful. "I recognized you. Would you rather hang than live? What's your secret?"

He snatched off the black mask. The Bishop's eldest son stood revealed.

"Good God!" cried Hare, recoiling from that convulsed face.

"Brother! Oh! I feared this," groaned John Caldwell.

The rustlers broke out into curses and harsh laughter.

"Damn you Mormons! See him! Paul Caldwell! Son of a Bishop! Thought he was shepherdin' sheep?"

"Damn you, Hare!" shouted the guilty Mormon, in

passionate fury and shame. "Why didn't you hang me? Why didn't you bury me unknown?"

"Caldwell! I can't believe it," cried Hare, slowly coming to himself. "But you don't hang. Here, come out of the crowd. Make way, men!"

The silent crowd of Mormons with lowered and averted eyes made passage for Hare and Caldwell. Then cold, stern voices in sharp questions and orders went on with the grim trial. Leading the bowed and stricken Mormon, Hare drew off to the side of the town-hall and turned his back upon the crowd. The constant trampling of many feet, the harsh medley of many voices swelled into one dreadful sound. It passed away, and a long hush followed. But this in turn was suddenly broken by an outcry:

"The Navajos! The Navajos!"

Hare thrilled at that cry and his glance turned to the eastern end of the village road where a column of mounted Indians, four abreast, was riding toward the square.

"Naab and his Indians," shouted Hare. "Naab and his Indians! No fear!" His call was timely, for the aroused Mormons, ignorant of Naab's pursuit, fearful of hostile Navajos, were handling their guns ominously.

But there came a cry of recognition—"August Naab!"

Onward came the band, Naab in the lead on his spotted roan. The mustangs were spent and lashed with foam. Naab reined in his charger and the keen-eyed Navajos closed in behind him. The old Mormon's eagle glance passed over the dark forms dangling from the cottonwoods to the files of waiting men.

"Where is he?"

"There!" answered John Caldwell, pointing to the body of Holderness.

"Who robbed me of my vengeance? Who killed

the rustler?" Naab's stentorian voice rolled over the listening multitude. In it was a hunger of thwarted hate that held men mute. He bent a downward gaze at the dead Holderness as if to make sure of the ghastly reality. Then he seemed to rise in his saddle, and his broad chest to expand. "I know—I saw it all—blind I was not to believe my own eyes! Where is he? Where is Hare?"

Some one pointed Hare out. Naab swung from his saddle and scattered the men before him as if they had been sheep. His shaggy gray head and massive shoulders towered above the tallest there.

Hare felt again a cold sense of fear. He grew weak in all his being. He reeled when the gray shaggy giant laid a huge hand on his shoulder and with one pull dragged him close. Was this his kind Mormon benefactor, this man with the awful eyes?

"You killed Holderness?" roared Naab.

"Yes," whispered Hare.

"You heard me say I'd go alone? You forestalled me? You took upon yourself my work? . . . Speak."

"I did."

"By what right?"

"My debt—duty—your family—Dave!"

"*Boy! Boy!* You've robbed me." Naab waved his arm from the gaping crowd to the swinging rustlers. "You've led these white-livered Mormons to do my work. How can I avenge my sons—seven sons?"

His was the rage of the old desert-lion. He loosed Hare, and strode in magnificent wrath over Holderness and raised his brawny fists.

"Eighteen years I prayed for wicked men," he rolled out. "One by one I buried my sons. I gave my springs and my cattle. Then I yielded to the lust for blood. I renounced my religion. I paid my soul to everlasting hell for the life of my foe. But he's dead! Killed by a wild boy! I sold myself to the devil for nothing!"

August Naab raved out his unnatural rage amid awed silence. His revolt was the flood of years undammed at the last. The ferocity of the desert spirit spoke silently in the hanging rustlers, in the ruthlessness of the vigilantes who had destroyed them, but it spoke truest in the sonorous roll of the old Mormon's wrath.

"August, young Hare saved two of the rustlers," spoke up an old friend, hoping to divert the angry flood. "Paul Caldwell there, he was one of them. The other's gone."

Naab loomed over him. "What!" he roared. His friend edged away, repeating his words and jerking his thumb backward toward the Bishop's son.

"Judas Iscariot!" thundered Naab. "False to thyself, thy kin, and thy God! Thrice traitor! . . . Why didn't you get yourself killed? . . . Why are you left? Ah-h! for me—a rustler for me to kill—with my own hands! A rope there—a rope!"

"I wanted them to hang me," hoarsely cried Caldwell, writhing in Naab's grasp.

Hare threw all his weight and strength upon the Mormon's iron arm. "Naab! Naab! For God's sake, hear! He saved Mescal. This man, thief, traitor, false Mormon—whatever he is—he saved Mescal."

August Naab's eyes were bloodshot. One shake of his great body flung Hare off. He dragged Paul Caldwell across the grass toward the cottonwood as easily as if he were handling an empty grain-sack.

Hare suddenly darted after him. "August! August!—look! look!" he cried. He pointed a shaking finger down the square. The old Bishop came tottering over the grass, leaning on his cane, shading his eyes with his hand. "August. See, the Bishop's coming. Paul's *father*! Do you hear?"

Hare's appeal pierced Naab's frenzied brain. The Mormon Elder saw his old Bishop pause and stare at the dark shapes suspended from the cotton-woods and hold up his hands in horror.

Naab loosed his hold. His frame seemed wrenched as though by the passing of an evil spirit, and the reaction left his face transfigured.

"Paul, it's your father, the Bishop," he said, brokenly. "Be a man. He must never know." Naab spread wide his arms to the crowd. "Men, listen," he said. "Of all of us Mormons I have lost most, suffered most. Then hear me. Bishop Caldwell must never know of his son's guilt. He would sink under it. Keep the secret. Paul will be a man again. I know. I see. For, Mormons, August Naab has the gift of revelation!"

CHAPTER XXI

Mescal

SUMMER GLEAMS of golden sunshine swam under the glistening red walls of the oasis. Shadows from white clouds, like sails on a deep-blue sea, darkened the broad fields of alfalfa. Circling columns of smoke were wafted far above the cottonwoods and floated in the still air. The desert-red color of Navajo blankets brightened the grove.

Half-naked bronze Indians lolled in the shade, lounged on the cabin porches and stood about the sunny glade in idle groups. They wore the dress of peace. A single black-tipped white eagle feather waved above the band binding each black head. They watched the merry children tumble round the playground. Silvermane browsed where he listed under the shady trees, and many a sinewy red hand caressed his flowing mane. Black Bolly neighed her jealous displeasure from the corral, and the other mustangs trampled and kicked and whistled defiance across the bars. The peacocks preened their gorgeous plumage and uttered their clarion calls. The belligerent turkey-gobblers sidled about ruffling their feathers. The blackbirds and swallows sang and twittered their happiness to find old nests in the branches and under the eaves. Over all boomed the dull roar of the Colorado in flood.

It was the morning of Mescal's wedding-day.

August Naab, for once without a task, sat astride a peeled log of driftwood in the lane, and Hare stood beside him.

"Five thousand steers, lad! Why do you refuse them? They're worth ten dollars a head to-day in Salt Lake City. A good start for a young man."

"No, I'm still in your debt."

"Then share alike with my sons in work and profit?"

"Yes, I can accept that."

"Good! Jack, I see happiness and prosperity for you. Do you remember that night on the White Sage trail? Ah! Well, the worst is over. We can look forward to better times. It's not likely the rustlers will ride into Utah again. But this desert will never be free from strife."

"Tell me of Mescal," said Hare.

"Ah! Yes, I'm coming to that." Naab bent his head over the log and chipped off little pieces with his knife. "Jack, will you come into the Mormon Church?"

Long had Hare shrunk from this question which he felt must inevitably come, and now he met it as bravely as he could, knowing he would pain his friend.

"No, August, I can't," he replied. "I feel— differently from Mormons about—about women. If it wasn't for that! I look upon you as a father. I'll do anything for you, except that. No one could pray to be a better man than you. Your work, your religion, your life— Why! I've no words to say what I feel.

Teach me what little you can of them, August, but don't ask me—that."

"Well, well," sighed Naab. The gray clearness of his eagle eyes grew shadowed and his worn face was sad. It was the look of a strong wise man who seemed to hear doubt and failure knocking at the gate of his creed. But he loved life too well to be unhappy; he saw it too clearly not to know there was nothing wholly good, wholly perfect, wholly without error. The shade passed from his face like the cloud-shadow from the sunlit lane.

"You ask about Mescal," he mused. "There's little more to tell."

"But her father—can you tell me more of him?"

"Little more than I've already told. He was evidently a man of some rank. I suspected that he ruined his life and became an adventurer. His health was shattered when I brought him here, but he got well after a year or so. He was a splendid, handsome fellow. He spoke very seldom, and I don't remember ever seeing him smile. His favorite walk was the river trail. I came upon him there one day and found him dying. He asked me to have a care of Mescal. And he died muttering a Spanish word, a woman's name, I think."

"I'll cherish Mescal the more," said Hare.

"Cherish her, yes. My Bible will this day give her a name. We know she has the blood of a great chief. Beautiful she is and good. I raised her for the Mormon Church, but God disposes after all, and I—"

A shrill screeching sound split the warm stillness, the long-drawn-out bray of a burro.

"Jack, look down the lane. If it isn't Noddle!"

Under the shady line of the red wall a little gray burro came trotting leisurely along with one long brown ear standing straight up, the other hanging down over his nose.

"By George! it's Noddle!" exclaimed Hare. "He's climbed out of the cañon. Won't this please Mescal?"

"Hey, Mother Mary," called Naab toward the cabin. "Send Mescal out. Here's a wedding-present."

With laughing wonder the women-folk flocked out into the yard. Mescal hung back shy-eyed, roses dyeing the brown of her cheeks.

"Mescal's wedding-present from Thunder River. Just arrived!" called Naab cheerily, yet deep-voiced with the happiness he knew the tidings would give. "A dusty, dirty, shaggy, starved, lop-eared, lazy burro—Noddle!"

Mescal flew out into the lane, and with a strange broken cry of joy that was half a sob she fell upon her knees and clasped the little burro's neck. Noddle wearily flapped his long brown ears, wearily nodded his white nose; then evidently considering the incident closed, he went lazily to sleep.

"Noddle! dear old Noddle!" murmured Mescal, with far-seeing, thought-mirroring eyes. "For you to come back to-day from our cañon!... Oh! The long dark nights with the thunder of the river and the lonely voices!... they come back to me.... Wolf, Wolf, here's Noddle, the same faithful old Noddle!"

August Naab married Mescal and Hare at noon under the shade of the cottonwoods. Eschtah, magnificent in robes of state, stood up with them. The many members of Naab's family and the grave Navajos formed an attentive circle around them. The ceremony was brief. At its close the Mormon lifted his face and arms in characteristic invocation.

"Almighty God, we entreat Thy blessing upon this marriage. Many and inscrutable are Thy ways; strange are the workings of Thy will; wondrous purpose with which Thou hast brought this man and this woman together. Watch over them in the new path they are to tread, help them in the trials to come; and in Thy good time, when they have reached the fulness of days, when they have known the joy of life and rendered their service, gather them to Thy bosom in that eternal home where we all pray to meet Thy chosen ones of good; yea, and the evil ones purified in Thy mercy. Amen."

Happy congratulations of the Mormon family, a merry romp of children flinging flowers, marriage-dance of singing Navajos—these, with the feast spread under the cottonwoods, filled the warm noon-hours of the day.

Then the chief Eschtah raised his lofty form, and turned his eyes upon the bride and groom.

"Eschtah's hundred summers smile in the face of youth. The arm of the White Chief is strong; the kiss of the Flower of the Desert is sweet. Let Mescal and Jack rest their heads on one pillow, and sleep under the trees, and chant when the dawn brightens in the east. Out of his wise years the Navajo bids them love while they may. Daughter of my race, take the blessing of the Navajo."

Jack lifted Mescal upon Black Bolly and mounted Silvermane. Piute grinned till he shook his earrings and started the pack burros toward the plateau trail. Wolf pattered on before, turning his white head, impatient of delay. Amid tears and waving of hands and cheers they began the zigzag ascent.

When they reached the old camp on the plateau the sun was setting behind the Painted Desert. With hands closely interwoven they watched the color fade and the mustering of purple shadows.

Twilight fell. Piute raked the red coals from the glowing centre of the camp-fire. Wolf crouched all his long white length, his sharp nose on his paws, watching Mescal. Hare watched her, too. The night shone in her eyes, the light of the fire, the old brooding mystic desert-spirit, and something more. The thump of Silvermane's hobbled hoofs was heard in the darkness; Bolly's bell jangled musically. The sheep were bleating. A lonesome coyote barked. The white stars blinked out of the blue and the night breeze whispered softly among the cedars.